HIS SALVATION

Rescue Me
Book 3

KENZIE YOUNG

Published by Blushing Books
An Imprint of
ABCD Graphics and Design, Inc.
A Virginia Corporation
977 Seminole Trail #233
Charlottesville, VA 22901

His Salvation
Kenzie Young

eBook ISBN: 978-1-63954-531-5
Print ISBN: 978-1-63954-532-2

Foreword

Author Note and Trigger Warning

This is book three in the Rescue Me series. As always this book will have sexual content included. This book deals with tough topics as do all of my books. This one deals with the struggles of an interracial relationship—I myself am in one —so these are based on my personal experiences. The FMC is black and Hispanic and the MMC is Japanese. (To my family: whatever you're thinking, shut it down). This deals with PTSD, grooming—not from the MCs—which leads to an obsessive ex who turns violent, and cheating—not from the main characters.

There is a degradation kink, but we like that a little bit over here so it's okay. There are conflicts with the main characters with miscommunication and commitment issues that get resolved eventually. There will be talk of racism but it's in a teaching moment. There is a slight panic attack due to being stuck in a small space, but it's an easily distractible issue. There is no 'other woman' drama, per se, but there is a moment but it's not long. I like drama so there's plenty of it.

There is also trauma and from the beginning we get a little more in depth about the guys and their capture, especially from the different points of view. My work is dramatized, but I won't lie, I do add my life experience into my books when it comes to intense topics such as race and mental health.

As always please take these warnings to heart and take care of your mental health at all times.

Thank you!

~KY

Never settle for a man who puts you second. Find a man who'll call you his good little whore and get you cake pops when you're stressed.

P.S. To my family, turn back, it's about to get weird.

Prologue

FIVE YEARS *ago*

Caden

A fist comes down on me again making me grunt in pain. "Tell me what I want to know!" is shouted at me, though muffled I can hear the slight accent that laces the words. Leaning my head back against the wall, chains attaching me to the wall, I cough. He moves to walk away, clutching the keys in a fist, gritting his teeth. I had to get him to drop them. I had to piss him off enough to make him distracted. So, I did the only thing I knew how... I taunted him.

"Fuck... you," I gasp out. The man in front of me curses again slamming his steel-toed boot into my side, possibly cracking one of my ribs as he did so. I wouldn't be surprised at this point. But he keeps kicking me, eventually dropping the keys, and makes me a gasping mess. The man leaves, cursing at me as he goes, but I couldn't really hear him. I'm looking down at the dirt around me, and spot what I was looking for. Stretching out my leg, I slowly cover the metal key ring and pull it closer until it's close enough for me to bend down and grab it with my teeth. Leaning down, I strain my neck and grab the keys nearly shouting in relief, but I calm myself.

When I sit up I take a breath, slowly pushing myself up with my feet and angling my head back just enough for my hand to grab the key. The muscles in my neck, shoulders, and back straining and tightening to the point of pain. But I knew if I stopped now we were fucked. Pushing through, my left hand twitches and I grasp the key before gasping out a breath I didn't realize I was holding. Moving forward, I quickly unlocked the cuff on my right hand but stopped as I heard the door open. My heart quickens and the guard from before comes in and sees me holding the key. Our eyes meet briefly and he smirks tsking at me before slamming his boot down on my left hand forcing me to drop the key.

The bone cracks under the pressure, snapping. I scream out, the pain is almost too much, but I can't stop now. If I do we'd all die. With my right hand free, I grab the chain and hit him in the knee with it, buckling him to the ground. He cries out as I stand, slamming my own foot into his face as I saw him do to Drew, over and over again. He goes for the gun at the waist of his pants, but I wrap the chain around his neck, pulling as hard as I can as he struggles, slapping uselessly at the ground. I don't stop until I hear an audible crack of his neck and he goes limp. Leaning back against the wall I take a breath.

I really hoped to hell the others were alive or I was going to be pissed as fuck. I glance at my mangled hand and grimace. I lean over and grab the key and unlock the cuff letting it fall with a soft *thud*. Hissing out a breath I pull my hand to my chest. "You bastard. If I never get to jack off again, I swear to God, I'm bringing you back from the dead and killing you again," I tell the corpse beside me.

Now, I know jacking off should not be the main priority right now. It's not, not really, but it's been nearly eight months since I've seen my fiancée Xena, and I've missed her so much being here. Trapped in what is essentially a dirt grave. Shaking my head, I scoop up the gun and keys before making my way down the weird ass cave system. It's been seven days. I haven't seen the others in three of the seven. The last time I saw them, Sorrow was basically dead, and Drew's face was cut to hell. Max was unconscious and I wasn't even sure he was breathing when I was dragged away.

What if they were dead? No, I couldn't have those thoughts. We had this plan; I'd let them drag me away for interrogation then I'd find a way to get the keys. I did that. I did my part, they just needed to do theirs and stay alive. I heard coughing and I followed the sound where I saw Sorrow hunched over throwing up.

"So?" I croaked out. The blond man turned at my voice and I nearly fell over in shock. His once clean-shaven face was sporting a small beard, his cheeks were hollow and dotted over with sweat and his face was red as if he were sick. I moved as fast as I could to get to him, wincing with each painful step I took.

"Cade?" he coughed out.

Nodding, I helped him into a sitting position ignoring the vomit next to us. "Where're the others?" I ask.

"Don't know. They took them somewhere. Max screams. All he does is scream." Sorrow rocks back and forth, his body shaking. "So loud. So damn loud."

Closing my eyes, I lean my head back, cursing the fact we are in this situation. It was supposed to be a cut and dry mission. Come in, save the missing Americans, then get out. Not a fucking set up.

"What happened to your hand?" Sorrow asks after a moment, his voice devoid of any emotion.

I look down at the bruised swollen appendage in question. "Jackass broke it. Killed him." Sighing, I pull away, and say, "We need to get Max and Drew. Can you walk?" He nods and slowly climbs to his feet, holding his side that had shrapnel in it.

"If I slow you down just leave me. Understood?" Sorrow says, getting into his commanding position.

I roll my eyes. "Don't be stupid. We are all leaving here." Even if it's in body bags, I don't add, but we both know what I mean. Sorrow grabs a chain from the ground and wraps it around his hand, almost like makeshift brass knuckles. We move in sync down the tunnels and hear screams. We rush forward where Max is getting shocked with what looked like a cattle prod, burning the skin off of his body as another guard doused him with water. Sorrow and I move forward, Sorrow taking the one with the water and me going for the cattle prod. He turns on me, hitting me with the prod, but adrenaline moves through me, making the pain nothing more than a sting that I'll probably feel later. I grab it, snatch it out of his hands and slam it down on his temple knocking him to the ground.

"Where's the other one?" I demand.

The guard shakes his head. Over this bullshit, I pull the gun out and put a bullet between his eyes. Ending all talk. I turn to gaze at Sorrow and he's hitting the bastard with his chain linked fist. "Sorrow, we need to find Drew." Sorrow drops the man, breathing deeply. He gives me a clipped nod and I walk toward Max who is looking at me warily as if I would harm him.

"You look like Caden. But he's dead," he whispers.

Shaking my head, I unlock the chains catching him before he falls to the ground. "Not dead. Well, not yet at least. We need to get Drew. Do you remember where Drew was taken?"

Max shakes his head, breathing deeply. "Hurts. Everything hurts."

"I know, but we need to get the fuck out of here. Can you walk?" Max shrugs and takes the hand Sorrow holds out to him.

"Never again. I quit, I want to go home," Max says, running a shaky, bloodied hand over his face. I couldn't agree more. I never wanted to do another mission in my life. Not like this. Never again. But now wasn't the time to reflect on what our lives would be like after this. There would be no 'after this' if we didn't get moving. Taking the lead, I moved forward, holding the gun in my right hand cursing the fact that my left hand was my dominant hand. We move through the tunnels looking this way and that, we can't find Drew and dread sets in. Was he dead? Were we too late?

But then I heard it, grunting. I move forward and I see Drew getting hit over and over again in the stomach. His head is bent low, and I honestly can't tell if he's breathing or not. There's at least five men in there, using different weapons on him and his entire body was bruised from head to toe. Lifting the gun, I go to shoot the one who's pounding on Drew just as an explosion happens, sending us flying. I curse as one of the guards lands on top of me, his body taking the brunt of the explosion. Then everything turns to complete chaos. I hardly know what's going on before I slip into complete oblivion.

The sound of beeping is loud in my ears as I slowly wake up. "Don't move too much," a deep voice says to me.

Blinking open my eyes I stare into the dark brown eyes of

my teammate. His face is pale as he stares at me and pushes his glasses up his face. "Spence?" I croak out, my throat dry as hell.

"Hey, Cade. How do you feel?"

Scoffing, I wince. "Like I was run over. Over and over again." I glance around the room and see I'm in the hospital. The walls are white and drab with nothing but the monitors and bed in here. "Where am I?"

Spencer leans back, pushing a hand through his hair, staring at me with worry. "We're in Washington. We were in a hospital in Afghanistan, but we moved you closer to home."

"The others? Where are the others?" I ask. I move to sit up, but Spencer stops me with a hand on my shoulder.

"They're fine. Ravi and Sam are with them now. Sorrow and Drew needed surgery, but they'll live. Max had to have a few skin grafts from the burns and some stitches." His jaw clenched as he told me this. I don't blame him, what happened there was fucked up. I wouldn't wish this on my worst enemy. I sink back in the bed and let the pain meds lull me to sleep.

The next time I wake up I see her. Xena. My beautiful Xena. Her black hair is pulled up in a tight bun pinned at the nape of her neck. I always loved that hairstyle, especially when I took it down and wrapped my fist in it. She was always in control with her hair like that, but with it down it gave me the power. The power I often craved.

"When we got the call I was so scared," she says when she notices I'm awake.

I shake my head. "No. I'm fine."

She scoffs, "If by fine you mean practically dead, I guess so."

"It's okay, Xe. You know it takes more than a little beating to take me out." I try teasing but her lips pull into a thin line. I gaze at her and notice her ring finger is bare. "Where's your ring?" I ask.

She shakes her head. "I gave it to your mother. I'm sorry, Cade. I can't do this anymore. You put your life in danger all the time. What about my life?"

My mind is reeling at this. What is she even talking about? "What the fuck are you talking about?"

Xena winces, she hates when people curse. She deems it as trashy. And I did my best to never swear in front of her. But what the actual fuck? "I'm sorry, Caden. I met someone else. I just couldn't stand the idea of you never coming home again."

I stared at her for a moment before finding the right words. "So, you cheated on me?"

"Caden," she pleads.

"Answer my goddamn question, Xena. Did you cheat on me?" I demand.

She's silent and when I see her brown eyes fill with tears I already know the truth. "I'm sorry."

A bitter laugh escapes before I can stop it. "No, you're not."

"I am," she whispers.

"If you were sorry you wouldn't have fucking done it!" I shout. "Who was it?"

She shakes her head. "Caden, please, I'm sorry."

"Who was it?"

Swallowing hard, she says, "Louis."

I sat up in the bed then, wincing as pain moved through my body. But I didn't care. "My best friend since middle school, Louis?" Nodding, she stares up at me, pleading with her eyes. Usually I would melt at that, wanting to give her whatever she wanted, but not anymore. No, my heart was shuttering closed, turning to stone.

"Get out."

"Caden, let's talk about this, please. You have to see it from my point of view!" she begs.

"Your point of view? What view is that? A selfish bitch who cheats on her man then comes across the world after he's been tortured and ends it? That fucking view? Fuck you, Xena. Fuck you. I hope you and Louis have a miserable fucking life together," I snap, tears burning in my own eyes. I've spent my life with this woman. From middle school until now when we were nearly thirty and this is how she fucking thanks me? By sleeping with my best friend?

"You don't mean that, Cade," she says, grabbing her throat defensively. God, I hate when she does that. As if she's worried I'll strangle her or some shit. No, I was done, done with the manipulative tactics, the betrayal. I was done with her.

Nodding, I stand. "I do mean it. I mean every fucking word of it." I pull the IV out of my arm, ignoring the blood seeping out, and stalk forward. She shrinks back, but I just move to the door pulling it open forcefully. "Now get the fuck out of my face before I call security," I grit out, my vision blurring from the onslaught of pain. So much pain. I didn't know what was worse, the pain from my battered and bruised body or the pain from my shredded heart. I saw Ravi come down the hall with concern on his face. He sees Xena and me standing, and his eyes widen.

"Caden, you should be in bed," he starts.

I shake my head. "Get her away from me. Now, Ravi. Get her out of my face!" I'm yelling at this point. I've never raised my voice to Xena before, my parents taught me to always respect my partners, but I couldn't help it.

"I need to ask you to leave. He shouldn't be in distress and you're making it worse," Ravi says, blocking Xena's view of me.

"I'm really sorry, Caden," she says, walking out the door.

Leaning my head out, I yell, "Fuck you, bitch!" Ravi turns to me, and I fall into him, sobbing. He tenses for a second and wraps his arm around me, holding me up so I don't fall to the floor. It wasn't the torture and captivity that changed me this day, it was the woman who so cruelly stomped on my heart. Leaving me alone in the darkest point of my life, never to love again. Or so I thought.

Chapter 1

Rory

Water was heavy against my thighs, rushing into the car as it slowly sank to the bottom of the river. I was trapped, drowning not only in river water but sorrow. Sorrow for not telling Caden how I really feel, and for the fact I will never see my friends again. Then I hear it, the maniacal laugh beside me, overpowering the sound of rushing water.

I turn in the seat and see Anthony sitting in his seat laughing his ass off as if our current predicament was something to laugh about.

"You're insane," I gasp out, horrified.

"And you're going to die." He laughs again. "No one is going to save you. Not your silly little friends and not that idiot boyfriend. You had it all when you had me, but you threw it all away, and for what?"

11

I couldn't think about that right now, no, I had to think about surviving.

The car was filling fast, so I did the only thing I could think about doing and unbuckled my seatbelt. The water was ice cold, but I had to ignore the sharp pain as I sank lower into the water. Without sparing Anthony a glance, I take a deep breath and move toward the window. The current was stronger than I thought, but I had only one chance to do this, or I was dead. But Anthony seemed to be anticipating my move because he grabbed my hair as I reached the window. His grip was brutal and yanked strands from my scalp as he pulled me back.

"And just what the fuck do you think you're doing? You think you can get away from me?"

"Let me go!" I all but shout, but he doesn't. Not that I expect him to. Struggling against him, I grip his wrist with one hand and twist my body the opposite way, twisting his wrist as I went. It wasn't enough to break it, but it was enough to hurt him for a moment. Now was my chance! With shaky hands I pushed myself out, letting the strong current pull me out. I was free! The thought was short lived as clarity sank in, reminding me I had to swim to the surface. Pushing myself up towards the surface was harder than I thought. The fact that I had to reach with my hands and kick with my feet was difficult, but I did it. With my lungs protesting every inch of the way.

Panic was setting in as I swam upward and I felt something tug on my foot. The closer I got to the surface the more I was pulled down. Instinctively I knew it was Anthony. He could hold his breath under water for like eleven minutes and he wasted no time bragging about it while we were together, but here I was at least four minutes in and the world around me was going hazy. I was running out of time. That's when my resolve started to hit me, I couldn't go out like this. Not being murdered by my ex-boyfriend. If Delaney could drive with a knife in her stomach, and Caden could survive a week of captivity, then I could survive this swim.

It's shocking to my system leaving me sinking until I force myself to swim up towards the light, but I'm not a strong swimmer. Never have been, and I know when I'm running out of air. I can feel my lungs burning with each burst of energy I use up trying to swim towards the surface. As I break the surface I take a gasping breath, before I'm pulled down into the water again. Water fills my mouth and nose as I'm pulled down by my ankle. I panic, fighting for my life as I kick at whatever has me. My arms are burning as I swim higher and higher until I'm back on the surface coughing, and trying to get the loose tree branch I see. I can hardly breathe as I pull myself out of the water and onto the branch. A part of me hopes Anthony didn't make it, but as I glance into the dark water and see him break the surface I knew I didn't have enough time.

Groaning softly, I push myself up and take off into the woods.

Chapter 2

ONE MONTH *ago*

Caden

Flames burned through the walls as I rushed through the building. This old building was moving ominously as if it was built on a prayer and straw making the flames burn faster than I would've liked. But that didn't stop me from powering through and adrenaline from coursing through me. I lived for this shit, the excitement and energy that runs through my veins as I do something that could potentially kill me but then coming out on top. I knew I was safe; I knew my crew had my back. I trusted them with my life, and they trusted me with theirs.

"You with me, Cade?" Ravi asked, coming up beside me.

Smirking, I nod. "I live for this shit, man." Shaking his head he moves forward while I move in step behind him. I heard it first, the soft yowls of an animal. Almost a whine, but the crackle of the fire muffles it. Hell, I don't even think Ravi hears it.

"Did you hear that?" I ask. Ravi tilts his head to the side to listen then shakes his head. "It's an animal. I think it's trapped." Veering off the mark I moved further into the house. Ravi curses behind me the radio static turning loud in my mask.

"Sato, I'm going to kick your ass."

Chuckling, I move deeper into the building, following the forlorn cries until I find a skinny cat huddled in the corner of a vacant room which the flames were starting to surround. Cursing, I moved closer, taking the ax I held and moving some of the broken wood away, hoping like hell the floor held a little longer. Taking a steady breath, I shuffle closer so I'm close to the cat.

"Hey, buddy," I say hoping it can hear me. The little soot colored cat yowls louder making me wince. "Yeah, I can see how this isn't an ideal day for you. But, I'd really appreciate it if you didn't scream as I try to grab you, okay? Can we do that?"

In response the little beast literally screeches. Okay, so small talk wasn't for him. The floor cracked and I cursed, pouncing forward and grabbing the animal by the scruff and pulling it from behind the wooden beams. It hissed and clawed at my gloved hands, but I paid it no mind as I ducked under the beams that started crashing to the ground.

"Caden, where the fuck are you?" Ravi snapped in my ear. Pulling the cat to my chest I hold it tight.

"Coming in hot, boss man," I say, running down the stairs. I usually would've been cautious, but I was running out of time. "Did you get the woman out?" I ask, breathing heavily.

Ravi sighs. "Yes. She's being transported as we speak. Hurry the fuck up. We are hosing as much as we can to no avail." Just as he finishes his sentence I burst out of the building nearly falling on my ass. Panting for breath I held up the cat to show Ravi, who took a step back as if it would attack him.

Then I remembered what happened a few months ago and had to stifle my laughter. He narrowed his eyes at me, then shook his head. "Get it some oxygen or something."

Saluting him sarcastically, I made my way to the truck where some of the others stood hosing down the building. "Is that a cat?" Logans, a gangly new hire, asked. I looked down at the bundle in my arms, noticing how it no longer struggled against me and sat silently, its small sides heaving for breath. Cursing, I moved past the kid and got to an EMT where I could put an oxygen mask on its face. Pushing my own hat off my head I shake out my sweat slicked hair and grab the closest tank and mask.

Pressing the mask to the little face I counted silently to myself before pulling it away and pressing my fingers to the tiny fluttering pulse. "Hell," I mutter. I couldn't let the cat die now. Not after we struggled to get it out of the building. Moving the mask back to its face I counted again. I don't know how long I stand there before the cat draws in a big, labored breath, letting me know it was slowly getting the hang of breathing. Relief swept through me. Why I cared so much about a stray cat, I didn't know, but hearing those yowls reminded me too much of my own time trapped and feeling hopeless. Thinking I was about to die in one of the worst ways possible. I couldn't let that happen to an innocent animal. I sit with the cat, rubbing its singed fur and murmuring words of encouragement to it as the rest of the crew contains the fire. It was mid-September and the weather was cooling off a little bit making it a habitual time for homeless people to find shelter in abandoned buildings hoping to stay warm in the winter months.

The only issue is some of them start little fires in the old, abandoned buildings. So, mix old, abandoned buildings with a fire and you got the kindling for a recipe for disaster. Exhibit A: the old schoolhouse on the outskirts of Houston. A hand settles on my shoulder making me tense until I see Ravi.

"We can call it a day. Get the cat to a vet or something. Nirvana wants to go help out at the bakery and, well, since you wanted to play hero, you can come with us. Since you're doing good deeds and all." Scoffing, I scooped the cat up in my arms and make my way to the truck.

"Does she still feel guilty?" I ask, hefting myself up into the back. Ravi sighed, settling in beside me. His girlfriend, Nirvana went through a lot a few months ago. So many secrets came out after her sister's death, on top of Nirvana being bipolar and not taking care of herself. So, in the midst of that, Layla put off her grand opening and Nirvana has been working overtime to help Layla out at the bakery while also trying to open her own non-profit that helps kids who are part of the LGBTQ+ community to feel safer.

Staring out the window he nods. "She blames herself for the push back dates."

I tsk under my breath, running my thumb over the cat's head. "That's ridiculous. She had no control over what happened. Layla would rather be there for her friend than a bakery. Nirvana needed them."

I can still remember the sound of her screams. That raw anguish and pain was something I knew. I've seen it before. But then watching Ravi hold her after she had to be physically pried from her lifeless sister's body... Shaking my head, I sigh. That was something altogether different. "What time?" I ask.

Glancing at the time on the truck he says, "Five thirty?" That gave me two hours. I could make it to the clinic, drop the cat off, and then get home to shower. Nodding in agreement I lean my head back, trying to erase the sounds of screams from my head and the smell of death from my nose.

Finally leaving the station, I take my duffle bag and my little rescue and make my way to my car, a 1973 second generation Camaro, and deposit my bag before climbing into the driver's seat. The cat took it upon itself to claw its way up my torso and sit perched on my shoulder, rubbing against my neck. The fur on its back was charred and smelled strongly of smoke. Its breathing wasn't as perfect as I'd like, but I didn't hear wheezing so that should be a good sign. I picked up my phone and searched for the closest vet clinic to my house and plugged the directions into the GPS. After ten minutes I was parked outside the clinic.

"All right let's go see if you're okay. I don't even know what you are yet, but don't worry I'm sure they'll find out. I don't know you like that and they are professionals so it won't be as weird. Think of it as a yearly physical. Except you were almost charred to a crisp." I had no idea why I was talking to a fucking cat, maybe I finally lost my mind. Too many sleepless nights and one too many fires going to my head making me slowly lose brain cells.

Sighing, I climb out of the car and tug the animal off my shoulder and make my way inside. The receptionist looked up at me and smiled. She was younger than me by a couple years with bright green eyes and blonde hair. She looked me over head to toe and her eyes lit with interest. Making my way to the counter I paste on a smile.

"Hi. Um, I found this little guy in a fire, and I need to make sure it won't have serious issues. I gave it some oxygen because it wasn't breathing very well. It's a stray. This is the closest vet clinic I can find that takes walk-ins."

The receptionist, who's nametag said, Nancy, nods and smiles. "Just sign in. Dr. Sanderson should be done in a minute. I can take him on back and give you a call whenever we're finished."

Nodding, I quickly signed in and put my information on the sheet watching as the cat was taken from my view. For some unexplainable reason panic seized me at the thought of the little creature being out of my line of sight. Forcing a deep breath, I turn on my heel and head home to shower and change clothes.

Chapter 3

RORY

Turning onto the busy road I sigh, flexing my hands then proceeding to shake them. All day they've been numb as if I put them in a freezer or sat on them for too long. Not to mention this constant headache I've had. On top of the fact that I was irritable as hell. But I promised Layla I'd come help at her bakery today and I planned to keep that promise. Even if I'd rather be home curled up in bed with an ice pack on my head and a heated blanket wrapped around me. Sighing wistfully I pull into a spot in front of the shop and park.

I shiver as I open the car door, pulling my coat closer to my body. I hurried to the shop and pulled open the door where I heard Nirvana and Ravi bickering already.

"It doesn't go there," she says, pointing at the corner of the room as Caden and Ravi move an old jukebox, attempting to follow Nirvana's directions. Huffing in irritation she points again. "There, you've got to move it to my left, not your left."

Ravi drops his side, and Caden almost topples over while glaring at his friend. "Pixie, we've moved this damn thing six times."

Nirvana glared at him with blazing blue eyes, and I decided to cut in, "Vana, honey, what's going on? It was fine where it was."

She shrugs. "They're not doing it right. Layla's shop has to be perfect." Stopping next to her I study her drawn features. These last few months have been hard on her, and I know she feels guilty and blames herself for the shop not opening. Even though we've all told her it isn't her fault.

"How about if I do it? Would that help?" Nirvana looked up at me, her eyes narrowing. The men stood taller, their chests puffed out. As if they were offended by the mere suggestion.

"We can do it just fine. We just need a break is all," Ravi said, dropping a hand to Nirvana's shoulder and rubbing gently.

She shakes her head and says, "We have to help her get it up and running soon or she'll lose this place before it even gets started."

Tsking, I step towards her. "She's not going to lose this spot, Vana. She has iron clad contracts that won't allow her to be kicked out. Everything is fine. Okay?"

Inhaling deeply, she nods. "Okay." Looking up at Ravi she grins and says, "It was still on my left not yours." He shakes his head but his own little smile peeks through as he wraps an arm around her shoulders and moves her towards the display case, leaving me alone with Caden. Feeling awkward, I focus my gaze on the jukebox. It still feels a bit weird being around them. First there was Delaney falling for Sorrow, and now

Nirvana with Ravi. Not that it bothered me. Both women deserved to be loved as fiercely as these men loved them. I was happy for them. But it was strange integrating from the little family we had to include them and the other men.

Chancing a glance at Caden, I study him. He was taller than many men I knew, including the man I was seeing. His hair was thick and a dark brown almost black. His skin was golden and covered in black ink, from his neck down to his hands. As if he could feel me looking at him he looked up from his phone, his dark brown eyes settling on me. He smiles, showing straight white teeth and a small dimple on his cheek. I feel myself blush and nearly curse. I was not checking him out. Nope. He may be attractive, I mean I wasn't daft enough to think otherwise. Plus, I was seeing someone. I was only looking so intently because I've never truly been alone with him before.

Sliding his phone in his pocket, he crosses his arms over his muscular chest. Making the fabric of his black sweater stretch over the taut muscles. Swallowing hard, I took a step back.

"Hey Ro Ro. I didn't know you were coming today." The way he said it with an easy smile had my heart turning and butterflies erupting in my stomach.

Forcing my own smile, I reply, "Yeah, I made a promise."

He nods in understanding and leans against the jukebox. "I got roped in. I was told there would be food, but it seems as if I was lied to."

He pouts dramatically and it surprises a laugh out of me. "Food usually comes after the work is completed." The numbness enters my hands again. With irritation I shake them out.

Caden stares at me. "Are you okay?"

I nod, fighting off a sudden wave of dizziness that suddenly plagued me. "Yeah. I just had a long day," I mutter.

He hums under his breath, never taking his eyes off me. I turn away, uncomfortable with how long he stared. My phone buzzed in my pocket making me breathe a sigh of relief for the distraction. Pulling my phone from my coat I saw a message from Anthony about a case he wanted me to prepare questions for and how he couldn't meet me for dinner.

A pang of longing went through me. These last few weeks he'd been more distant than usual only texting or calling for work... or a quick fuck in his office between classes. Not even a good fuck, at least not anymore. He was currently my professor for my pre law class, the last class I need to graduate from law school. I've done it all, I finished college at a four-year university getting a bachelors in political science and government. In high school I took a course that allowed me to get an associates degree as a paralegal at the local community college, which was where I met Anthony for the first time. He was the TA there working through his own law studies and now here I was. His student... again. And working under him as a paralegal assistant. I wasn't even a normal paralegal. I was the assistant. The one who got coffee while doing most of the work.

Sighing, I didn't respond. It didn't matter if I did or not. He knew I'd get it done even if that meant losing sleep. Which was most nights. Leaning against the jukebox I press my head against the cold glass, letting it soothe some of the ache that was continuing to build. That tension that felt like it was seconds from snapping.

Closing my eyes, I take a deep breath. It didn't work though, dizziness hit me swiftly and with a vengeance until I was sinking to the ground. Or I would have if strong arms hadn't caught me. Then there was nothing. Just complete darkness.

Chapter 4

CADEN

I glance over at Rory from the side of my eye, watching as she puts her head against the glass of the jukebox. Her face was oddly pale considering her normally dark complexion. Her normally bronze brown skin was almost gray, her honey brown and moss green hazel eyes were glazed over with discomfort, and she shook her hands four times without even noticing.

Her satin black curls were piled on top of her head out of her face. Then I see her eyes roll back in her head and she starts to fall forward. Cursing, I leap forward and catch her before she can hit the checkered floor.

"Fuck," I mutter, tapping her cheek lightly. "Rory, wake up." I press my fingers to her pulse and find that it's steady, a little fast but nothing too concerning. "Shit. Ravi!" I called. Not even wanting to know where those two wandered off to. The sound of footsteps drew my attention as Ravi came into view, his brows furrowed.

He gazed at me then Rory on the floor and cursed. "What the hell happened?" he asked.

"I don't know. One minute she was leaning against the jukebox the next she was fainting," I say.

The shop door opened, and a long-suffering sigh sounded behind us. "What the hell happened?" Drew repeated as he came inside the bakery. His gruff voice was a welcome sound at that moment.

"Fainted," I said, lifting Rory into my arms and moving towards the back of the shop towards Layla's office. There was a worn leather couch there that I gently laid her on.

"How long has she been out?" Drew asks, coming in with a black bag.

I mentally count in my head and reply, "No longer than two or three minutes."

He nods, setting the bag on the floor. He pulls out a little bottle, opens it, then wafted it under Rory's nose. She comes to quickly, swatting at his hand. "What the hell?"

Glancing around her she sees the three of us and her eyes widen. "I've seen this scene before and I wasn't impressed," she mutters. My mouth twitches in amusement as she glances around herself in confusion.

"You fainted," I say and offer my hand. She takes it and I pull her up to sit.

Pressing the heel of her hand to her head, she winces. "Damn. That's embarrassing."

Leaning back, Drew stares at her with impassive eyes. "How do you feel?"

"Like bulls are running through my brain using my skull as a battering ram."

He nods and takes out a blood pressure cuff, lifts the sleeve of her coat up, and wraps it around her small bicep. The sound of the machine was loud in the tiny office as we waited for the machine to read her blood pressure. It read

140/90. My brows furrow as I watch her shake her hand and flex her fingers.

"Are your fingers numb?" I ask.

She shakes her head. "Tingly."

Drew searches his bag again and pulls out a smaller black bag. "When's the last time you ate or drank anything, Rory?" he asks, setting up a glucose test strip.

Rory shrugs. "I don't know. This morning, I think."

Taking her hand in his, Drew uses an alcohol wipe on her index finger before pricking it with a needle. Hissing out a breath, she says, "Warn a girl first."

"It was a little poke," he says and sighs, putting the strip to her finger letting it read her sugar levels. The machine beeps and Drew stares at it for a second then at Rory. "Your sugar is at 50."

Rory runs a shaky hand over her jean clad leg and asks, "Is that bad?"

Drew stares back at her stunned. "Well, it's not good. When's the last time you went to the doctor?"

She shrugs. "I don't know." She takes her phone out of her pocket and scrolls through her notes app. "Um, four years ago," she says and nods. "Yeah. Four years ago. I had my first pap smear."

We're silent for a moment, and she looks at us with wide eyes. "What? I don't have a lot of time."

Drew sighs. "You are supposed to get a pap smear when you turn twenty-one and then physicals every year. A pap is every three years. Are you sexually active at all? Are you caught up on vaccines?"

Rory shrugs, turning a slight crimson. "I'm fine. And yes, but with one person. Just one."

She goes to stand but wobbles on her feet. Placing a hand on her shoulder I push her back down onto the couch. Not that it took much effort when she was so weak.

Sighing, Drew looks at Ravi. "Can you go find an orange juice and a cookie or something?" Ravi nods and leaves the office.

"I think I'm just tired really," she says.

Drew stands. "You'll make an appointment with a primary doctor tomorrow." It's a demand nothing less.

Rory's eyes go to Drew. "I don't have one."

Sighing in exasperation, Drew said, "Have none of you heard of going to the doctor? Is that just not a thing you do? Jesus Christ. You're like grown toddlers."

Rory shrugs. "Not everyone can afford to go to the doctor. Or they just don't take you seriously."

Drew sighs. "I have a doctor I can send you to. But you have to go. And you have to find your own gynecologist, there's only so many I know." My eyes widened at the offer. I've known Drew a long time and have never seen him so bent out of shape for people before. Irritated, yes. Pissed off, of course. But caring? Never. Not really.

She swallows hard. "Okay. Thank you."

He grunts and drops the kit in her lap. "Check your sugars when you wake up and after you eat. Then before lunch and dinner then after. Then one last time before bed. You can find strips at any drug store, but it has to be the exact one." Turning to me he sends me a pointed look and says, "You stay with her and make sure she checks her levels after thirty minutes." Pinning her with one last stare he says, "I mean it, Rory."

She nods at him. Trying not to laugh, I sit on the couch staring at Drew as he packs his bags muttering about irate women. After he leaves Rory turns to me and says, "He should work on his bedside manners."

I huff out a laugh and reply, "That's as polite as he can get I'm afraid."

Sighing, she leans her head back. "Figures." We sit in

relative silence, then the door opens, and Ravi walks in with a small shopping bag.

He drops it on my lap and says, "Nirvana said these were your favorite." With that he turns and leaves the office, closing the door behind him. Opening the bag, I pull out a pack of Chips aHoy Crunchy and a bottle of orange juice.

"Soft ones are better," I say, twisting off the top and handing it to her.

Rory scoffs, taking small sips before opening the small box and offering me one. I shake my head and lean back watching her. "Everyone knows the crunchy ones are better. Especially if you dip them in milk."

"I hate to disagree with you, but I disagree with you. Chewy is way better. They're softer and soak up more."

Chewing thoughtfully, she shrugs and says, "I have this feeling you're not all that mad about disagreeing."

I laugh at that. "Nah, I'm not. Because everyone knows it's chewy."

Rolling her eyes she sets her cookies down. "Nope. Crunchy. The milk makes them soft, that's the point of a cookie."

"Why drown them to make them soft when you can already get the soft ones?" I ask.

Rory sputters for a second then narrows her eyes at me. "Because that's silly." She bites the cookie and glares at me. "No one wants a soggy cookie. Crunchy is a perfect balance with the milk and if you dunk a soft cookie all you get is wet paper in your mouth."

I stared at her for a moment and then threw my head back and laugh. "Wet paper?"

Nodding solemnly, she finishes her snack and juice and sits back. "Have you ever felt paper when it's wet? It's honestly the worst feeling in the world. I can't stand it."

"I can imagine."

Tilting her head back she stares at the ceiling sighing softly. "What does low sugar imply?"

I stare at her for a moment then shrug. "It can mean a lot of things. Not enough nutrients from lack of eating. Unhealthy lifestyle leading to diabetes. It could be hereditary. Or it can be a hormonal thing. It's not the end of the world if you do have it. It's manageable. But I'm not a doctor so I can't tell you for certain until you get labs done and research it."

Sighing again she looks at me. "It sounds like the end of the world to a woman."

"Why?"

Shrugging, she replies, "Because I'm only twenty-eight and shouldn't be dealing with this. I watch my weight, I exercise… sometimes. I don't indulge in too much unhealthy food. I don't know. It feels like I did something wrong."

Leaning forward I touch her hand softly, ignoring the slight heat I feel. "It's not the end of the world. It'll be okay. Just try not to Google things. It makes it worse."

Slowly moving my hand away from her, I forced a smile. I need to change the subject, so she doesn't overthink too much. "How's school?"

Groaning, she sits forward. "Dammit. I forgot I have to pick Rio up from school." She goes to stand but I stop her with a hand on her wrist. She stares down at me and arches a brow.

"You can't drive. You just fainted."

Shaking her head, she mutters, "I have no one else to pick him up."

Cursing, I grab the trash and glucose kit. "I'll drive. You can sit in the passenger's seat."

"Caden, that's not—" I narrow my eyes at her, and she stops.

Satisfaction burned through me as she nodded. I'm not

even sure why I want to make sure she's okay, but I know I want to. Smiling, I throw an arm over her shoulders. "Good. Now, let's go. Or your brother is going to be stranded."

Chapter 5

RORY

Letting Caden lead me from the bakery is awkward. Not that I mind being under his arm. I don't. But I do feel odd because I am trying to hold my breath to ignore his spiced lemons and honey scent. It's warm and welcoming, but manly at the same time. It was difficult to explain, and I really wanted to lean into him and inhale. But here I was, holding my breath as he led me to a cherry red Camaro. He opens the door for me and helps me into the leather seats.

"You all right?" he asks, setting the bag in my lap.

I nod and take a breath as I clumsily fiddle with the seat belt. My hands were still tingling and shaking making it more difficult to grab the belt. Tsking, Caden ducks his head into the car and takes the belt from me. He leans over me and buckles it before grabbing the top and tightening it around my chest, making me suck in a sharp breath. His fingers brush against the side of my neck, sending heat pulsing through me.

"Good?" he asks, his voice deeper and husky.

"Yes," I say on a breath. He smiles at me, flashing perfect white teeth before he eases away and closes the door. I watched as he walked to the driver's side of the car and saw him responding to someone. Turning in the seat I see Ravi standing outside talking to him. Caden flips him off and climbs into the car, locking me inside with him.

"What was that about?" I ask.

Caden starts the car, letting it roar to life before he peels out onto the road. "Oh, Ravi was telling me to drive carefully," Caden replies and grins at me, grabbing the gear shift.

"I like this car," I mutter, running my fingers over the soft black leather.

Caden grins. "Thanks. I rebuilt it a few years ago. Gave it some modern touches and reupholstered the seats. Now she drives a lot better."

He sounded proud of it and a small smile spread on my face. It was cute seeing him talk about his car. But then my gaze went to his hands, to the tattoos there. I watched the way his fingers flexed whenever he shifted gears or when he turned the wheel. It sent a wave of desire through me that I automatically shut down. No. I can't have these thoughts. No.

"Where to Ro Ro?" he asks, drawing me from my less than innocent thoughts. Clearing my throat, I gave him the address to my brother's school. We sit in comfortable silence until we get to the school. Caden parks in the empty lot and I sigh when I don't see Rio. "Is he here?"

I nod. "Yes. I'm only ten minutes late," I mutter. I open the door and stick my head out staring out at the empty school until I see movement. Narrowing my eyes, I see my brother and a girl making out against the building. I whistle loudly drawing his attention. "*Amonos,* Rio," I snapped.

Rio glares at me and pulls away from the girl, straightens

his clothes and helps her straighten herself out before walking her to her green Honda Civic. I can see Caden trying not to laugh, and I glare at him. "Don't you dare laugh."

Caden shrugs. "I mean, he's a teenager."

Caden climbs out of the car and pushes his seat forward for Rio to get in the back. He immediately stared at me and started arguing with me. "You're so embarrassing, Rory. She's never going to talk to me again."

"You're at school. You come here to learn not to stick your tongue down a girl's throat." I turn and glare at him. "You better have been respectful, Rio, or I swear I'll come back there and teach you some manners."

He rolls his eyes. "Please. You were late, I should tell *mamá.*"

Caden doesn't start the car right away, but turns to my brother, his eyes darkening. "Your sister fainted. That's why she's late."

Rio stares at me in horror. "*¿Estás bien?*"

"*Sí.* I'm fine, Rio. Let's just get you home."

Rio didn't look convinced, but he stopped arguing and buckled up. I thought it was going to be a quiet drive but, of course, Rio had other ideas. Leaning forward Rio stared at Caden. "I'm Rio. Who the hell are you?"

Gasping in horror, I turned in my seat. "Rio!"

Caden just laughs. "It's fine. I'm Caden Sato. Ravi and Sorrow's friend."

Rio's brows furrow before he snaps his fingers. "You were there when they were destroying that house. Vana's boyfriend, right?"

Caden nods. "The very same."

Rio whistles. "I still can't believe he jumped through a fire to save her. Shit's badass."

"Rio, language," I admonished.

"What? It's just us." Rio smiles at me and leans closer. "So, Caden what do you do?"

Caden glances at me and I mouth *sorry* to him but he just chuckles under his breath. "I'm a retired pararescue. Now I work as a firefighter."

Rio leans forward again. "That's so cool. Did you used to go into war? Did you rescue anyone? What was it like?"

"Rio."

"Rory," he counters. Rolling my eyes, I point towards our exit.

Caden takes it and answers Rio's questions. "I did rescue people. It was intense at times."

I glance at him, and I see the way he swallows hard. I know he was one of the four who were captured before being saved and I couldn't imagine what that was like for him and the others. Steering the questions away from pararescue, I asked, "What's it like as a firefighter?"

He gazes at me with a small smile of thanks on his face. "It has its moments. Today during training I rescued a cat. Poor thing was singed to hell."

Rio grimaces. "Is it all right?"

Caden nods. "A vet currently has it. Hopefully I'll hear back soon. But it just happened today so it may be a few days."

Rio nods and turns to me. "Rory loves cats. She had this really fat one once upon a time, named him Eggnog."

I felt my face heat up as I glared at my little brother. "He was shaped like an egg. Calling him just egg felt mean." Caden laughed at my expense and Rio joined him.

Rolling my eyes, I crossed my arms over my chest trying to be mad, but a small smile was tilting up my face. "Oh, it's there." Caden pulled up to my parents' moderate sized house where my brothers Nico and Marco were sitting and talking while drinking a beer. Watching the car as Caden pulled in.

"They don't look happy," Rio said in a whisper.

I shook my head. "I was late, they probably thought you were kidnapped or something."

Rio reared back and glared at me. "Me? Kidnapped? Please, Rory. If anyone were to get kidnapped out of any of us it's you."

I gasped. "I would not."

"You so would. A kid could come up to you crying and you would go with them willingly."

"Get out of the car, Rio."

Rio laughs, grabbing his bag and Caden gets out of the car and moves the seat up so he can climb out. "Thanks. It was nice to officially meet you, Caden."

"You too, Rio," Caden said.

Caden moved his seat back and sat down staring at me. Not caring that my three brothers were watching us, or that my parents came out, watching as well. "I should be going," I mutter, my hand going to the handle.

He shakes his head, his black hair falling into impossibly dark eyes, fanned by dark lashes. "Not until I check to make sure your sugars are at a better level."

I started to protest, but he has the kit out of my lap and is already setting things up. "Your brother is quite the character," he says conversationally.

"They all are," I agree, watching as he rips open the alcohol wipe with his teeth. Swallowing, I held my hand out to him. Uncaring that my entire family is watching me right now. His touch is gentle and sure, making it easier to let him prick my finger. With a steady hand he brings the monitor to my hand and lets the strip collect the blood before pressing the wipe to the small drop.

"One seventy. It's a little high but better than before. Drink some water, eat some, and get some rest. Don't forget what Drew said."

I nod, taking the kit. "Thank you."

Caden smiles easily at me. "No need to thank me, Ro Ro. It's what friends are for. Just make sure you're careful."

"I will. Good luck with your cat."

He laughs. "I'm sure it'll be okay." I smiled at him and gathered my bag of trash and the kit before climbing out of the car, finally steady on my feet. I walk towards my family and sigh when I see them eyeing me with different looks of curiosity and overprotectiveness.

"Hello to you, too," I mutter sarcastically.

My mother's eyes drift to the car and as Caden backs away, she lifts her hand, stopping him. Panicked, I whipped my head towards her. "*Mamá.* What are you doing?"

"I'm inviting your friend in for dinner, *mija,*" she says casually, brushing her long black and silver hair from her face, smiling widely at me.

I glance at my dad with wide pleading eyes. "Dad, you have to stop her."

He wipes a dark hand down his face, trying not to laugh, I can tell. "I'm sorry, honey. But you know once your mother has an idea in her head she just goes with it." My mom waves her hand and I wince as the car door opens.

I glare at my brothers, but their eyes are on Caden as he walks towards us as if he has not a care in the world. I glance up at the darkening sky, praying that the ground opens up and swallows me whole.

Chapter 6

CADEN

I was pulling away as I saw Rory's mother wave at me, making me stop the car. I glance at Rory and I see her mother smile, and motion me forward. Curious, I pulled back into the driveway and turned off my car before climbing out and walking up to the group. Rory looks up at the sky and mutters under her breath making me want to laugh.

"Good evening," I say.

An older version of Rory steps forward, smiling widely. "Hello. Welcome to our home. I didn't realize Rory had other friends outside of the girls."

Arching an eyebrow at her, I turn to Rory who mutters something in Spanish. "*Mamá,* you know that's not true." Grimacing she turns to me, and starts introductions, "Um, Caden, this is my mother, Maria and my father, Deon. These are my brothers, Nico and Marco. This is Caden." I shake their hands, meeting their eyes as they study me, as if gauging my intentions towards their sister and daughter.

"It's nice to meet you all," I reply with an easy smile.

Maria smiled wide. "Would you like to stay for dinner? I made pozole."

"I'm sure Caden has things to do," Rory hedged, her hazel eyes pleading.

A gentleman would've followed her lead. I wasn't a gentleman, far from it. So, I shook my head. "Dinner sounds good."

Rory's eyes widened, her gaze strayed to mine and narrowed, and through gritted teeth she responded, "Great." Turning on her heel she walked into the house, leaving the scent of vanilla and lavender in her wake.

Rio stepped beside me. "You're in for a real treat."

Maria shook her head. "Come come, Caden. I hope you don't mind spicy food."

I shake my head. "Not at all. It's my favorite."

I follow them into the house and as soon as I step inside my nose is assaulted with the smell of spices. My stomach grumbles with hunger; but my eyes wandered through the home. The house was bigger on the inside than I thought it would be. Filled with the memories of their family. A large red couch sat backed against the wall, sitting directly in front of a TV. In the center of the room, a soft brown colored coffee table sat atop a colorful rug. I turned my back to the living room, looking at the walls lined in years of framed memories. As my eyes trailed and analyzed all of those pictures, my gaze was snagged on a picture of a baby. Walking closer I see that the tiny baby is Rory. She was wearing a white dress with a beautiful floral pattern, and what looked like hand-woven lace if I had to guess. Atop her small head, she wore a red flower.

Footsteps sounded behind me, drawing my attention.

"Ahh, that's Rory when she was turning one. It's called a *huipil*, a traditional garment. They're worn on special occasions, to me her birth was the occasion," Maria says, a smile evident in her voice. I glance at the picture seeing all the people surrounding behind her and smile.

"We have something similar in our culture. A kimono. But there's different types worn for different celebrations," I explain.

"What is your culture if you don't mind me asking?"

Smiling, I respond, "I don't mind. I'm Japanese."

Maria nods, smiling back at me. "Beautiful culture."

"As is yours. So many beautiful colors and language."

Maria hums under her breath and points at another family picture, "Deon's family is different. A mix of cultures. Some of his family comes from the Irish, while others are of Native descent. His mother's side is from the Congo, Deon is first generation American like my children."

"My family as well." I pause, "Well, my father is anyway. He is from the Tohoku region. Same as my mother, but her family moved to the states when she was around ten."

"Are they in Texas?"

Shaking my head, I turn to her. "No, ma'am. They live in California."

"Dinner is ready," Rory calls out, stopping our conversation.

Maria tsks but smiles fondly at her daughter. "*Mija*, did you get out the toppings?"

Rory nods. "Of course." Ducking her head back into what I presume is the kitchen, I follow after her mother.

Maria leads me towards the dining room and motions me to sit in the seat next to Rory and Nico. "So, Caden, what is it you do?" Deon asks as Maria dishes out a delicious smelling stew into the bowls.

"He's in pararescue and a firefighter!" Rio pipes in

before I can say anything. Not that I mind. The kid seemed excited, and I didn't mind him answering. In all honesty, talking of my time in the service made my skin break out in a cold sweat. It made the tattoo on my back burn and breathing next to impossible.

"Firefighter?" Marco says, his deep voice silencing the room. I glance at him, and he regards me with dark eyes.

"Yep," I say, staring at him.

"Why'd you leave pararescue?" Nico adds on.

Rory shifts beside me, grabbing a plate of garnish. "Here. Put this on top. It's good, I swear." Taking the plate, I stared at her bowl and copied what she put in it before passing it to Nico who watched me with the same intensity. It felt like an interview of some kind. Not that I wasn't used to it.

Xena's brothers had done the same, only I'm not seeing Rory romantically. In fact, I should've taken her out to eat, but for some reason I wanted to see her squirm. Well, how the tables have turned. Not that I have anyone to blame but myself and my cocky ass attitude. Now I know for next time.

Clearing my throat I say, "My contract was up." Not a lie. Technically it was up, but at the time we all discussed signing on again. Wanting to help people and serve our country. That was until that last mission that left us all fucked up. Hell, my hand was busted up so bad I still struggle with pain in it. Not that I'd tell anyone. The scars were still on them, covered by black ink that gave me the illusion of them being gone. As if that would wipe away the memories.

But they didn't. "How long were you serving?" Deon asks.

"I did a six-year contract at first, then signed on to another six-year contract, so twelve altogether. I went in when I was nineteen."

Maria tilts her head and asks, "How long have you been out?"

"Five years almost," I say.

Rory looks over at me, her dark brow raised. "Damn, I didn't think you were that old."

I stared at her for a moment then laugh. "I'll take that as a compliment."

She snorts. "Don't go getting a big head now. Then you'll rival Marco's."

Offended, Marco threw a radish at her. "Hey. It's not like it's any less bigger than yours."

Rolling her eyes, she took the radish and ate it, staring at her brother. "It is not. My head is full of knowledge. That's why it's big, it has to make room for my brain."

Marco scoffs, "Liar."

Rory shrugs. "Whatever you say, *hermano.*"

I glance at Rory, grateful for her taking the questions away from me. Redirecting it to something else. She meets my gaze briefly and nods towards my bowl. I look down and dig in, letting the spices coat my tongue. The flavor was something I've never tasted before, and it was delicious. We ate in comfortable silence with some bickering from the siblings before we finished dinner. Rory stands and grabs my bowl before I can offer to help. Her and Maria leave the dining room leaving me alone with the men.

"What are your intentions with my sister?" Marco asks, after they are out of ear shot.

I turn to the man, meeting his eyes head on. "We're just friends. She wasn't feeling well earlier when she had to pick up Rio from school, so I offered to bring her to get him and bring her home."

They watched me intently, as if trying to see if what I said was true. It was. I wasn't one to date. I slept with a woman once or twice then moved on. I didn't do relationships. Not anymore, nor will I ever again. That ship has sailed along with the remnants of my heart that Xena shattered.

Chapter 7

RORY

I rinsed out the bowls and handed them to my mom to put in the dishwasher before wiping down the counters. "Caden seems nice," *Mamá* hedges after working in silence so long.

Sighing, I turn to look at her. "We're friends. That's all." Even that was debatable. We were acquaintances to the highest degree. These last few months have been crazy, dealing with everything with Nirvana. We haven't had a moment's peace. In fact, I don't even think as a collective we even knew the meaning of peace. Hell, I worked in one of the most demanding fields there was, on top of law school. There was no time for me to have peace. That just simply didn't exist in my world.

"I'm going out of town in a few weeks," I say, changing the topic.

Mamá glanced at me. "Where are you going?"

"There's this networking event for the office. It's their way to discuss cases, education, and relax at a nice hotel." I put the lid back on the pot and turned the stove off. "It's good to go because I can meet new people. I graduate in June so it's the best thing I can do."

She nods, twisting the towel in her hand. "Do you need me to water your plants? Or your brothers?"

I smile. "No, it's only for two days. I'll take care of everything before I go. I do have to go though. Maybe Caden will bring me to get my car, I have a lot of work to do tonight. I'll be over this weekend for Aunt Frida's birthday."

Wrinkling her nose she nods. "Yes. I forgot your father's sister was coming this weekend. You should invite your friends. Maybe it'll do them some good after everything with Vana." I nod. My mother would often be the girls go-to when they had no one else. Especially Delaney and Nirvana because they oftentimes didn't have their own mothers to rely on. Between her and Louise they raised us as best as they could.

A slight knock on the wall distracted me as Caden came into view. "I'm sorry to interrupt but I've got to get going. Thank you so much for dinner. It was amazing."

Mamá beamed up at him. "Thank you. Your company was welcome. I hope to see you soon."

Caden smiled at her and nodded his head in agreement before turning to me. "Would you like me to drop you off at your car?"

I could tell he wanted to make sure I wasn't going to faint at the wheel. I felt a lot better, still tired, but I knew I could drive home. "I'd appreciate it. Thank you." I hugged my mom and kissed her cheek before moving out of the kitchen towards the living room where my dad and brothers were sitting watching TV and laughing.

"I'll see you this weekend," I call out, grabbing the bag I brought inside.

Dad stands with a grunt; I don't even think it hurts to

stand it's just something he's always done that makes me smile. "Getting old on me," I comment, walking into his outstretched arms. Dad's arms wrapped around me in a tight embrace as he whispered in my ear, "Caden seems like a great guy."

"He's a good friend," I say emphasizing the word friend. Dad laughs as he lets me go as Caden walks into the room. "Ready?" he asks. Nodding, I follow him out to his car. He moves to the passenger's side and unlocks it first, opening it for me so I could slip inside.

I thank him and settle into the seat as my mom comes outside with a grocery bag and stops Caden. She holds it out with a smile. Taking it graciously, Caden smiles back at her and bows his head slightly. I swear my mother swoons a little bit as Caden walks to his side of the car and climbs in.

"Leftovers?" I guess.

He nods and carefully sets it in the back before buckling up and starting the car. "It's been a while since I've had a home cooked meal I didn't make."

I stare at him as he pulls away from the driveway. It was dark now so I couldn't really make out his features other than the shadows I saw when we passed a streetlight. He looked relaxed but I saw his jaw tighten slightly. "I'm sorry they pressed you about your work."

He hums under his breath. Keeping careful attention on the road. His hands clenched on the gear shift and steering wheel before he answered, "It's okay. They didn't know. Thank you for redirecting the questions. It was becoming... too much."

I turned away from him, taking a breath. "I understand. They aren't usually so intrusive." Not normally at least.

Caden laughed softly, the sound husky and deep. "They are protective. They asked me what my intentions were with you."

Groaning, I cover my face with my hands. "Oh God. I'm so sorry." I could die of embarrassment. I was going to kick their asses.

Laughing harder now, Caden turns onto the street where the bakery was. "I think it's nice. I've done that with guys my sisters have brought home."

Turning to glare at him, I huff out a breath and ask, "Why do guys do that? What's the point?"

After parking he turns to me and explains, "We have to know the women in our lives are taken care of. It's practically a law."

"It is not."

He nods solemnly. "It is. We get the rulebook when we're born."

I grin at him and climb out of the car with him following after me. "They need to redo it because you all act like cavemen." My gaze goes to the bakery, and I see people inside. "What's going on?"

Caden glances at the window. "Oh, Spencer's high school friend came to visit."

My brows furrowed. "I didn't realize he had other friends."

That makes Caden laugh, tossing his arm over my shoulders he leads me forward. "Now who's casting stones?" he comments, making me remember my mother's own comment about my friends.

"Touché," I say. We move up to the bakery and Caden opens the door letting me enter first. All eyes turn to us, and I swear my face turns bright red as if I did something wrong.

Nirvana moves towards me, her blue eyes worried. "Are you feeling better?"

I nod. "Of course. Just a bit tired, nothing more." My gaze moves over the room landing on a tall man with steel gray eyes and a neatly trimmed beard. His dark black hair was styled neatly on his head and his arms were covered with a multitude of tattoos and scars I could easily see.

"Right," Nirvana whispers beside me.

I turned to her. "What's his name?" Moving deeper into the store I stop beside Delaney and Ophelia who stood to the side while the men talked. I watch as Caden joins them. Spencer introduces them and the two shake hands talking as if they've known each other their entire lives. Layla slides up to me and hands me a steaming cup of tea.

"That's Elijah, Spencer's best friend from high school," Ophelia says. We stand off to the side watching the men as they talk, all holding coffee cups I didn't notice they had until Spencer hands one off to Caden.

Wanting to keep myself busy I take a tentative sip of my tea, my eyes on them. But my gaze somehow falls on Caden again. Taking in every inch of him. The way his black tattoos are more pronounced on his olive skin, the way his long fingers grip the cup he's holding. I swallow another sip of tea feeling suddenly thirsty.

"Is it just me or is it extremely attractive watching men drink coffee?" Delaney finally asks.

Nirvana sighs and says, "Oh thank God. I thought I was going into heat or something. This shouldn't be as attractive as it feels."

We all muttered in agreement. "It makes no sense," I say.

"It's because they are usually so strong and watching them do something mundane just makes them seem more approachable," Ophelia says.

I hum under my breath, but it feels different than that. But maybe I'm just going into heat like Nirvana so eloquently put it. Shaking off those thoughts I ask, "Where's Sera?"

"Work," they say in unison, still watching the men.

Biting back a laugh I turn away before my own

hormones betray me, and announce, "My aunt's birthday is this weekend. You're all coming."

"We are?" Layla asks, drawing her attention away from Spencer and his friend.

I nod. "Yes. Everyone is going to be there. I'll need some form of entertainment aside from the arguing that we all know is bound to happen." I bat my lashes at them, hoping to sway them my way.

But as usual they just stare making me groan. "Please. Derrick will be there, and my brothers already hate him. Can you imagine me being alone?" I haven't seen my Aunt Sheryl or Derrick in years because they always were traveling to his side of the family. So, the idea of seeing him now made me nervous. I don't want him to say anything that could send any of my brothers spiraling out of control.

Nirvana winced. "Shit. They haven't been around in years."

I nod. "Exactly. Please, I need you." Turning to Ophelia I add, "Louise is already going to be there."

Clicking her tongue, she nods. "Oh, all right. I'll be there. I can't say no to Maria's food anyway." Sagging with relief I smile at them.

They were always there for me. Especially in times like these when I would deal with extended family I didn't want to be around. My phone vibrated in my pocket. I pulled it out and saw around thirty texts from Anthony about the case. Cursing, I hand my tea over to Nirvana, "I've got to go. I have case reports to look over for tomorrow."

Delaney's eyebrows furrow before she asks, "Can't Anthony do it? You do most of his work anyway."

I shake my head. "It comes with the job, Lane. I'll see you guys this weekend." I wave to the guys and make my way towards my car. My phone vibrates in my hand and as I look down I see Anothony's name flashing on the screen. I sigh and answer, "Hello?"

There's a silence then, "Hello? I've been trying to reach you all day and all I get is a hello?" he snaps.

Climbing into my car I roll my eyes. "I've been busy, Anthony. I do have a life outside of work."

There is another bout of silence that stretches so long I almost hang up until he speaks, his voice low and hollow. Emotionless. "Rory, we have a case that needs work. You want to be a lawyer, but you won't put in the work. How would that look for you?"

I lean over, pressing my head against the steering wheel. "Anthony, you have another paralegal. I've had a long day and I have to pull an all-nighter to get the rest of these questions done." Not that it was technically my job since I was a glorified assistant. Tension and stress built inside of me, knotting up my muscles and making my head throb. I could only do this for so long. I was exhausted and wanted a break. "If Claire doesn't start pulling her weight," I start, swallowing hard, "I think I might need to find employment elsewhere."

Anthony sighs through the phone, gentling his tone he says, "I can't do this without you, Rory. You are what keeps me going. If you want to take Claire's spot I'll willingly talk to Stanley."

A part of me wanted to jump at the opportunity to move up. But I knew he was only placating me because I was fed up. I was tired of being their errand girl. I was tired of doing all the work. But then I was raised not to quit. Never give up. I just had to graduate and take the bar and I'll be fine.

"How about this, we can talk about it more tomorrow at lunch?"

Shaking my head I sat up, turning the key in the ignition and starting the car. "I can't. I have something I have to do tomorrow afternoon."

He hums under his breath. "Afterwards meet me at the office and we'll get an early dinner." He didn't give me a chance to decline before hanging up. Cursing, I tossed my phone into the passenger seat and pulled away from the bakery. The drive home was silent, full of my thoughts running rampant. Wanting nothing more than to crawl into bed and sleep until the next night, but I knew I didn't have that luxury. Pulling up to my apartment building I finally feel my body relax a little bit. Grabbing my stuff from the passenger seat I make the seemingly never-ending trek up to the building.

Wind blew my hair into my face and moved my clothing harshly against my body. It was early August, and the air was humid with stifling heat. Sighing, I stared up at the starry sky wanting nothing but a break that I wasn't afforded. Groaning, I maneuvered my books to one arm, and put in my building code to open the lobby door.

"Oh dear. Here, let me hold something," a sweet, soft voice said, offering to take my books from me. The heavy weight was lifted from me as I came into the lobby looking at one of the teenagers who lived a floor above me.

"Bria! I didn't know you were home," I say, closing the door behind us as I study the girl. She was shorter than my five-eight and slender. Her olive skin shone under the overhanging lights of the lobby and her silky brown curls hung loosely down her back. However, it was the slightly rounded bump under her shirt that gave me pause.

"You're pregnant?" I ask, dumbly. It was obvious she was. At seventeen she was slender and showing.

Bria blushed and I immediately apologized, "I'm so sorry! I just haven't seen you in a while. How do you feel?"

Giving me a small smile she shrugged. "It's okay. It's been a minute and I understand the shock. I was shocked too."

"Are you back living with your mom?" I asked, taking my books from her.

Bria shook her head. "No. Mom moved out a while ago. Me and Preston live there now. Preston is my boyfriend. He's getting some dinner from the Chinese restaurant across town, I was craving an eggroll."

I laugh and move towards the stairs. "Sera used to crave the strangest things when she was pregnant with Darcy."

Bria fell into step beside me. "Yeah? Like what?"

"She used to like onions with strawberry jelly and pickles wrapped in those sour straws. It was a mess."

Laughing, her nose wrinkled. "I can't imagine eating that."

"How far along are you?"

She rubs her small bump and smiles, her brown eyes shining with love. "I'm turning four months tomorrow. We are having a little boy."

We stopped at my door, and I smiled at her. "Congratulations. If you need anything let me know."

She nods and leaves with a small wave leaving me watching after her. When she disappears from view, I unlock my door and enter my apartment. I kick off my shoes and lock the door behind me, before making my way to the living room where I unceremoniously drop the books on my coffee table. They hit the wood with a small thud.

"Stupid books," I mutter, leaning over to turn on the lamp on the end table, lighting up the room in a soft glow.

Plopping down on the worn green sofa I groan, sinking deeper into the cushions. Letting my body relax just for a minute. Only I don't realize how exhausted I really am before I sink into a deep sleep.

Chapter 8

RORY

The shrill sound of an alarm has me shooting awake. As I sit up I groan, feeling a twinge of pain in my neck. Sunlight peeked through my black curtains blinding me momentarily as I searched where that alarm was coming from. Using my hand to block what I could of the sun I look down at the ground where my phone lay on the floor. Scooping it up I press the screen ready to turn off my alarm when I see the time. It's nearly noon.

"Noon?" I shout and jump from the couch. Fuck, fuck, fuck. I was late. I was so late. Cursing, I stumbled towards my bedroom. I hated being late. I pull at my clothes as I step into my bedroom and find a simple burnt orange dress and black cardigan hanging in my closet. I toss the clothing on my bed and rush towards the bathroom to brush my teeth and pull my hair into some sort of order.

"This is what happens when you don't do what you're supposed to do, Rory. Now look at you, late with a crick in your neck," I scold myself under my breath. I brush my teeth quickly and pull my curly hair into a top knot before rushing into my bedroom again to throw on my clothes before running back out to the living room and scooping up my books, keys, and phone.

I'm a panting mess by the time I run out of the apartment and down the stairs. Papers are flying around me, escaping the books. Groaning in frustration, I stoop low and grab them.

"Son of a bitch," I curse, feeling on the verge of tears as the books tumble from my hands and down the stairs with an ominous *thunk thunk thunk*. I was tempted to just turn my ass around and go back into the calm and peaceful confinement of my apartment and curl into a ball on my floor watching overly dramatized telenovelas. But I couldn't. With a huff I rushed downstairs to where my books landed in a pathetic little heap.

Bending low I pick them up, trying my best to keep the papers as neat as possible before dejectedly going to my car. This day couldn't possibly get any worse could it?

The answer... it could. The day could get worse. As I sit in the waiting room of the doctor's office, thirty minutes from my office, I stare at my dead phone. Unable to check emails, messages, or anything because I didn't plug the damn thing in before falling asleep. The sound of a door opening drew my attention as a small auburn headed nurse called my name, "Rory Flores-Phelps?" Tiredly I stand and move over to the woman who gives me a warm smile. "Good afternoon."

I nod and follow her to a scale. "If you'll please step up here," she asks. I do and stare down at the numbers as they bounce from high to low to high to low before finally settling on a number that was probably less than desirable for someone of my height, but I was too tired to care. Following after her I zone out, blocking out the sound of her voice as she explains what the doctors are going to do. Blood work, a glucose test, all the terms I'd rather not listen to.

"It's not uncommon for someone like you to get diabetes at this age," she says conversationally, drawing me back into the conversation.

"Someone like me?" I ask, glancing around the white and pink room.

The nurse nods. "You're underweight for your height, and people of color are more than likely to have diabetes being hereditary in their families. Especially in the black and Hispanic communities."

I stare at her, my eyebrow raised, and she turns red, blue eyes going wide in shock. "N-n-not that it's bad. Well, being underweight is bad. But statistically people of color have a higher rate of diabetes, high cholesterol, and heart disease. I mean around 12.1% of black adults and 11.8% of Hispanic adults are diagnosed with it which doesn't seem like much in the grand scheme of things, but it is very common." She was rambling nervously as she checked my blood pressure.

I didn't respond, what could I say? So we sat in awkward silence until finally the machine beeped.

"Your blood pressure is higher than it should be," she says.

I snort humorlessly. "Today hasn't been the best of days."

Nodding slowly, she rolls up the cuff and sets it on her cart before turning to me. "I'm sorry. I sometimes ramble when I don't mean to. If I offended you please know I truly did not mean to."

I send her a small grin. "If I got offended by every offhanded thing I'd be a weeping mess the majority of the time." Not that it mattered. People would say anything they wanted. It wasn't lost on me. I've been in Texas for twenty-eight years. I've lived through the backhanded comments, the outright racism, the prejudice. I've been through it all. But in this instance I don't think she meant it in a malicious way. More of an awkward spout of facts that she thought I should know. We sit in another bout of silence as she sets up some test tubes readying for blood work.

"I figured you'd send me somewhere else," I mutter.

Shaking her head, she opens an alcohol wipe and says, "I was told we had to get these done faster than normal." Humming under my breath I roll up the sleeve of my cardigan. Drew must've had a lot more pull than I thought he did. I watched her movements as she gently lifted my arm and tied the tourniquet on my bicep tightly.

"What do you do?" she asks.

Grimacing in discomfort, I take a breath and stare at the eggshell yellow ceiling. "I'm a paralegal assistant. I'm in law school."

"Really? My mom always wanted me to be a lawyer."

I gaze back at her. "Why? A nurse is a much more important job."

She shrugs and takes off the band, and draws the blood into the tubes. I didn't even feel her press the needle into my vein. "Money. Nurses don't make nearly as much as a lawyer would."

"Money isn't everything. Not when nurses and doctors are needed more now."

"That's what I told her. But she said it doesn't really count because I'm in a doctor's office. I don't really make an impact when I do basically clinical work. It would be different if I worked in the hospital."

"Don't downplay what you do. Your work isn't any less important." She sends me a grateful smile before removing the needle and pressing a gauze pad to it and taping it down.

"Thank you. For what it's worth you seem like you'd be a great lawyer. There're not enough women lawyers in the world. Although my sister's lawyer, Anthony Lincoln, was able to help her with a domestic abuse case. But I think he had a woman partner."

I wince inside. I remember that case. I'd never met the woman who suffered so much from the abuse she lived through, but I did set up the questions. I had looked over all the evidence proving he was abusive and one blackout away from killing her. Anthony was able to get her a twenty-year protective order and full custody over their infant twin sons with no visitation and full child support. Setting her up for a safe and free life.

After she cleaned up after herself she turned to me with a wide smile. "It was nice to meet you. Again, I am truly sorry for my blunder."

"What's your name?" I ask.

"Andi."

I nodded, sending her the first genuine smile I had all day. "Thank you, Andi. For everything."

She nods, grabbing her cart and test tubes before moving towards the door. "Dr. Martin will be with you shortly." I thank her again watching as she leaves the room, closing the door behind herself. I don't know how long I sit there looking at the different pamphlets before a knock sounds on the door.

"Come in," I called.

The door opened and an older black woman with graying hair came into the room, a kind smile on her face. "Good afternoon, Miss Flores-Phelps. How are we today?"

"Just Rory, please. I'm doing okay."

Dr. Martin pulls up a chair and flips through the chart.

"So, Drew told me a little bit about what's going on. Fifty is low for blood sugar. You actually want to be between 70 and 140 for a healthy blood sugar level. Have you always had issues with this?"

"No. I mean I have times when I get dizzy and really thirsty but sometimes I'll forget to eat or drink."

Dr. Martin watches me intently, nodding her head every now and then. "I see. Typically, adults who are being diagnosed with diabetes it's type two. It can have a lot to do with exercise and diet. But you seem to be a little underweight. Your cholesterol is normal, your white blood cells are normal, but your A1Cs are concerning. It's not as common for adults to be diagnosed with type one diabetes but it's not unheard of. From my understanding you don't go to doctors much." She pauses, then asks, "Does anyone in your family have diabetes?"

I nod. "My grandmother had it. She enjoyed eating when she was around family."

"You can eat what you like in moderation, make sure your diet is healthy and you exercise. This is manageable, Rory. As I said, it's not the end of the world. To stay healthy includes going to the doctor when you need to."

I nod my head. She sighs and continues, "As women we have to be on top of our doctor appointments. All of them. Don't be afraid to advocate for yourself." She stands and listens to my heart and breathing before telling me about insulin, and how I could get a pump after a year, and how to check my sugars. The information was daunting and overwhelming, but she assured me she'd be available for questions and gave me my first dose after checking my sugar and waiting a few minutes before going to get me an apple and juice. When she comes back she smiles, handing me some pamphlets and the fruit.

"How about we make an appointment for three weeks

from now to see how you're doing? If you need me sooner don't be afraid to make an earlier appointment."

I nod. "Thank you."

Her warm hand squeezes my arm, and she says, "It's not the end of the world, Rory. It's manageable. I sent in a prescription to the pharmacy you gave Andi so you should be good to go."

I thanked her softly and left the room, stopping at reception to make my next appointment. When I'm done I make my way to my car. After I start it I'm able to plug my phone into the charger before I make my way to the office. I'm lost in thought as I drive, passing the different businesses. People are going back to work from lunch. I didn't get a chance to work on the new case and I knew it would push it back. Rubbing my face, I sigh. There was no use dwelling on it. Maybe Anthony can help. Nodding to myself I pull into my parking space and make my way to the office. There aren't many people here, either still out to lunch or already back to work leaving the front mostly empty. I wave to some partners and attorneys as I pass, making my way down the dimly lit hall. The walls held different pictures of employees, of the owners, and the floors gleamed from the fresh polish.

The offices and conference rooms were on one side of the building while the other side had file rooms and a law library. I make my way to the last office at the end of the hall and pause when I hear talking and laughing.

From outside the door, I listen. "Yeah, I have a dinner meeting tonight with the paralegals for this new case, so I'll be home late, sweetheart," I hear Anthony say. My heart drops and my stomach tightens.

"Anthony, we talked about this. You said once I got into the second trimester you'd start easing your workload a little bit," a woman said, a clear pout in her voice.

Anthony whispers to her, cooing to soothe her, "I'll be

home tomorrow night in time for dinner with your parents. I promise you. This is a big case and I need to get the interviews settled and make a plan for witness statements. I have to work as much as possible to be able to take a few months off with you once our baby is born."

I nearly gasped out loud as shock, hurt, and betrayal course through me. He was married. Turning on my heel, I rush away from the office as tears prick the backs of my eyes. How could this happen? How could I not know? Shaking off those thoughts, I rush out the building breathing hard as I literally run to my car. I don't even pay attention to where I'm going until a car honks at me, drawing me out of my thoughts. Wiping at my face, I apologize and move forward to where my car is parked.

Climbing in, I sit stoic and numb. What the hell? Tears are falling down my face in earnest now. I can hardly process what I had just overheard. With a shaky hand I grab my phone and unlock it looking for the number I need. I sniffle, trying to calm myself down but when he answers I break down.

Chapter 9

RORY

I don't know how long I sit in my car, staring off into the distance before the passenger door opens. The books that I had in the seat were moved to the floorboard in the back.

"Oh, Ro," he says on a breath, climbing into the car. Fresh tears fill my eyes as his strong arms wrap around me pulling me into a tight hug. "What happened?"

I don't speak for a long while, I just let him hold me before I pull away and look up, meeting hazel eyes much like my own. "I messed up, Nico. I messed up badly. I gotta go to Planned Parenthood. I made an appointment for today. I need to go." Nico stares at me for a moment, before his gaze goes to the window just as my door opens.

"Get in the back, Rory." I glance up at my older brother and I nod, letting him help me into the backseat as Rio rushes towards the car to climb in. Marco takes my place at the wheel.

"You're all here?" I sniff, wiping my face with the sleeve of my cardigan.

Nico turns to me with his serious eyes. "You called me crying, Rory. Of course we'd come."

Rio nods. "You never cry." Love for my brothers welled inside of me.

Swallowing hard I say, "Please take me to Planned Parenthood. They close at seven and it's already four-thirty." My brothers gaze at each other but don't ask me any more questions as Marco pulls away from the office. The first thirty minutes are silent until I finally mutter, "I went to the doctor today."

"Are you okay?" Rio asks. "I know you said you fainted yesterday, but I just figured it was because you were tired."

Nico's head whips to the side and he glares at our youngest brother. "She fainted and you didn't think to tell *Mamá* or Dad? Hell, even us?"

I leaned forward and put my hand on his arm. "It's okay. He didn't really know what happened. I have diabetes. Type one." I sigh. "I might have something else with the shit luck I've had today."

Marco clears his throat and asks, "Are you going to tell us what happened?"

Embarrassment filled me. "I fucked up. I've been seeing this guy for a while. I went to see him at work, and I found out he's married." My brothers draw in a collective breath. "And his wife is pregnant."

"Shit, Ro," Rio says.

"Language, Rio," Marco scolds. His hands were tightening on the steering wheel as he directed his next question to me, "How long is a while, Rory?"

I shrug, suddenly uncomfortable with the question. "Since I was seventeen."

Their heads snap towards me, and Marco starts to swerve

off the road before straightening. "What the fuck do you mean since you were seventeen? How the hell could we not know?" Nico demands.

"It was on and off. No one knows."

Rio sighs. "Not even your friends?"

Shame fills me. "No. Not even them." I don't know why I didn't confide in them. I never had that issue before. But I guess maybe a part of me was ashamed. He was older than me. That maybe they'd think I got decent grades because of him. Maybe self-consciously I had something to prove. Not only to the people in my life, but to myself. The rest of the ride is tense and silent until we get to the doctor's office. It was starting to get dark but there was still almost an hour left until they closed. They were able to squeeze me in at the last minute, which doesn't usually happen. And even though it was getting dark there were protesters standing outside holding signs and chanting.

"Hell," Nico mutters.

Nerves move through me, at the speculation they will pin on me. The assumptions. "Can you walk with me? Please?" I ask.

They don't even hesitate to climb out of the car and wait for me. Taking a breath I climb out. Then I hear them. *"Abortion is murder!"*

My brothers make a protective barrier around me as we walk forward only to be stopped by a red-faced woman pushing a sign of a fetus in our faces. "Murderer!" she shouts.

I step around her, trying to ignore the things she says but she presses on, drawing the attention of guards who move to open the door.

"Murderer! Baby killer! I hope you burn in Hell!"

Something snaps in me. It could be because I was starving, my head hurt, and the guy I was with for years happens to be a married jackass. The day has weighed on me too long, and I can't take it anymore. My normally composed nature vanishes as this woman waves her sign in my face.

Gritting my teeth, I push it away from me. "Shut the fuck up," I snap.

She freezes, her eyes wide. "Excuse me?"

"I didn't stutter, lady. You're sitting here waving some sign in my face acting as if you know why I'm here. You don't. This isn't just for abortions, you'd know that if you stepped out of whatever propaganda group you're in and did some research. Google is there for a goddamn reason, use it."

She scoffs, embarrassment tinging her red cheeks. "Who comes here this late in the evening other than to cover up their murder?"

"Not that I owe you an explanation but since you're concerning yourself with my pussy I'll elaborate. I just found out the man I've been seeing is fucking married. Now, I'm sure your pea-sized brain can figure out what that means. If you can't, I'll help. If he's so comfortable fucking someone behind his wife's back there's no stopping him from sticking his dick into any hole that let's him. Now, if you'd so kindly get the fuck out of my way, so I can get tested for every disease known to man, I'd really appreciate it."

The woman doesn't say anything as she steps out of our way allowing us to enter the building. It's just like the doctor's office Drew sent me to only little to no people. I signed in quickly and sat between my brothers, waiting. My heart is pounding so fast that I fear they could hear it. They don't say anything, but I don't miss the looks they toss my way and at each other.

"Rory?" a voice calls. I stand on shaky legs and make my way to the back room alone. Almost as if I'm heading to my doom. And it very well could be.

Chapter 10

CADEN

I'm panting and the sound is loud in the silent room, followed by the pounding of my footsteps as I push myself to do another mile. Sweat covers my body as I run on the treadmill. The burning in my legs and chest made me move faster, ready to hit that twenty-mile mark. Music played in my ears, loud and fast-paced. Just how I liked it. I was on edge lately. I didn't know why I started having nightmares again. I had successfully pushed them from my mind. Yet now they were back with a vengeance. A shadow passed over me catching my attention. Something dark and angry rose in me until I ripped my headphones out of my ears and wrapped the cord around their neck.

The only problem is that the treadmill was still moving, sending us toppling to the ground. Not that I cared. I used the momentum to my advantage taking the person to their back ready to quickly end it. I raised my fist sending it flying, only it was caught mid-air. "Caden!" the person snapped, coming into focus. Blinking rapidly, I stared down at Ravi's green eyes before gazing at the headphones I had wrapped around his neck.

Horror washed through me, and I scurried back. "Fuck. Ravi, I…" I start but I don't have anything to say. I was fine one moment then the next it was blank. Ravi stood slowly, watching me intently as if he was ready for me to strike at him again.

"You're okay, Caden," he says softly.

I shake my head taking a deep breath. What did I just do? I could've killed him. "I don't know what just happened."

Keeping me in his sights, Ravi turned off the machines and grabbed a spray bottle and paper towels. "You thought I was an enemy." It was a statement. One I couldn't really refute. It was as if just seeing him close was enough to send me back. My hand ached with the memory.

"What are you doing here?" I ask, sticking to a safer topic as I watch him spray down the machine.

Ravi doesn't answer right away, silently he just wipes the entire machine down. As if he were bracing himself for what he was going to say.

When he was finished he tossed the towels and turned to me. "He left, Cade. This morning."

Staring ahead I sigh. "We aren't there to back him." I'll never understand why Sam decided to do another tour. But it didn't sit right with me that we weren't there to watch his back.

Ravi sighs and sits on the ground next to me. "We can't know what goes through his brain. He sent out a text when he was already in transit and then he went radio silent. Spencer can't even track him."

I stare ahead tapping my fingers on my raised knees. I saw the message; it was vague and to the point. Nothing to show that something was amiss. Just a standard message, almost as if it were automatic. "It just doesn't sit right. We all agreed to retire."

Ravi nods. "We did. But he does his own thing."

That was true. We all did. "What did you think of Spence's friend?" I ask, instead. That was a safe topic.

"Seems decent enough. The women sure fawned over him though," he grumbled.

Smirking, I stood. "Worried he might steal Nirvana out from under you?"

He scoffs and says, "I'd kill him before he even had a chance."

Laughing, I shook my head. "Who would've thought the little blonde would cause so much blood lust?" Ravi was a reserved straightforward man, he said what he meant and didn't hold back. Especially not with the woman he chose as his own. Anything threatened or harmed her he'd take care of it, no matter what. Hell, the crazy bastard broke his hand smashing a window open for her and ran through literal fire to get her.

"She told me about this party Rory's parents are throwing this weekend."

I hum under my breath. "Yeah, Delaney was talking to Sorrow about it this morning." I move towards the locker room and pull my shirt over my head.

"Are you going?" Ravi asks, leaning against the wall as I pull the little blue locker open.

"I don't know, depends on if I have a shift or not. I think I can pick up the cat tomorrow afternoon."

Ravi looks at me. "You're going to keep the cat?" His tone is incredulous, it's almost laughable.

Keeping my back to him I shrug. "I know you have a certain… affinity to the feline group. I can't very well leave the animal alone."

He sighs. "What about when you go out of town? You leave in three weeks. Or did you forget?"

I wince at the mention of leaving. I was going back home for my sister's wedding to her longtime boyfriend, Xander. My ex-fiancée's younger brother. I haven't seen them in four years. Since the last mission. Even then I didn't really see them. I've called them of course, but seeing them in person hurts too much. I didn't want them to see the scars I've tried to hide behind ink. I don't want to see their sympathy and the inevitable tears that are bound to fill my mother's eyes. But I'm not going to miss my little sister's wedding. Even if I have to encounter seeing the one woman who broke my heart.

"I'll see if Drew or Max will check on it. Feed it occasionally. Or do an automatic feeder and waterer."

Ravi nods. "Are you going to see her?"

I shrug and reply, "Her brother is the groom. It's been four years. I'm over it."

He scoffs, watching me with a deep scowl. "She broke something in you, Caden. You were nearly inconsolable when she visited you that first time." I don't respond right away as I grab my shampoo and soap.

"It was years ago, and I did get over it. They're happy so that's good for them." At first I cared though. I was hurt, I was angry. Those first few years I was fucking any woman I could find. Trying to ease the pain they caused me. Not just my fiancée but also my best friend. Now, I had no feelings. Stripping off the rest of my clothes, I step into my shower shoes, head for a stall, and pull the curtain closed. Turning, I started the water letting it heat up as hot as I could take and ducked my head under the steady stream.

"When do you leave?" Ravi asks, drawing my attention. His gaze was focused on his phone, his brows furrowed in concentration.

"A few weeks. October first through the tenth," I say, squirting some shampoo in my hand and rubbing it through my hair.

Ravi sighs. "That's nine days. Can a cat be left alone that long?"

Ducking my head back, I rinse the soap before turning to him. "You offering to take it in until I get home?"

He grimaces, shoving his phone in his pocket. "No. Nirvana would never want to part with the thing. Not to mention Gran."

Laughing, I say, "Is that why you're here? Hiding from the women in your house?"

Ravi sighs. "I don't know how long I can handle another audiobook. I swear if I hear the word 'thrust' or 'sheath' again I will shoot the damn stereo."

Not being able to hold it in anymore I laugh. "You got her to listen to them."

Tossing his hands up he grunts in defeat. "I figured she'd listen to the Bible or some shit. Now she and Nirvana have little dates and listen to this shit."

Shaking my head, I finish the shower and point to my locker, "Pass my towel." Huffing, Ravi moves to grab it and tosses it over his shoulder to me. Catching it I wipe at my hair before wrapping it around my waist. "So, you're hiding from a horny old woman? That's what I got from this."

"God, she shouldn't even be interested in it." Ravi shudders.

I dry off and dress quickly before sitting on the bench and putting on my shoes. "I hate to be the one to tell you this, Ravi, but I'm pretty sure your Gran fucked before. If she didn't, your ass wouldn't be here." Glancing up at him, I swear he physically turned green.

"No, she's a born-again virgin. I refuse to believe otherwise."

Shaking my head, I lean back. "Are you meeting someone here?"

That took his mind off his Gran and woman making him insane as he nodded. "Max. He wants a spotter."

As if on cue the tall redhead walked into the locker room. Tension runs off him in waves. "Hey," he mutters, opening a locker with more force than necessary. I glance back at Ravi who shrugs.

"You good?" I ask.

Max grunts under his breath and pulls out his earphones and phone. "Let's go, Banks. I don't have all night."

Ravi arches an eyebrow. "When did I become your bitch, Casen?"

Max sighs up at the ceiling before forcing himself to relax. "You're right. I apologize."

"That's better." Ravi nods before turning to me. "Make sure you figure this cat mess out before leaving." Together, the two men walk to the door before Ravi stops again to look at me over his shoulder. "You know, maybe you should bring a date to the wedding. Then you won't have to worry about the ex being there to begin with." With that they exit the room, leaving me with those parting words. I had thought about it, but I wouldn't know who to bring. I don't go past two dates before moving on to the next woman. This was a ten-day affair that was halfway across the country. Shaking those thoughts away, I grabbed my gym bag and phone. I didn't have time for this right now. I had a cat to see.

Chapter 11

CADEN

Staring down at the little ball in the cage made my heart hurt for the little guy. An IV stuck out of the little arm taped in pink and yellow medical tape. "She's a strong one," the nurse said, smiling up from where she petted the cat.

"Her? It's a girl?" I ask, staring at the gray ball. Slowly, as if knowing she was being watched, she blinked open bright yellow eyes. "Hi, little one," I say, my voice low.

The nurse smiles, her pale face turning red slightly. "She's able to go home with you Monday. The doctor would like to keep her over the weekend for observation. He's still not a hundred percent comfortable with her breathing yet."

Nodding, I turned to the woman, she was different from the other nurse, her hair darker and eyes an amber brown. She was cute and a part of me wanted to take Ravi's advice, but I didn't want her to get the wrong idea if I asked her on a date. Plus, she seemed younger than I would've liked. Sighing at the stupidity of my thoughts, I nod and turn back to the little bundle. "I'll see you Monday." The nurse looked a little disappointed as I went to leave with a wave, but for some reason I couldn't find it in me to feel bad.

I leave the clinic and climb into my car. I have no destination in sight, so I drive around aimlessly lost in my own thoughts until I get to a small bar outside of Houston. I park and climb out. One beer wouldn't hurt. Moving towards the bar, I open the door, and as I walk in I'm hit with warm air and the sound of country music. The bar itself is minimalistic with red booths and black floors. Beer lights and posters hang on the walls with one side having a large bullhead hanging on it. Moving towards the bar I sit on one of the cracked stools and stare ahead until a man steps in front of me.

Glancing up I meet Rory's oldest brother's stare. "Ah, the new friend," he says, tossing a white towel over his shoulder.

"The older brother," I say.

Marco stares at me for a moment before leaning forward. "What brings you to this part of town?"

Shrugging, I answered honestly, "Was driving around, saw a bar, and decided to get a drink."

Marco stares for a moment before nodding. "What will it be?"

Tapping my fingers on the bar, I tilt my head towards the glasses. "Whatever's on tap is fine." Nodding, he turns his back towards me and grabs a glass filling it up with Budweiser before sliding it over to me. I thank him and take a healthy swig letting it burn its way down my throat before placing the glass back down.

"Rory is here," he says randomly, watching me closely.

"Is she?" I ask.

Marco nods. "She's not doing too good." My brows wrinkle in concern.

"What's wrong?" He doesn't answer, just points to a lone

booth in the back of the bar. I finish off my drink and stand, moving towards the back where I see her sitting alone picking at a basket of fries without really eating them. "Ro Ro," I say, sliding into the booth across from her. Her hazel eyes snap up to meet mine and they look more green now and red rimmed as if she had been crying.

Hastily she wipes at her eyes. "What are you doing here?"

"I came for a drink," I say, studying her intently. "Are you okay?"

She sniffs and nods. "Never better."

Bracing my arm on the table I lean forward. "I don't want to call you a liar… but you're crying."

Her eyes narrow as she glares at me. "I am not. I never cry. Ask my brothers."

"I'm asking you." I lean forward, meeting her gaze. "What happened?"

Shrugging, she tosses the fry she held into the basket. "Drew was right. It's diabetes. I guess I owe him a fruit basket," her gaze moves away, "and you."

Tsking, I wave her comment away. "I doubt Drew would take anything from you. Nor would I. You needed care. I'm glad you were able to figure out what was causing your issues."

Hugging her arms around herself she sighs. "I thought type one was rare. Now here I am walking around with a pouch of needles. If my mom finds out she'll think I'm dying or something." Staring at her I know it's more than that. Where the diagnosis can be challenging and difficult to take, the way she's hugging herself and rocking slightly back and forth I know it's something else. I opened my mouth to say something, what, I don't know, but a strange need to comfort her flooded me.

"Tell me what else is going on," I say gently.

Rory sighs and runs her finger over the table, tracing small circles on the table. She braces herself and I wait patiently for her to speak.

"The guy I was seeing turned out to be a total asshole. He's married and the wife is pregnant."

I suck in a breath and stare at her. I can see the way she's hurting and I stand before I realize it and sit directly beside her pulling her into my side and holding her to me. She tenses for a second, but then relaxes against me resting her head on my shoulder.

"I feel so stupid," Rory mutters. 'I should've known better."

I tug on the ends of her hair forcing her to look up at me. "Stop that. You didn't know what he was like or that he was married. It's no one's fault but his own."

We sit in silence for a few moments before Rory pulls away from me and looks up at me, her eyes brighter and less sad than when I came in.

"I wish I could just kick his ass," Rory states randomly.

"Just throat punch him, and it should be fine," I tease.

Rory scoffs, "The only thing I do is kick and that's the best there is."

"Well kicking can only get you so far," I agree, taking a sip from my beer. "Show me a fist."

I watch as she makes the most atrocious fist in mankind. Her thumb is tucked under her fingers which is a sure way of getting the damn thing broken.

"My God, Woman, are you trying to break your hand?" I reach over towards her and take her small fist in my hand and gently take her thumb out and position her fist just right. I try to ignore the tingling that travels up my body, but I feel Rory gasp against my side. I stare at her and see her eyes widen. I lick my lips and lean closer to her. Her eyes go to my mouth before jumping to my eyes.

"Your brothers should've taught you a proper way to hold a fist," I whisper.

"Maybe I didn't want to scare you with my non-existent moves," she taunts just as softly.

"Someone should teach you, Ro Ro." I find my thumb rubbing against the soft skin of her hand.

"Then teach me."

Chapter 12

RORY

I stare up at Caden and my heart is pounding. Did I just say that? Teach me? What the hell is wrong with me? I know it's probably because I'm heartbroken over Anthony, I know that's the case, but with Caden currently beside me and his finger gently stroking figure eights over the top of my hand it's causing me to have a lapse in judgment. Do I want to kick Anthony's ass? Of course I do. Do I know how? No, no I don't, but I shouldn't spring that on a man whom I barely know but here I was. Waiting with my breath being held for an answer.

"I can help you with that, Rory."

I swallow hard and nod my head. "Okay," I whisper.

"Is tomorrow good for you?" Caden asks.

I groan and shake my head. "No, tomorrow is me and the girls day. We are going to hang out and catch up."

He hums under his breath and moves away from me making me wish he'd grab my hand again and hold it longer.

To rub his thumb back over the top. Wait, what? No. No, I need to stop having these thoughts.

"How about I give you my number and you call me when you're ready?" Caden suggests.

"Sounds good," I say and take my phone out of my pocket and hand it to him to put his number in it. He types it in then I hear his phone ringing as he dials the number making sure we both have each other's numbers.

"There now you have my number." He stands and stares at me for a moment. "Don't get into too much trouble tomorrow *Chīsai doragon*." And with that he walks away leaving me breathless and wondering what the hell just happened.

Caden

I can feel her eyes on me as I leave, and I wonder to myself what the hell just happened. Did I really just offer Rory self-defense lessons against her shitty ex? And how bad was he that she needed self-defense? My fists clench at my sides at the thought of what she must have dealt with with this creep. I walk to my car and climb in and head to the only place I can think of. It doesn't take long for me to get to S Security and head inside after I'm done parking. All I see is Max when I walk in, typing away on his computer.

"Hey, man," I say sitting in the chair across from his desk. Max looks up with bright blue eyes and nods at me.

"What's up, Cade?"

I shift in my seat and clear my throat. "I need you to get some information on someone for me."

Max arches a red brow before turning in his seat to fully stare at me. "And who might that be?"

I shift again suddenly uncomfortable with the intense way he is staring at me. "Rory," I say, finally.

"Rory," he draws out and I give a stiff nod. "You know this is a violation of privacy right?"

"What's a violation of privacy?" Spencer asks, walking into the office with Elijah and Sorrow behind him.

"Our boy here wants information on Rory," Max says, having way too much fun with my tiny request.

"What? Why?" Sorrow asks. Over the last two years he's become protective of the other women thanks to Delaney being their best friend. She also has a mean streak when it comes to her girls. But after tonight I want to know more about Rory. Not because I'm interested in her romantically or anything because I'm not. I don't date. Ever. No matter how beautiful a woman is all I can offer is a fuck and that's it. Granted it will be a good fuck but it's a fuck all the same. And Rory doesn't strike me as the type to do a quick fuck, especially after her break up with the married ex.

"Huh, Lorelai," Max says randomly.

"What?" I ask, getting out of my thoughts.

"That's Rory's legal name, Lorelai," Max elaborates.

"Huh," is the chorused response from the other men, who are now crowded by the computer.

"She graduated top of her class in college, studied as a paralegal in community college while she was a senior in high school. And she's on track to become fully licensed in the summer after she takes the bar. She finishes law school around May and her grades are impressive," Spencer reads off.

"She has three brothers and both parents are still alive and married," Max continues. But that's stuff I already know. I know Rory or rather Lorelai is brilliant. That's not what I want to know, it's the little stuff. What are her dreams, what's her darkest secret? But I guess that's something I'd have to ask her, but being in her presence does something to me and I don't know why.

"How long have you been interested in Rory?" Sorrow asks, not listening to the others.

I sigh. "I'm not interested in her the way you think. I'm just helping her out with something." Not technically a lie, I am helping her, but I can never be into her in a romantic way and Sorrow knows that. After being held captive, and knowing that Xena cheated on me, I swore off all women and I planned to keep it that way.

Chapter 13

RORY

I sat in my car at the rage room and sighed. On my phone were the test results that could change my life for the worse. But I took a deep breath and opened the lab results and nearly sagged with relief as I saw the word *Negative* highlighted at the very top. Tears, I didn't realize I was holding in, began to freefall as the words weighed down on me, the severity of my situation finally sinking in. I should've known better than all of this and it's my fault for getting so caught up in a man rather than doing what I was supposed to do.

A knock on the window startled me causing me to drop my phone as I glanced up at Nirvana who was looking at me with concern. I forced a smile and reached over for my phone before climbing out of the car.

"You're crying. Why are you crying?" Nirvana demands staring up at me with a fury only she can possess, which makes me laugh a little.

"It's nothing, just had an overwhelming day," I answer

not ready to disclose how much of an idiot I am. But that doesn't matter right now. Now, I just want to spend some time with my friends and smash a bunch of random shit to feel better. Nirvana loops her arm through mine and skips forward like a ball of energy as she leads me to the other girls.

"Are you all right?" Delaney asks, seeing my puffy red eyes. I've always been an ugly crier so there's no way for me to hide them.

"Allergies," Nirvana answers for me before I can come up with an excuse.

The other women look skeptical, but they drop it for the time being and for that I'm grateful. We walk into the small storage like area and see a small woman at the counter flipping through a magazine. When she looks up at us as we move closer to the counter.

"Six today?" she asks counting us before she grabs coveralls and masks for us. "Everything should be in the room for you. There's a Bluetooth speaker connected to the wall, and you can listen to whatever it is you want to for the next hour. We grab the clothes and quickly change, everything oddly quiet before we head into our room with two cars and some small appliances.

I twist my neck, relieving the ache that has grown there since my test results, and I connect my phone to the Bluetooth and play *River* by Bishop Briggs. Without waiting for the others, I let out a scream I've been needing to let out and slam my baseball bat onto the windshield of the car. I watch it splinter and everything I've been holding in for days comes out. The anger, the betrayal. All of it. I slam the bat down again, smashing the side windows and breaking them into millions of pieces. It was therapeutic just like the time we destroyed Nirvana's family home, but this time felt different.

This felt freeing in a whole other way, releasing demons I personally didn't know I had.

"Rory?" Layla's voice sounds behind me but I was too far gone. Screaming out my frustrations with work, with Anthony, with life. I was just so done, so tired of the emotional turmoil that surrounded me day after day. I was pissed that I had to get an STD scan and even more pissed that Anthony could cheat on his pregnant wife with me. I screamed again and hit the hood of the car.

"Lorelai!" I heard shouted and I finally stop, dropping the bat before falling backwards to sit in my own misery. Ophelia steps closer to me and leans down on her haunches to stare me in the eye, her dark eyes seeing way too much for my liking.

"Sorry," I breathe out.

"Don't apologize, you clearly needed to let that out," Delaney says, sinking down beside me with a little groan.

"Do you want to tell us about what just happened?" Sera asks, leaning against the crowbar she held.

I take a deep breath saying, "I have been seeing Anthony since I was seventeen and just found out he's married, and his wife is pregnant." There is a stunned silence before Layla breaks it.

"What the actual fuck? Rory, are you okay, did you kick his ass?"

I laugh a little and shake my head. "No, apparently I can't even make a proper fist, as Caden so eloquently put it 'I'd break my fucking thumb'." I mock in a deep voice.

"When have you seen Caden?" Nirvana asks, her interest piqued.

I feel myself blush. "Um, he found me crying at my brother's bar. I told him a little about Anthony and I said I wanted to kick his ass. Then he asked me to make a fist and he said it was wrong, so I may have asked him to teach me to kick his ass if the need ever arrived."

"Is he?" Delaney asks.

"He said he would." Before we could say anything else there was a loud crash outside causing us to all jump into action. I ran outside and was shocked that there were two cars smashed together.

"Someone call 911!" I shout before running across the busy street ignoring my friends' shouts of me to come back. But I couldn't. I could see a child in the back seat, and I knew I had to do something. I made it to the car and saw how bad the wreck was up close. The car was caved in on the passenger's side and the sound of kids crying was loud in the air. That on top of the smell of gasoline dripping. I looked under the car and saw the gas and smoke piling high into the air.

"Shit," I muttered as a sense of urgency rose inside of me. I went to the side of the car where a woman was driving and unconscious as her kids tried to wake her up. "Hey, hey it's going to be okay." I try to be soothing but it's difficult with my heart racing and the sound of people rushing forward to help the other people. The sounds of sirens were heard in the distance and all I could think was Caden was coming. He could help better than I could, but for the time being I began getting the kids out of the car and to the side of the road where the girls were waiting to protect them until help could get to their mother. But I could see the woman was in pain, coming to after passing out. I lean into the window and ask, "What's your name?"

She gasps for breath and says, "Louisa."

"Hi Louisa, your kids are fine, are you hurt?"

"My arm." Without thinking I climb into the backseat of the car and climb over the console and climb into the front passenger's seat.

"Here, let me see if I can stabilize your arm so there is not a lot of pressure on it." I undo my coveralls and pull my shirt over my head, uncaring that I'm in just my bra as I rip the material and reach over the console to wrap the shirt over her neck as gently as possible and make a makeshift arm sling, so her arm doesn't move.

"I didn't mean to crash," Louisa cries out as I move her arm back into place across her chest. "I forgot to take my meds today. I was in a hurry. I had to get the kids to their doctor's appointments, and I just couldn't gain control of my seizure."

"Hey, hey, hey. No one could've predicted this. I don't think anyone else was injured too badly and all your kids are safe with my friends. We got them out and you're next." Just as I say that the firetruck stops beside us and the first thing I see is dark eyes.

Chapter 14

CADEN

I am sitting in the rig cleaning it when the alarms go off making me jump into action. I suit up as fast as I can and jump back into the rig beside Ravi as we put on our headsets.

"What do we got?" I ask as adrenaline runs through my veins at the thought of action. These last few days have been more training but today was the real thing.

"Head on collision on the interstate across from the rage room. Was called in as soon as it happened," Ravi explained. It doesn't take us long to get to the scene of the accident but when I see it I know it's going to be a bad one. The front end is smashed to hell along with the passenger side of the other car. But it's the other woman in the car that has my breath stopping in my lungs.

"What the hell is she doing?" I mutter under my breath as we come to a full stop. I jump out and run over to her.

"Rory?" I question and she turns, and I see relief in her hazel eyes. Her hand is gentle on the other woman's shoulder as she sits beside her inside the car. "You're here," she breathes out. "Um, this is Louisa, she's a thirty-five-year-old woman who had a seizure while driving and wrecked into the passenger side of the other car. There were three kids in the back seat, but I got them out of the car before you came and got them over with the others. There are no physical injuries on them as they all had seatbelts on. I know I probably should've stayed put, but there's gas leaking. I was scared to move Louisa because I don't know how to support her neck." She's rambling as if she's nervous, but a sense of pride fills me at her quick thinking.

"Rory, you did good," I say, moving her gently out of the way. "Go sit with the kids. I'll get their mom out and into an ambulance."

She nods slowly and goes to climb through the back seat but stops when Louisa grabs her hand. "No, you can't leave. Please don't leave me."

Rory grips her hand tightly and leans into the car. "You're in good hands, Louisa. I'll be right over there with your kids making sure they're okay. They are worried about you and knowing that help is here will help them feel a little better."

Louisa nods her head sending brown hair flying around her as she slowly lets go of Rory's hand and lets her back away and move towards her kids. I turn back to Louisa and say, "Hey Louisa, I'm Caden. Can you tell me what hurts?"

"My head and back hurt a lot. My arm is aching too. I can't move it. Rory put her shirt on it." I didn't even notice that as Rory was wearing coveralls, but the level of thought she put into helping a stranger was on another level I never knew truly existed in people. Not with the life I've lived. But that was a thought for another time, when I wasn't working, because I couldn't afford a distraction right now.

"Okay, on a scale of 1-10 where is your pain level?" I ask.

"I've had three kids naturally, so I'll say it's a strong six right now."

I chuckle and take the bar Ravi was holding and pry open the door, before he moves in to pull her from the car as EMTs come over with a gurney. The whole process doesn't take long as we deal with the gas leak and the cars are towed away. My eyes move to where Rory is standing with the other women, she says something to the others before coming towards me.

"I'm sorry for getting in the way earlier."

"You did good, Ro Ro. It was dangerous, so don't do anymore hero shit. It almost took ten years off my life seeing you at the wreck," I say teasingly, but I meant it. Seeing her standing there in those coveralls and holding Louisa's hand had my nerves wrecked.

"I'm sorry," she whispers.

"Don't apologize, *Chīsai doragon* you did what you had to do. You were a badass." And I meant that. Not many people would've helped, they'd be too busy gawking at the sight in front of them. But not Rory. She jumped into action. Was it terrifying? Hell yes, but I admired the fuck out of her for it.

"Do you want to get a drink with all of us after your shift tonight?" she asks.

I stare into her eyes; I should say no. I really should, but I find myself nodding. She beams up at me, her smile wide and I knew I made the right call. I tap her chin gently, and head back to the rig where Ravi is watching me intently. I don't say anything to him because I don't want him to get the wrong idea. Luckily he doesn't say anything, and we head back to the station.

It took me an hour to get ready for the bar that we were meeting the girls at, and nerves went through me. Why the hell was I suddenly nervous to see her? It's not like I had feelings for her. We were just friends. Shaking those thoughts out of my head, I headed to my car and climbed in. It doesn't take me long to get to Marco's Bar from the station, but it does take me a minute to catch my breath and get the courage to go into the bar. When I do, I see her. Standing alone at the bar with tight black jeans on and a white t-shirt that shows off her curves. I walk over to her, and she turns to look at me, her eyes bright and smile wide.

"Hey!" she calls.

"Hi, Miss hero," I tease and see her cheeks turn a slight shade of pink that has my heart rate kicking in.

"You're the real hero. I saw the way you cut her out of the car, plus you put out that little fire." She waves her hand through the air and smiles at me. "You're a real hero and should be proud of what you do."

If only it were that easy. I enjoy what I do, but all my life I've been told I'm too reckless, too stubborn, and should settle down. But I didn't want that, nor do I want to be stuck at a boring job that'll have me wanting to rip my hair out.

"What's going on in that head of yours?" Rory asks, leaning over to grab two waters before passing me one. I take it gratefully and take a sip, so it gives me something to do other than focus on the penetrating stare that is Rory.

"Life," I finally say.

"It can be shitty sometimes," she says, nodding her head sending curls bouncing around her face.

"That it can."

We stand in silence before she asks, "Have you always wanted to be a firefighter?"

I think about it for a second then shrug, "I've always wanted to help people. Like I've told you before."

"That's true, but there's other ways to help people. A nurse, a doctor, a veterinarian, things less dangerous."

"Maybe I like the danger," I tease but that's not true. Well, not all the way true.

I take a sip of the cold water letting the liquid soothe my suddenly burning throat. "It's freeing. The adrenaline I feel is freeing. Like free falling from a cliff."

"That sounds incredible," she whispers.

"What about you, why a lawyer?"

She turns her head and I follow her lead seeing the other women laughing with Sorrow and Ravi.

"I did it for Delaney and Nirvana. Their lives have been so tragic, the hurt they had to endure was so unfair, and I know they deal with it every single day. If I can help someone get out of those situations, I will."

"That's admirable. I'm sure they are proud of you," I say. "I know I'm proud of you."

She looks at me and smiles softly. "Thank you, Caden. I really needed to hear that."

"What's your job like?" I ask, because I want to get to know her and not from the basic stuff I learned during my search of her.

"I'm switching away from being Anthony's assistant to a new lawyer's paralegal this week."

"Is Anthony the ex?" I ask, squeezing my water bottle a little tighter.

She nods. "That's the one. The one whose ass I want to kick."

Laughing, I ask, "When are we going to do that by the way?"

"Do what?" Ravi asks, leading Nirvana towards the bar.

"Kick my ex's ass. Caden is going to teach me self-defense tomorrow if he's free."

"We should teach all of them self-defense based on their

pasts. It would be good just in case someone isn't there to protect them," Ravi mutters, thinking to himself as he looks at Nirvana as she gets the bartender's attention.

She looks over her shoulder at Ravi and sends him a small smile before grabbing a bottle of water and beer. "What are we talking about?"

Ravi takes the beer she holds out and says, "Self-defense for you guys just in case you need it."

"I think that's a great idea," Rory says, glancing at Delaney.

So that's how I got roped into doing a self-defense class for all the women. I wasn't upset that it was no longer going to be just me and Rory, not in the least. Nope, it was better this way. Now, I wouldn't be tempted by her. Not that I was, but now there was a guaranteed line there I won't cross. I can't cross. I just have to keep telling myself that.

Chapter 15

CADEN

Today's the day I promised Rory to give her self-defense lessons. Rory and the other women that is. The other men are here with me, and we are just waiting for the women. I stand by the wall going through some throwing knives before sheathing one at my side. I want the women to become well acquainted with weapons when they need them. I hear footsteps and turn as Rory comes in wearing a pink sports bra that makes her skin shine and matching leggings. I take a deep breath as she comes near me.

"Good afternoon," she says with a warm smile.

"Hey, are you ready for this?" I ask.

"Yup. Never been more ready to learn how to kick someone's ass before," Rory says, bouncing on the balls of her feet. The other women arrive soon after Rory and stand in a line before me. I nod approvingly.

"All right. You all know why you're here," I start. "Self-defense is very important, especially as a woman. Men are the number one cause of death in women around the world. So, you need to learn how to protect yourself with whatever it is you have on hand. When fighting a man you need to go for the weak spots. The eyes, the throat, and the groin."

"What if they are way taller than you and you can't reach their eyes or throat?" Nirvana asks, her tone serious.

"Then go for the groin and or the shin, it will distract them for a moment giving you time to grab a weapon. Which is whatever's closest to you," I answer. "Now, I want to separate you into pairs. Sorrow you are with Delaney, Ravi you're with Nirvana. Layla you're with Drew, Sera you're with Spencer, Ophelia you're with Max, and Rory you're with me."

Was it stupid to put Rory with me? Probably, but I wanted to be the one to teach her. She wanted me to teach her, so here we are and damn it if I didn't want to know what it felt like to have her hands on me.

"Elijah, you'll be back up if anyone gets hurt, but you can also let us know if there's anything else we need to know or teach." I know he's a detective, Spencer told us that when we met, although I was sure there was more to him than that, but it wasn't my business. Rory stands in front of me and swallows hard. "I'm going to come at you, and you have to stop me," I instruct. She nods and I lunge at her already catching the fist she was sending my way and turning her into me with the little knife pressed against her throat. It was a fast move, one I have perfected over the years.

I can feel her breath quicken as I step back holding the knife away from both of us. "You have to be quicker than that, Lorelai," I say.

Her eyes narrow. "How do you know my full name?" A smirk finds its way to my lips as I see that hint of fire inside of her.

"Doesn't matter. Pay attention. I'm coming at you

again." I lunge forward and she does something I don't expect. She starts screaming at the top of her lungs. Panicked, I grab her and cover her mouth with my hand. She fights against me and bites down on my hand hard before she turns in my arms and knees me between the legs. I curse and fall down, and she gasps in surprise as I lay groaning on the ground. I hear a collective *ooh* from the men, and I know I'm done for. I'll never live this down as long as I live.

"Oh my god! Caden, I'm so sorry!" Rory kneels beside me, her face full of anguish, but she did exactly what she was supposed to do. She protected herself even if that meant I would get hurt in the process.

"It's okay," I groaned, still cupping myself between my legs. It hurt like hell, but pride swam through me. "Maybe we can go to knife throwing next," I suggest causing Rory to give a slight laugh as she holds a hand out to me and helps me up. I grimace at the pain and limp towards the throwing board waiting for her to follow me.

"Is throwing knives a good self-defense mechanism?" Rory asks.

"Of course not, but it's fun," I say seriously. She nods her head as if she understands. I can tell she knows I'm just bullshitting her, but she plays along.

It's just the two of us at the throwing board and I pull the knife out and toss it at the cork board hitting it directly in the middle. "It's like darts, hold your elbow straight and throw at a ninety-degree angle and you'll hit your mark."

Rory nods and takes the knife from the board, lines herself up with the board, and throws it as accurately as she can, hitting it just below the target in the wall. "Not bad," I say encouragingly.

"So," I start, "how are you doing after everything?"

Rory sighs and grabs the knife again. "It's fine. Well, as

fine as I can get. Anthony doesn't know anything is wrong. I haven't seen him, and I just put in a request for a transfer. So, I won't have to see him at work, but I still have to see him at a dinner being hosted by the company."

"You don't want to go to the dinner?" I ask, taking the knife from her and placing it back into her hand the correct way, before I line her arm up so she can take the shot.

"Not really. All my peers will be there, so will he."

That makes me stop and think about what Ravi said in the gym about bringing a date to my sister's wedding. If I can help her with her little problem she can help me with mine.

"Maybe we can help each other out," I say as the idea begins to solidify in my head.

Rory

I stare at Caden arching a brow. "How can we help each other?" I ask genuinely curious.

"I need a date for my sister's wedding, and you need someone for your dinner. We can both help each other out." The idea does sound appealing. I don't want to have to go by myself to this dinner and showing up with one of my girls might send an odd message or show that Anthony broke something in me. Which he didn't. Not in the slightest, but I didn't want to face him like that, especially alone. Something about Caden made me feel confident in myself and my capabilities as a person. Not just the lowly assistant. The loser who dated a married man by accident. No, I was here to gain that confidence back and I was. Just by being in Caden's presence. I don't understand why I feel so comfortable in his company, but I won't complain.

"Okay, how would this work?" I ask.

"Monday night come to my apartment, and we can discuss it in detail," Caden says, nodding his head as he goes. He holds out the knife to me, a beautiful piece with words engraved on the handle and a dragon along the blade in a beautiful display that had me in awe. I didn't realize it was a dragon at first, but it's beautiful.

"Take it, practice throwing it, and when you come back for more training it will be easier."

"I can't take this, it's beautiful. What if I break it?" I ask, holding the hilt out to him.

"Take it. You did a great job today and we can talk more on Monday." With that he called time on everyone before leaving. Leaving me alone with this beautiful knife and a thousand questions.

Chapter 16

RORY

I stare blankly at the screen in front of me, watching the cursor as it blinks over and over again. After last night I put in a formal request to be transferred to someone else or I would be sending in my two weeks' notice. Little did I know, Anthony had already had me moved to someone else. A public defender who had two cases under her belt. I didn't mind, but it irked every nerve I hardly had to no end.

"Bastard," I mutter, rearranging my hair so it sat neatly on the nape of my neck. I had two hours before I had to be at Caden's apartment in order to discuss our situations and see if we could come to a comfortable conclusion. But I also had to find a way to get back at Anthony. I glanced at the binder where the questions and answers for the latest witness sat, and I smirked before grabbing it and erasing all of the answers before emailing Claire.

She never bothered to actually meet the clients and those she did meet complained about her unprofessional behavior and how rude and condescending she could be. I quickly typed out the email explaining my departure and she now had to ask the witness questions before the next interview stage. Then I emailed the witness about being re-questioned by someone new in order to have an accurate depiction on what happened. To be honest with everything going on I forgot about it all until this very moment.

Once satisfied and the emails were sent, I turned off my computer, and muted the notifications on my phone. With a small smile, I stood and grabbed my bag before slipping on my shoes to go to Caden's. And for some reason the thought made the constant pressure in my chest ease a little bit. These last few days had been slow and tortuous as I waited to see Caden. I have no idea why, it's not as if we were together and I was a teenage girl with her first crush. Caden was a friend. A good friend and I just enjoyed being in his company. I head out of the office and stop as a figure steps in front of me. I take a step back as Anthony crowds into me.

He goes to kiss my mouth, but I turn my head and look at the wall. As he steps back the smile that was on his face falls. "What's wrong?" he asks, as if he doesn't have a wife at home.

For some reason his obliviousness pisses me off and I push at his chest, pushing him away from me. "As if you don't know," I sneer.

He looks confused and hurt at my rejection and normally I would feel bad, but not this time.

"How about the fact that you're fucking married!" I snap at him, watching as the color drains from his face.

"How, how'd you—" he stammers.

"I came to your office a week ago and she was in there with you. And heavily pregnant. How could you do that to not just me, but her, too?"

"I… we aren't exclusive. We never were, Rory. We were just having a little fun."

Anger boils over in me as I lift my hand up and slap him across the face. His head reels back, and he stares at me shocked and angry. That makes two of us.

"Don't try and downplay what we did. You're a cheating, lying asshole and we both deserve better than you."

"You won't say anything to her," he snaps, grabbing onto my arm tightly and shaking me. I grimace at the pain I feel and try to push him off of me, but his grip tightens.

"Let me go," I demand. But he doesn't.

He gets into my face and sneers down at me. "You'll keep your mouth shut, or I'll give you a reason to keep it shut. Do you understand me? Who is going to believe a lowly whore like you compared to me? Someone with a good career, a wife and baby. I'll be damned if I let you ruin it because you couldn't keep your legs closed."

Tears threaten in my eyes as he speaks, but I don't let him see he's getting to me. Instead, I yank my arm free and head out of the office to the one person who's been nothing but kind and caring towards me. To the place I feel safest. To Caden. To whatever plan he had up his sleeve that I would inevitably agree to because I just couldn't help myself.

Chapter 17

CADEN

Crouching down, I turned on the PlayStation waiting for it to load before moving back and typing in the Netflix password to set up the movie. "You're such an old man, Cade," a voice sounded through the speaker of my phone.

Tsking, I turned and looked down at the camera where Jade and Amani were both sitting and watching as I struggled with the damn controller. "It takes time. Hush so I can concentrate. You're distracting me."

"Did you at least fix the food before this?" Amani asks.

"Of course I did. It's warming on the stove," I mutter as I finally load the movie on the TV. Smiling in triumph, I stand and dish up my food before plopping down on the couch ready to play the movie. As soon as I get comfortable however, there is a small knock on my door.

"What now?" Jade asks, eating a spoon full of ramen.

Huffing, I set my bowl down and head to the door without answering my sisters. I open the door and stare down in shock as Rory gets ready to knock again. "Oh," she says and startles, her hand falling to her side swiftly. "Sorry, am I late?" she asks, her voice hesitant.

"Late?" I question before my eyes widen. "Shit! I forgot… I um…"

She gives a small smile and says, "It's okay I can come back if you'd rather do this another day."

Shaking my head, I pull her inside. "No. No, it's fine." I watch her as she bends slightly to pull off her shoes revealing socks with a gavel and briefcase on them. "Nice socks," I tease, the tension easing out of me.

Rory glances up at me and smiles. "Nirvana got them for me last Christmas. They are my most treasured possession."

I laugh and lead her to the living room. "Are you hungry?"

Rory bites her plump lower lip, snagging my attention before she nods slowly, "A little bit, but I don't want to intrude."

I wave my hand. "No intrusion. I'll just be a minute." I grab my phone and make my way to the kitchen before setting my phone down to see my sisters looking back at me with wide grins.

"I didn't know you'd be having a girl join you," Jade teases. I can feel my cheeks heat up before I scowl at them.

"She's a friend."

"A friend that you cook for," Amani added skeptically. I don't answer right away as I make some spicy Tteokbokki and ramen with cheese before I open the fridge to grab an egg and the jar of kimchi, that my mom walked me through how to make last weekend. It takes me a few minutes to make before I'm putting it into a bowl with a fork and walking back to the living room where Rory is sitting primly on the couch.

I hand her the bowl and she looks at it with curiosity before looking at me. "What is this? I've never had it before."

"Spicy Korean rice cakes. Tteokbokki is what it's called. My sisters and I have a movie night once a month where we eat food from the movie that is chosen."

Rory gasps and asks, "Why didn't you tell me I was intruding on a sibling day?"

I laugh again. "It's fine. Stay." I set the phone down to introduce Rory to them, "Rory, these are my sisters Amani and Jade."

Rory smiles and waves. "It's nice to meet you both. I'm sorry to intrude, I didn't know."

Amani waves her concern away. "It's fine. I hope you like scary movies though." Rory looks at me and I see a slight smile on her mouth before I lean forward to press play on the controller. The movie starts but I find myself staring at Rory as she takes a bite of the rice cake.

She hums softly and goes for another bite before turning to me. "This is really good, thank you, Caden." I smile at her and get comfortable and eat my own food while watching the movie. We sit in comfortable silence watching as the movie gets more intense as it goes on and I feel Rory scootch a little closer to me pulling her knees up to her chest and resting her chin on her knees.

"Do you think you'd survive the zombie apocalypse?" she asks randomly, turning away from the movie to glance at me.

"Of course. I know how to fight and have a straight, always accurate shot."

Humming under her breath she leans her head back and replies, "I don't think I'd want to. I just imagine the smell and it just doesn't seem worth it to me."

"I'm pretty sure everyone just breathes from their mouth at that point," I comment, staring at her.

She shudders dramatically. "No thanks. Plus, what about

hygienic products? Medicine? The pharmacy would be the first thing raided after a grocery store and gas station."

My mouth twitches in amusement. "You've thought about this long?" I ask.

"Ever since the movie started," she replied.

I shake my head, smiling as we fall into silence again watching until the end of the movie. I can see tears brimming in Rory's eyes as she turns away from me to wipe at them.

"You didn't tell me how sad it would be," she accused half-heartedly. I chuckle before bumping my shoulder gently against hers, then stand grabbing her bowl.

"I didn't know. I'm going to put these in the sink so we can talk, okay?"

She nods before standing. "Where's your restroom?"

Pointing to the hall, I say, "First door that's open." Nodding, she moves down the hall leaving me alone with my thoughts. How I wanted to pull her against me when I saw tears brimming her hazel eyes, or the small smile she got when she was talking. Sighing, I head to the kitchen. I didn't need to have these thoughts. Not when I needed her to be my girlfriend for ten days next month.

I busy myself with the dishes and don't even realize my sisters are still on the call until Jade says, "She's pretty. Different from Xena."

"Don't say her name in my presence again, Jade," Amani said and sniffed, making me smile slightly.

"She's going to be our sister-in-law. We've got to be respectful for Mom and Dad."

I hear the bathroom door open and quickly wipe off my hands before grabbing my phone. "I've got to go," I whisper and hang up before they can say anything else just as Rory rounds the corner.

"Your sisters seem nice," she says.

I huff out a laugh as I lean against the counter, watching her as she twists a small ring on her middle finger I didn't notice before now. "Are you okay?"

"Yes. I'm just not sure how to start this conversation," she replies.

I nod and reply, "That's fine. I'll talk and you interject when you see fit."

She smiles and leans forward. "Deal."

Swallowing, I push a hand through my hair, and begin, "You need a date to your lawyer school thing, and I need a date to my sister's wedding, as I told you before. But it is for ten days and in California. Now, before you say anything I am capable of footing the bill. You won't need to spend any money. I will cover for you as any decent boyfriend would." She opens her mouth but stops before saying anything. "I'm aware you've just come out of a difficult relationship so this will be strictly platonic, but on the outside we will seem like a real loving couple."

"Fine. But there must be rules."

"I wouldn't have it any other way."

Her hazel eyes narrow before she says, "No sex. That's how things get complicated. No flirting with other women in front of me. It may be fake, but I won't be disrespected by another man."

"I would never do that to you, Ro Ro."

"And," she starts, "No bad pet names. If I hear as much as a pookie or care bear I will castrate you and gift your balls to Nirvana for Christmas without a second thought."

My mouth twitches but I nod holding out my hand. "Whatever you say *Chīsai doragon.*"

Hesitantly she places her hand in mine and says, "No rule must be broken."

"Haven't you heard the saying rules are meant to be broken?" I tease, shaking her hand.

"Caden." It's a warning. One that makes me grin.

"As you wish."

"So, it's a deal?" she clarifies.

"It's a deal." One I hope I never regret.

Chapter 18

RORY

I stare at my new cubicle. It was a barren, pale beige box. Nothing more nothing less. I placed my box of belongings on the desk and stared out of the small window watching the leaves on the trees subtly fall to the ground. It was seven in the morning, and I packed my things from my old desk before anyone would be here at nine. I was meeting my new attorney today, a woman named Kaila who was a public defender.

I heard her before I saw her. The soft *click clack* of her heels were loud. I don't know what to expect when I meet her until she says, "Dude, there's some guy in the lobby who was glitter bombed and I honestly don't think I've started my day in such a bright way in years."

I turned and met her head on, her eyes were a dark brown matching the color of her hair that hung in loose waves down her back and she wore a bright smile. "I'm sorry, what?"

She nods. "Yeah, I guess he fucked with the wrong person and got a package that as soon as he opened it, boom!" She motioned a bomb exploding with her hands. "Glitter everywhere."

I covered my mouth trying not to laugh. "Who was it?"

She shrugs. "Your old attorney, Anthony. Anyway, I'm Kaila and today we've got a shit ton of meetings. We are meeting a client who was arrested for a traffic violation which she swears she didn't commit. I know you would usually do the questioning as a paralegal, but I want you to see how I like things. My assistant Vanessa is on her way now."

She takes out her phone, glances at me, and asks, "How do you take your coffee? Also, are there any health issues I need to be aware of? I like to have all the information in case shit hits the fan. Also, we are doing a mock trial on the 18th so be ready for that."

I'm taken aback at her request and quickly rattle off my coffee order. An iced latte with low sugar caramel and Splenda. "I'm diabetic. So, I have certain times when I take my insulin."

She hums. "My dad had diabetes, so I get it. Just set alarms and we'll work with it." Putting her phone in her pocket she asks, "Anything else?"

I swallow hard. "I know it's a little last minute, but my, umm, boyfriend has a family wedding on the first through the tenth of September, so is it possible to get that week off?"

She nods. "Should be fine, but I'd like to ask to set up at least one meeting during if that is possible. Will he be there at the," she uses air quotes, "gathering"?"

"Yes, he is my plus one."

Kaila sits at her desk and motions for me to sit. "When do you graduate?"

"Usually in May but this year it's June, I had a later start."

"When do you plan on taking the bar?"

I hesitate, clasping my hands in my lap and answer, "I planned for July."

Nodding, she leans forward. "Good. Be sure to study and have all your ducks in a row. But if you need to, never feel bad for taking a break. It doesn't expire so you have all the time in the world."

Another pair of heels sounded in our direction. "Cedrick sent the footage Kai! And it is absolute gold!" The excited woman put a tray of coffees down and turned to me with a wide smile. "Hi, I'm Vanessa." She was a bubbly, happy woman with wide green eyes and red hair that reminded me of the rising sun.

I blink and stand shaking her hand. "I'm Rory. It's nice to meet you."

"Okay enough chatting, we have business to attend to," Kaila says, handing me my coffee and grabbing her keys as Vanessa grabbed a pile of folders. I follow after them and stop when I see the glitter covering the floor and I smile, knowing he'll be covered in the stuff for weeks to come.

After a long day, I received a message from Ophelia inviting me to dinner at Sorrow's place. So, here I was sitting in the driveway for a moment before climbing out and heading to the door. I held up my hand to knock, but I didn't get that far before the door was pulled open. Sorrow stood there wearing an apron with bright pink oven mitts all over it.

"That's an interesting fashion choice," I say before I can help myself.

He rolls his eyes and motions towards the house. "Everyone is inside."

"Thanks, I do like the apron. You look very domesticated."

He snorts. "Shut up and go inside." I nod, take off my jacket and head inside where the others are laughing and talking. I glance around the room looking for Caden when I see him in the kitchen flipping something in a pan. I can't help but stare at the way his back muscles flexed with each movement.

"You've got a bit of drool happening," Sera said, coming up beside me, causing me to jump.

I glare at her, and she smiles. "Didn't Louise teach you not to sneak up on people," I hiss.

"She might have, but we both know if she did I didn't pay attention." Sera holds out a drink to me. I sip it, letting the fruity concoction coat my tongue, and sigh softly as the tension of the day finally eased out of me.

"Thank you." Sera looks at me intently, seeing more than I would like her to see, but that's how they all were. Attuned to everything we did or felt.

"Are you feeling okay?"

I nod, sipping at the fruity drink and letting it soothe me before I went to sit beside Nirvana and Ophelia. "Which one of you did it?" I ask in a low whisper so the others didn't hear me.

Nirvana glances at me. "Did what?"

"You know what."

Ophelia arches a neat black brow and asks, "What is it you think we did?"

"The glitter bomb on Anthony at work today."

The two of them exchanged looks before bursting into laughter. "Oh man! I wish I could've been a fly on that wall," Nirvana said, wiping under her eyes. "Honey, I'm crazy but my brand of crazy doesn't include glitter. I'm a set a house on fire type of bitch."

Glaring at her I say, "Well, who did it then?"

"Yeah, that was me and Delaney," a deep voice said behind me.

I turn and gape at Caden as he sets a small plate in front of me. "You sent him a glitter bomb?"

He nods. "He made you cry. He deserved that and more." For some unexplainable reason that sent my heart fluttering and heat to rise in my cheeks. He stares at me for a minute making me forget everything but him in the moment. He sent me a dimpled smile and I found myself smiling back and pulling my phone out.

"I have the lobby footage of him opening it. Want to see?" Caden's smile widened as he plopped down beside me and threw an arm over the couch behind my shoulders, not quite touching me but close enough that I could feel his warmth. Swallowing hard, I press play on the video Vanessa sent me and Kaila. There's no sound but the picture is clear when the delivery man brought in the little box for Anthony.

Nirvana sat closer to me, basically leaning over my lap as she watched with wide eyes. Ophelia stood and moved behind the couch to see better just as Anthony unwrapped the box which exploded open spraying him with a huge amount of glitter. Nirvana burst out laughing first and we all followed suit as he had a tantrum. And that's what it was, a tantrum. He threw the box down and kicked it, shouting at those close to him while pointing. What sends me over the edge is when he kicks the box a second time, he misses, and falls back on his ass. I close my phone and burst into laughter with the others.

"D-Did you see how he fell?" Nirvana wheezed out, wiping under her eyes.

"Or his feet stomping?" Ophelia added.

We sober a little before laughing again.

"What the hell are you doing, Caden? You're on kitchen duty," Spencer says, coming into the living room, holding a whisk, and glaring at us. Caden glances behind himself before turning to me saying, "Send me that video. I need it as my screensaver." Laughing, he pats my knee as he stands, before walking towards Spencer and taking the whisk from him. I stare after him before sighing softly, almost wishfully. I shake my head and stuff my phone in my pocket.

I glance at Nirvana and Ophelia and catch them watching me intently making me chuckle nervously. "So what do you think this dinner is about?"

They don't say anything for a long moment, just keep staring, before Ophelia takes pity on me, shrugs and says, "Delaney said she had to tell us something."

"Ten bucks says she's pregnant," Layla says as she walks in with a box of cupcakes.

"Twenty says she's pregnant and eloped," I say jokingly."

Nirvana shakes her head. "Nah, they are totally adopting another dog."

Before we can make any more guesses Delaney calls out, "Dinner."

Chapter 19

CADEN

My eyes find her as soon as she enters the dining room, her eyes meet mine and she smiles softly. Just a slight tilt of her full lips as she sits down next to where my seat is. She pushes her hair out of her face and rearranges her utensils. I'm so caught up in watching her I don't even realize someone is beside me before I hear, "You do realize you could take a picture and look all you want."

I glance away and glare at Sorrow who is clearly enjoying tormenting me.

"Then I'd be a stalker, Sorrow."

He snorts. "Yes, because drooling in my kitchen makes it better."

I roll my eyes. "I was not drooling."

"Really? Then what's on your chin?" Glaring, I wiped at my face making him laugh.

"I miss when you didn't joke at other people's misery," I groan, my face heating slightly.

Sorrow laughed and shook his head. "Nah, I just like seeing the men, who vowed never to be in a relationship again, fall for a woman."

I roll my eyes. "Please, I never plan to fall for another woman." Besides, Rory would only be my fake girlfriend, nothing more. But he didn't need to know that. I grab the salad bowl and walk over to the table and set it in the middle of everyone before sitting down.

Rory glances at me for a moment before leaning closer. "After dinner I need to talk to you about something."

My heart speeds up and I nod. "Help me with the dishes, we can talk there without anyone around." She sends me one of those small smiles and nods.

As everyone settles into their seats I sigh wishing Sam was here with us. Since he left on another tour the table didn't feel complete, as my eyes zeroed in on Elijah I could see he was fitting in with us, but we didn't know much about him.

"Elijah, what is it that you do?" I ask, as plates are passed around.

The large man in question clears his throat taking the bread basket from Sera, "I'm a detective." The table goes silent as we all stare at him.

"A detective?" Drew drawls out.

Elijah nods. "I'm here to find a child predator. He's been out of reach for years."

Rory sits up beside me. "A predator? If you're here do you know where he is?"

Elijah looks at her for a lot longer than I care for, causing me to straighten in my seat, and I see Spencer beside him smirk before forking some salad as his friend answers, "No. Our last lead was in Texas, so I've been investigating while also seeing Spence. It's been a few years."

"How long have you known each other?" Delaney asks, biting into a piece of bread.

"Since elementary school. We were on the Little Leagues together. Been friends since."

We fall into easy conversation eating and talking before Nirvana speaks up, "Okay, the waiting is killing me. What's going on Laney?"

I glance up and stare at Delaney as she glances at Sorrow twisting her fingers nervously sending my nerves on high alert. "What's wrong?" I demand.

"Nothing bad. We just wanted to tell you all together. We're married," Delaney said softly.

"And pregnant," Sorrow adds, looking at his wife with so much love in his eyes.

Delaney swallows and stares at her friends with pleading eyes. "Please don't be upset. We plan to have a wedding eventually, but when we found out we were expecting I wanted to get married soon."

Rory stops her, "Lane, you don't need to explain to us. We're happy for you. Never think we'd be upset for doing what you felt was right."

"You're not upset?" Delaney asked, her voice wobbling.

We all shook our heads. I was happy for them, I always knew Sorrow wanted to marry this woman and it was only a matter of time before he did it. But this news explains his reaction to her at the party. I watch as Rory stands and goes towards Delaney and hugs her tightly. She smiles at Sorrow and congratulates him before pressing a kiss to Delaney's head gushing at how good of a mother she will be, and I couldn't agree more. Standing, I move over to the couple and hug Delaney. "Does this mean I'm going to be the fun uncle?"

She laughs, "Of course you are."

Pulling away I hug Sorrow. "Congrats man. I knew you had it in you." He scoffs but hugs me back before pulling away and looking at Delaney as she talks to her friends.

"Never been happier. I can't wait to see what she's like with our child."

I smirk. "Look at you all sappy. I knew it was only a matter of time," I tease. He rolls his eyes, but I could see the happiness shining in them. After a while I gather up the empty plates with the help of Rory and start the dishes.

We work in relative silence both lost in our own thoughts when she finally speaks. "Did you really mean what you said?" I arch a brow at her as I put the plate she hands me into the dishwasher.

"Be more specific."

She sighs. "I know at your house we made a deal. I got the time off of work, but I'm not sure how this is going to work. I only have one dress I'm wearing to the banquet, so I need to know the dress code."

"That's easy enough. Come to the station tomorrow during your lunch and we can go to the mall and find you something to wear. Or the boutique next to it. We'll find you a perfect dress. No worries, don't overthink it."

She nods slowly and bites her bottom lip. "Okay, but what about touching?"

My brows furrow. "Touching?"

"Yes. Like normal couples do. Should we have a signal or something? I read it in a book somewhere that they had a phrase."

I think for a moment and said, "Just put your hair behind your ear and I'll know to touch you. I'll nod and you can touch me."

Sighing in relief she nods. "Okay good. That works." We fall into silence again before she gasps. "You brought the kitten home today, right?"

I laugh under my breath. "Yes. I even named her."

She smiles. "What did you name her?"

"Skittles."

Her hazel eyes widened. "Skittles? Why Skittles?"

I shrug. "She came to me when I was eating them and it just kind of stuck. Fits her though, she has a little spattering of freckles on her nose."

She laughs. "That's cute. I like it."

I lean over after taking the last dish and shut the dish-washer before starting it and turning to Rory. "Thank you. I really appreciate you helping me with this," I hesitate for a moment before adding, "Just don't fall in love with me. Promise me that."

She nods. "I won't fall in love with you, Caden. I know it's all fake."

I nod, smiling, but a part of it feels forced as if I am lying not only to her but to myself.

Chapter 20

CADEN

I didn't sleep much the night before and was rewinding the rope when I heard a commotion. I stand slowly and move deeper into the station as I see Rory walk inside. She's a sight to behold. Wearing a tight black pencil skirt and red blouse with her hair pulled back showing her minimally made up face. She looked beautiful like an angel fallen from the Heavens. I shake my head. What the fuck? I wasn't supposed to see her as anything more than a partner.

I watch as her gaze moves around the station ignoring the men milling around before her penetrating gaze landed on me. "Oh, there you are. Are you ready?" she asks, her voice sounding huskier than usual.

"Yeah. Have you eaten yet?" I ask, getting my thoughts together.

She nods. "Yep, after I took my medicine. So I should be good."

I grab my wallet and stuff some candy into my pocket

before walking up to her. "What time do you have to be back?"

Glancing down at the dainty watch on her wrist she says, "An hour. So we have time."

I place my hand at the small of her back and lead her out of the station aware of the others, including Ravi, watching me. And I knew for a fact that Ravi would be pressing me for answers when I got back. Groaning internally, I lead her towards the small shop next door with high end dresses. Her eyes widen when she walks inside.

The store had an old rustic vibe with white wood and antler chandeliers which looked both country and chic at the same time. Rory's eyes roamed around the shop and a small brunette bounded over to us with a wide smile on her face. "Hello. Welcome to Cleo's. I'm Miranda. What can I help you with today?"

Clearing my throat, I motion towards Rory and say, "My girlfriend needs a dress for a wedding. No white."

Miranda's eyes move over to Rory, and she looks her up and down before nodding, "Okay, I have a few that might work for what you're looking for. Follow me, please." We follow after her and I'm sent to a chair as Rory is shown to a dressing room directly in front of me.

Sitting down and waiting I pull out my phone seeing texts from the group chat.

Ravi: *What the hell was that Caden?*

Spencer: *What did he do now?*

Ravi: *Rory showed up to the station and Caden looked at her with hearts in his eyes all googly like.*

Me: *I did not. I'm just helping her with something, not that it's any of your business.*

Sorrow: *Helping her?*

Drew: *How?*

Me: *Just going to a dinner with her where her ex is going to be.*

I felt awful lying but I didn't want them talking me out of this. I didn't get a chance to see their replies when the door of the dressing room opened drawing my attention and Rory stepped out wearing a pink silk dress, making her skin look like she was painted almost gold and shining brightly under the light.

"What do you think?" she asks.

I swallow thickly. "You look beautiful. But I think her bridesmaids are wearing pink."

She glances down. "It's a little too tight anyway."

My gaze went down her body, noticing how the dress hugged her slim figure and made her breasts nearly spill out of the top.

"Next one?" I croak out. She nods and goes back inside. She's in there for a while before she calls my name.

"Caden, can you come help me unzip this, please? It's stuck."

I stand and make my way towards the door. It opens slightly and I squeeze into the small room that smells like lavender and vanilla. Rory says, "It's stuck on the fabric, and I don't want to rip it. Can you help me?" I nod, turning her around so I can see the small zipper. My fingers trail down the gentle curve of her spine to the zipper and I steadily and meticulously take the scrunched-up fabric from the tiny prongs. I can feel her breathing hitch as my fingers brush her skin, but I ignore it as I pull the zipper down. When I finish I step back. "There you go."

"Thank you," she says as I leave the room. It goes on like that for thirty minutes, her trying on dresses we both hate, and as she tries on the last one I look around the shop until my gaze lands on a dress in the window.

I get up and look at it as Miranda comes to check on us. "Can she try this one?" I ask.

"Sure, I think it's the only one though. But I can get it for you." I nod in thanks, take my seat, and watch as she slips the dress to Rory. I wait in anticipation until she finally comes out of the dressing room. My breath catches in my throat as I watch her leave the room fully. She wore the dress I chose, a long silk emerald green dress with sleeves off the shoulders and a bodice that cinched in her waist, with a slit up the side. She looked more beautiful than I thought possible. It made the green in her eyes more pronounced.

"Wow, you look amazing," Miranda said, coming up to Rory with a pair of strappy gold heels and handing them to her to try on with the dress. "What do you think?" Miranda asks me drawing Rory's attention.

"Breathtaking," I say without meaning to. Clearing my throat I ask, "How do you like it, Ro Ro?"

"I love it. It's beautiful."

I nod and look at Miranda. "We'll take it."

Rory

I stand beside Caden as Miranda rings up the dress and shoes and I can slowly feel my blood pressure rise at the growing price. Before I can ask her to take off the shoes Caden already has his wallet out and is paying for it.

"Caden, I can..."

"Don't finish that sentence, Lorelai. Consider this a gift." He said my full name again and I make a mental note to ask him how he knows it.

I can't protest, there will be no point plus *máma* always said it was rude to deny a gift, so I nod and mutter, "Thank you." He smiles showing those dimples and I find myself smiling back. This shopping trip has been different than any

I've ever been on before. The entire time Caden told me I looked beautiful or gorgeous in them, but this new dress was different. I felt different in it. Confident. When Miranda was finished bagging the dress Caden grabbed it and slung it over his shoulder before pressing his palm into the small of my back. His touch was gentle, but I felt it to the very core of me. The slight burn that had me inhaling deeply to the possessive curl of his fingers. A move I don't think he even realizes he's doing.

It made me feel secure, treasured even if all of this was fake and I knew it was. But sadly, my brain wasn't catching up. When he walked me to my car I turned and looked up at him. "Thank you for today. I had a lot of fun and truly appreciate the gift." He gave me another smile that had my heart flipping inside of my chest.

"Anytime, Ro Ro. We should have dinner before your conference. So we can get more comfortable together."

I hum under my breath, clutching my keys in my hand. "It's coming up in the next two weeks so we can plan for a night. Maybe I'll come meet Skittles."

He chuckles. "I don't know if I can deal with my cat liking you better than me."

I shrug. "It's not my fault I'm lovable."

He leans closer to me brushing his lips slightly over my forehead, catching me off guard, "People are watching," he explains when I stare at him in confusion. "But if you insist I can make dinner or something."

I glance at him, my eyes going to his pink plump lips before meeting his dark brown eyes, "I'd like that. I'll call you because my work week is hectic so it might not be this week."

"Whenever you need me, Rory, I'll be here."

My lips tilt up. "A girl could get used to having a man at her beck and call." I'm teasing but I can see heat flash in his eyes.

"Be careful what you wish for *Chīsai doragon*." I swallow hard and lean up on my toes and kiss his cheek before climbing into my car, ignoring the heat pooling between my thighs. I didn't need to think of Caden like that, but seeing the way he was looking at me was becoming too much. I needed to focus. I wasn't lying when I said I had a lot on my plate with this new client and trying to get acquainted with the new attorney was taking a lot out of me. I'm so lost in thought that I barely realize I'm parked until someone bangs on my window causing me to jump.

I glance up and see an angry Anthony staring down at me, patches of glitter still coating his face and hands. I don't put my window down, but grab my bag and open the door hitting his legs when he doesn't back up.

"Sorry," I say, even though I wasn't the least bit sorry. In fact, it took a lot of effort from me not to laugh at him.

"You sent that shit to me," he snarled, grabbing my arm in a tight grip.

I turn on him, snatching my arm away. "I didn't do anything, Anthony. Whatever you have going on right now is none of my business."

"So you didn't sabotage my client? You didn't give Claire the questions? How is that not fucking me up?" He's basically shouting in my face now and it's making my blood heat up.

I glare back at him pressing my finger into his chest. "I told your client I will no longer be conducting the questioning which is only right. And Claire studied the same shit I did, if she can't come up with well-informed questions that's a her issue, not a me issue. Get over yourself, Anthony. I'm so sick and tired of your narcissistic bullshit."

He scoffs. "I made you, Rory. Or did you forget?" He gets closer to me, his voice barely above a whisper, and says,

"No one wanted to take a chance on a kid from a low income family the way I did."

"They also didn't want to fuck said kid either. Don't start something you can't finish, Anthony. You didn't make me, I made me. If you did make me you wouldn't be struggling the way you are now." With that I turn and head towards the office.

Chapter 21

RORY

Groaning, I turn off my laptop and press my shaky fingers into my eyes, trying to put pressure on them in an attempt to stop the oncoming headache. Today has been one of the worst days of my life. First with Anthony and then being yelled at and cursed at by a witness who thought that he'd be paid for answering our questions. How he came to that conclusion is beyond me.

"Hey, are you okay?" I hear Vanessa ask behind me.

I nod and reply, "Just tired." And late on my medication. I grab my laptop and shove it into my bag before making my way to the bathroom behind me. I glance around and look under the stalls making sure it was empty before going into the last stall. I sigh with relief when I sit on the toilet, grab my insulin, lift up my shirt to inject it into my belly before leaning my head back and taking a much needed breath. Which then caught in my throat when the bathroom door slammed shut and locked from the outside.

My skin crawled and my stomach dropped as I shoved everything back in my bag and stood. I waited to hear footsteps, but everything was eerily silent save my erratic breathing. Closing my eyes I counted to twenty before I slowly opened the stall door and made my way to the bathroom door and tried pulling it open. It didn't budge. I jiggled the handle before pounding on it with the palm of my hand.

"Hello?" I called out. No one came. That's when panic started to come in. For as long as I can remember I can't be trapped somewhere, or I panic. Or be in water because I suck at swimming but that's a story for another time. I was trapped. "Help somebody!" I couldn't breathe it felt like the walls were closing in on me. I pounded on the door, but no one came and as luck may have it the lights shut off leaving me in total darkness. Tears pricked the backs of my eyes as I sank to the ground and pulled my knees to my chest.

"Think Rory," I scolded myself. Sitting here crying wasn't going to fix my situation, I had to think. My gaze moved restlessly around the room until I saw the small window. I calculated in my head as I stood and made my way to the stall with the window and shut the toilet lid before standing on it. I put my bag on the ground before attempting to reach the window and pushing it open. The fear slowly eased out of me to be replaced with a seething rage that was boiling over.

"That self-righteous prick," I mutter. Because I already know it was Anthony who did this. He knew I hated being trapped, it was one of my biggest fears, yet here I was. Trapped in a bathroom of all places. Pushing open the window did nothing to lessen my anger, if anything it made it worse because there was no way I was getting through it without help and my balance in these heels was unstable at best, and break my neck falling at worst. Cursing, I slowly climbed down and opened my bag to fish out my phone. I debate on calling one of the girls, but I find myself dialing Caden's number.

It rings, once, twice, three times before he answers. "Rory."

I take a breath. "Caden, I…" I pause embarrassment and angry tears burning my eyes. "I need help."

"Where are you?"

With a shaky breath I say, "I'm stuck in the bathroom."

He's silent for a moment then asks, "Like without toilet paper stuck or stuck in the toilet stuck?"

That surprises a laugh out of me. "No. Not like that, I'm locked in and no one's in the office. And it's dark."

"Where's the office?"

"Like ten minutes from the station."

Caden curses, "Shit. I'm at home and that makes me like forty minutes away." My heart sinks and I sniff trying not to cry. "No, don't you cry, Rory," he commands, making me want to smile if the room wasn't suddenly getting smaller and smaller. "Okay, okay Ravi is still at the station. He'll be there soon. I'm turning around, Rory. I'll be there as soon as I can. Until then tell me how you got in such a predicament."

I huff out a laugh. "Fucking Anthony's immature ass. He's pissed at me because he thinks I sent the glitter bomb and he's just now realizing how incompetent Claire is."

"Damn it, this is my fault."

I shake my head even though he can't see me. "No. No, it's not your fault. Anthony is a controlling asshole. If things don't go his way he throws a tantrum." *But he's never used my fear against me,* I add in my head. And he hasn't, but I've never made him this angry before.

"I'm sorry I called you. I figured you were still at the station."

He sighs softly. "No, I was just covering a shift today. I'm sorry."

I rear back surprised. "Why are you sorry?"

"I wasn't there when you needed me."

I scoff softly, "Caden, this isn't your fault. I know better than to poke fun at a wounded man."

"Can you climb up?" a deep voice asks, making me scream, and drop my phone. I turn and see Ravi peeking his head into the window.

I'm gasping for breath as I stare at him. "What the hell, dude? Can't you make some noise?"

He shrugs and says, "To be fair I was always told it's rude to interrupt a phone call." His tone is dry suggesting he did make noise, but I didn't notice. I blush and stand grabbing my phone and hanging up on Caden with a hasty 'bye' before turning to Ravi.

"I'm sorry. It's been a long day, and I didn't hear you."

His gaze softens somewhat before he nods. "I get it. We all have those days. Can you climb up?"

Nodding, I take off my heels and stuff my phone into my bag before climbing up and handing them to Ravi who grabbed them and set them to the side. Swallowing hard, I braced my hands on the edge of the window and pulled myself up to the back of the toilet balancing precariously on the marble and my tiptoes.

"Grab my hands and I'll pull you out," Ravi instructs. I nod, breathe, and grab his hands letting him pull me through the window. The only problem, my hips get stuck.

I look back at my hips and laugh almost hysterically. "You've got to be kidding me."

Ravi glances at me cursing, "Well, damn."

I hang my head low and sigh. "I'm going to kill Anthony."

"Can you push yourself back in?" Ravi asks, moving

around the window. I shrug and try to push myself back through only to yelp in pain when my blouse is caught on something sharp, and it digs into my skin.

I stop and kick my leg in frustration. With nothing left to do, I glance at Ravi, "So how are things with Nirvana?"

His gaze comes back to me and something inside of him softens, melting away that tough exterior that he usually has. "She's good. We're good. Only thing is she's been watching a lot of *MythBusters* lately."

I let out a soft chuckle. "That was Aero's favorite show when she was younger. She used to make us all watch it with her. How's the shelter going?"

"Good. She's really making a difference. I know she wants to help Layla get her shop up and running first before going into it with all her heart."

"Is she still taking her medication?"

"Yes. We have a system that works for us." I want to ask what system but stop myself when I see a bright light flash our way. I glance to the side and see Caden step forward and I could almost weep with relief.

"What the hell?" he mutters.

I glance down at myself and wince. "So, I overestimated my hip span and should've done the Marilyn Monroe thing."

He arches a dark brow. "Marilyn Monroe thing?"

I nod seriously. "Yeah, you know, measure your hips then the window to see if you are able to fit." I should've and there was a part of me terrified of being stuck here all night. It was easy when Ravi was talking. Now, I could feel that sharp object digging into my skin and blood beading on my stomach.

Caden moves closer and glances at the window before peering down at me, his dark brows furrowed, as he asks, "Are you caught on anything?"

"I think a nail or glass. I can't tell."

He hands his flashlight to Ravi and moves closer, his fingers brushing my hip gently before he grabs the window-pane and pulls, splintering the wood.

I glance down gaping at the broken wood before glancing back up at Caden. "I feel like that should be sturdier." Caden's lips tip up as he and Ravi pull the pane out, before he grabs me and pulls me out of the window. I sigh with relief and hold onto him before I even realize I am. It's as if a weight has been lifted off of my chest making it easier to breathe, but he doesn't seem to mind as his strong tattooed arms wrap around me. I bury my head into his shoulder and breathe him in, letting his spiced lemons and honey scent surround me.

His hand finds its way onto my hair, stroking it. "You're okay. Everything is okay."

"He's a rat bastard. I'm going to kick his ass." His deep laugh vibrates against my ear until I pull away. "I can't believe he locked me in the bathroom." I shudder thinking about how long I could've been in there or why he even locked me inside.

Taking a deep breath, I slowly pull away from him before glaring at the window. "Can you believe I couldn't fit through?"

Caden scoffs and turns me towards him, so he could pull up my shirt to glance at the mark. "Looks like a nail. You'll need a tetanus shot."

"No thanks. I'm sure it's fine," I say trying to pull my shirt down, but he stopped me.

"Stop it. You could get an infection and with you being diabetic it might not heal correctly. So, you'll get it cleaned and a shot."

Huffing under my breath, I nod in agreement. "Fine. But I'm not happy about it." With that I slip my shoes back on and grab my bag before making my way to the parking lot where I see my car. Or what's left of it. The windows are smashed, and the tires slashed. I glance up at the sky and laugh.

"Rory," Caden says from behind me.

I motion to my car and ask, "Which one of you can pick a lock?" They exchange looks, "Well?"

"We both can. But maybe we should just call the police to file a report or something," Ravi suggests.

"Fuck the police. Who do you think they are going to side with? A white man or a Latina black woman that will be labeled as hot tempered?"

Caden sighs. "Okay, what do you need us to do? If it's killing him you're probably the first person they'll look to, no offense."

I wave it away and say, "None taken. Anthony is scared of snakes and we get little garden snakes all the time. It's September so we can probably still find some before the winter hits and they do whatever it is snakes do."

"I'll go find one, but I swear to God if I get bit I'm kicking Anthony's ass for the hell of it," Ravi mutters under his breath.

I watch as he walks away leaving me alone with Caden. "Can you squeeze through the window with me? We can sneak out through the bathroom door, if you can get it unlocked, and go to his office without getting caught."

Caden smirks, showing that dimple before nodding. "I haven't done this shit since high school."

I huff out a laugh. "I know I should be the bigger person and I will. But not after being locked in a bathroom and my car being destroyed. I can't let it go."

He nods understandably. "I get it Ro Ro. It's okay. We can be mature adults for the rest of our lives. I told you, whatever you need I was here, and I meant it."

I smiled, grateful he didn't chastise me or point out I'm

nearing thirty years old and should just press charges, but fuck that and fuck Anthony. Caden doesn't say anything, just takes my hand and rushes us back towards the broken window. Adrenaline rushes through me as he lifts me up and I ease my way back inside before he follows after me. We stand in the small stall together before he looks through the window where Ravi appears holding a rather large garden snake in his hands.

"How'd you find one so fast?" I was impressed.

"Doesn't matter, hurry up before the cops get called," he mutters. Caden nods and unlocks the stall door, pulls out a pocketknife, before heading to the bathroom entrance to get the lock open. I wanted to watch him work, but I needed to grab the snake. I reach through the window and grab the snake gently before Ravi could protest and hold it away from me. The tail curls around my wrist and it just kind of looks at me before trying to slither out of my grasp.

"Are you almost done, Caden?" I call out quietly.

"Yeah. Come on." I leave the stall and head out to Caden who does a double take at the snake I'm holding. "Did you really take the snake from Ravi?"

"Yes. Now, let's go." He opens the door and I step out first being mindful of the cameras. I don't know what to expect, but I didn't think I'd see Anthony's office light on, and the door cracked open. Nor did I expect to hear moaning.

"Harder, go harder," the whining voice of Claire panted as Anthony bent her over the desk and fucked her. It was... something I'd rather not see. My heart broke a little, but not for the reason a person might think. No, it broke because I now knew he had a pregnant wife at home, yet here he was fucking someone else while trapping me in the bathroom.

"Tell me did she cry when you locked the door?" Anthony demanded. Claire moaned and a sick feeling went through me. Caden glanced at me. I cursed silently, knelt low, and nudged the snake in the direction of the door.

"Yes. Yes, she cried and screamed."

I rolled my eyes, that was an exaggeration if I ever heard one. "Go on, little guy be free. I hope he pisses himself." I watch as the snake slithers towards the open door. I stand up and instinctively grab Caden's hand just as they start screaming for a whole other reason besides pleasure.

Chapter 22

CADEN

Rory grabs my hand as the pair start screaming as the snake moves into the room and takes off down the hall trying and failing to control her laughter. The door opens and a red-faced Anthony leaves the room butt ass naked.

"What the fuck, Rory?" he snaps.

She turns and flips him the bird. "Tell your wife I said she deserves better!" With that she takes off dragging me with her. Pride rushes through me as she just books it through the office and through the front of the building opening the door, so alarms go off, laughing the entire time.

"Ravi let's go!" she calls out running towards my car.

I laugh with her, my heart pounding from the adrenaline. I haven't felt this free and uncaring since I was younger. Xena wanted a mature man, someone who would fit on her wavelength rather than a man who went off to fight in war or fires. But today was different. First the dress shopping and now this. I never felt more alive, and it was all thanks to Rory with her easy laughter and a penchant for violence. It was perfect. Or crazy, I couldn't tell, but I loved every moment of it.

We jump in the car, and I see Ravi in his as he drives by waving at us, but I could tell he had questions that I'd need to answer, but for tonight I wasn't worried. Rory climbed into the backseat as I climbed into the driver's side and sped off laughing our asses off.

"Oh my god! Did you see that? I didn't think he'd be here and getting help from her of all people!" She gasped, leaning back in the seat. Her laughter was infectious, making me want to laugh with her. I drove around for a while before I turned into a little cul-de-sac, then pulled into Drew's driveway.

"Where are we?" she asks, leaning up in the back seat.

I turned off the car and turn to her. "I told you we had to get that cut handled." She looks down at her red blouse as if she forgot she was injured, and maybe she did, but I didn't. I may be a little overprotective, but I needed to make sure she was okay. She gives a little sigh, but nods and climbs out of the car. I follow after her and she looks up at me and narrows her eyes. "Only because you seem to take this fake boyfriend thing seriously will I accommodate you. Otherwise, I'd put a cute little Band-Aid on it and call it a day."

I chuckle, lead her to the door and knock three times so Drew knows it's me. He opens the door shirtless showing the abundance of scars that cover his body, scars that match my own. I wait to hear Rory's gasp of surprise, but she just tilts her head and glances past him where a dog is barking. A small smile tilts her lips. "You have a dog?"

Drew glances behind him at the golden retriever puppy. "Yeah. Her name is Goldie."

"Can I pet her?" Drew glances at me and I shrug. He sighs and moves aside so she can pass him, and she does without a single thought. "Oh, she's the cutest thing I've ever seen," Rory says in a whisper more to herself than us.

She pats her knee and the dog bounds over to her wagging her tail happily as Rory runs gentle fingers over her golden head. Goldie yaps happily as she's given attention. Drew looks confused as he pulls a shirt on and then glances at me.

"What are you doing here? And don't tell me it's to make friends with my dog."

"It's just a happy bonus that you have the world's cutest dog," Rory says.

I sigh and explain, "Rory needs a tetanus shot. I was hoping you could help."

He glances at her. "What did you do?"

Shrugging, she mutters, "My ex locked me in a bathroom, and I had to climb out the window. There was a little rusted nail that nicked my skin. No big deal."

Drew eyes me for a moment and I feel my face heat up. Was I being dramatic about a small cut? Probably. Did I care? Fuck no. Anything could happen from one small cut, and he knew it.

Sighing, Drew made his way towards Rory. "Let me see."

She glances at me before slowly lifting her shirt showing a small gash that looked worse than it probably was. "It's not bad. Do you even have tetanus shots here? How would that be possible or even legal?" Rory asks, but Drew doesn't answer, nor do I expect him to. He was one who did things his own way which is why I brought her here in the first place.

"I can give you the shot and clean it up. You need to keep it clean and put antibiotic ointment on it. Besides, you probably need the shot anyway."

Rory rolls her eyes, but doesn't argue as she takes her shirt off leaving her in a dark purple bra and her skirt. I glance at her, the expanse of smooth brown skin and the soft dips of her stomach making my mouth go dry.

Drew is clinical as he treats her, but I can't help feeling the need to rip his hand off her as he squeezes her bicep to inject the shot or the way he kneels in front of her to clean her stomach. My fists clench involuntarily as I watch them. But as Drew turns to look at me, his brows furrow before a small smirk plays on his mouth as he stands taking off gloves I didn't notice he put on.

"You should be good to go. Try not to climb through any more windows or anything."

Rory scoffs. "It wasn't by choice. The bastard locked me in the bathroom."

Drew hums under his breath and asks, "Why's that?"

Rory muttered under her breath and stood grabbing her shirt. "It doesn't matter but thank you for doctoring me up… again. At this point you should debate opening your own practice."

"Maybe one day."

Rory nods. "I'm sure you'll do great. If you ever need a dog sitter let me know."

"I won't," Drew states.

"You sure? You look like you could use a vacation," Rory mutters, petting the dog lovingly.

"Vacations are a waste of time," Drew comments.

"Geez. You must be fun at parties."

I step in before the two can argue anymore. "We should get going," I say, making that cocky ass smirk on Drew's face widen. I glare at him, but my eyes find their way back to Rory as she buttons up her red blouse. She glances up at that moment as I take in her slender form, and I feel my face heat up when I look away.

Once dressed, Rory walks over to me. "Ready?" she asks.

I nod and say goodbye to Drew before leading her back

to my car. It's silent other than her calling a tow company before hanging up and sitting back in silence. I don't say anything either, instead chancing glances at her from the corner of my eye. "You look at me a lot," Rory muttered, blinking at me.

My hands clench on the steering wheel. "I like looking at you, *Chīsai doragon*. You intrigue me."

"You're not too bad to look at either." Sitting up straight she sighs under her breath. "I think I should just go to my parents tonight. Nico can drive me to work in the morning."

"You sure?" I ask, taking the exit needed for her parents' house.

"Yes. I'll see you tomorrow if you want. You kind of owe me the whole story of your infamous ex."

Scoffing, I pull into the driveway. The drive wasn't long enough for my liking, but I didn't say that. My thoughts weren't working in my favor tonight. "I don't remember offering you the whole story," I say instead, because God forbid I tell her about this slight attraction that is building inside of me whenever I look at her.

Rory smiles, a serene little smile that had my heart pounding in overdrive. "You didn't, but I figured if I mentioned it you'd offer it up." With that she unbuckles her seat belt and leans over pressing her warm lips against my cheek before grabbing her bag and leaving my car. Leaving me feeling dazed and confused. Aroused. All from a simple kiss on the cheek. "Fuck, I'm screwed." The worst part is I didn't want to stop. I made rules and here I was mentally breaking them.

Chapter 23

CADEN

It took me an hour to get home. Tired and annoyed by my thoughts about Rory, I climb out of the car slamming the door harder than intended. Cursing, I stomp up to my house and unlock the door pausing halfway when I see a figure sitting on the couch.

"What the hell are you doing?" I demand. He turns and glares at me with deep green eyes.

"I can ask you the same thing," Ravi says, bringing a bottle of beer up to his mouth before taking a long drink. I sigh and step inside, closing the door behind me. I should've known he'd confront me.

"Okay, say what's on your mind then get out. You're probably scaring Skittles with your mere presence." I glanced around for effect, searching for the small kitten that was nowhere to be seen.

Ravi stands. "You named the cat Skittles? What are you, five?"

I glare at him, my fists clenching. "Hey, I don't judge your name so don't go judging my cat. She's been through enough."

He holds up his hands in surrender. "Fine. What the fuck are you doing with Rory?"

I shrug. "I'm doing what you suggested. I'm going to bring her to the wedding."

He sighs, pinching the bridge of his nose. "I told you to bring a date. Meaning a stranger who could help you relax or something. Not someone you know and can complicate things with."

Moving towards the kitchen, I open the fridge and grab a bottle of water before leaning over the counter, staring off into space. "I know. It's a mutual agreement. We have rules."

"What kind of rules?"

I twist off the cap of the water and sip it, letting the cool liquid soothe my suddenly dry throat. How was I going to explain this to him? The fact that I am going to pretend to be her boyfriend for this work event while she pretends to be my girlfriend while at the wedding. There were strict rules, no love, no touching unless at the event, and no sex. It complicates things and whether Ravi wanted to hear it or not, I wasn't a total dick.

He sighs and sits down at the counter. "Cade, you can't do anything remotely close to dating. Remember what happened after she came to visit you?"

How could I forget? Xena broke something in me, something I haven't been able to get back. Ravi was the only one who knew what really happened because he was there. Rory knew a little bit but not how far off the deep end I truly went. What led us to that moment in that recovery room.

Shaking my head, I stare at him. "We are just two friends helping each other out. Nothing more, nothing less."

"If that's the case then I can expect the two of you at this date Nirvana wants to do. Sorrow and Delaney are going. So the two of you can practice dating there."

"Then what will we tell the others?" I ask.

"Just say you went as friends because Rory really wanted to go," Ravi said.

"Fine. We can do that," I say with confidence I don't really feel.

Rapping his knuckles on the counter Ravi stood. "I hope you know what you're doing." With that he walked out of the house leaving me alone in the dimly lit kitchen. I sigh, bowing my head, I hope I know what I'm doing too.

There was no use reflecting on the past though. Not now. I stand up straighter and head to my room to get ready for bed.

The feel of hands grazed my back, and the sound of moaning filled my ears. It was the same dream I've had for years. The feel of Xena as she lay under me, holding me like she always did. Drawing me closer to her as I moved in and out of her slowly. Only this time I didn't see her under me. I didn't see the expanse of pale skin. No, I saw smooth brown skin. Dark curly hair sprawled over my pillows, and hazel eyes peered up at me. Taking me in.

"Rory," I breathe out.

"Caden. More. I need more," she groans, arching her hips up, taking me deeper as she wraps her legs around me. I brace my hands on the side of her head, staring down at her, taking in every inch of her. So beautiful, so perfect. So mine.

"Caden," she moans again, her voice taking on a breathy tone that had every ounce of my control snapping. Gone was the dream I was used to, one that became a constant companion over the years, replaced by a new one. One I embraced with open arms. One I knew was going to stay

with me for a long, long time. And I didn't give a fuck as long as I could hold this woman in my arms. My Rory.

Rory

Shifting on my feet, I stare at the clock on my desk. It's been two days since my little adventure with Caden and I haven't heard from him. He called once to say we had a practice group date and I was nervous, especially with lack of communication. Granted, I didn't reach out to him, but I was unsure how to broach everything. My banquet was coming up next week and I was getting nervous thinking about it and wondering if he was still coming with me. I guess I can ask him after our date.

"Rory?" A voice sounded behind me causing me to jump in my seat. I glance up and see one of the partners of the firm standing beside my desk. Her name is Wendy Prescot, and she scared the hell out of me. With her graying hair slicked back in a bun so tight I was pretty sure she walked around with a migraine most of the time, and a scowl so prominent it'd put every Disney villain to shame.

Swallowing hard, I nod. "Yes, ma'am?"

"My office. Now." Damnit. I was screwed. I was aware of the camera footage as it came up in this morning's meeting. No names were mentioned, but I know they saw me. Hell, I was hard to miss. As one of the only women of color in this place I was hard to miss.

I stand and wipe my hands down my skirt, before raising my head and following Prescot. The office she led me to had the other two partners and Anthony sitting in it, and I knew I was fucked. A part of me wanted to just apologize for what I did, but I knew I wasn't sorry. Not in the least.

"Have a seat, Miss Flores Phelps. We'd like to discuss what was seen on the cameras Monday evening," the older man named Walters said. His eyebrows were overlapping his eyes and it made me cringe internally as I sat in the seat beside Anthony. I crossed my legs and sat up straight waiting for them to continue, but they just sat in silence. I knew they expected me to speak, but I waited. They wanted me in here so they could start. I wasn't about to incriminate myself, especially for the likes of Anthony.

With a sigh, Prescot said, "What the hell were the two of you doing? One second everything is empty, then the next we see you running away with some man, and Mr. Lincoln comes out of his office, naked."

I see Anthony's face turn red from the corner of my eye and sigh. "I can explain," I begin and the three look at me expectantly. Clearing my throat, I sit up. "You see someone must've forgotten I was in the bathroom and locked me inside of it. So, panicked, I called my boyfriend because he's a firefighter and I knew he'd help me. At the moment I didn't know who else to call, so I picked him. He helped me get out, and I realized I left some important documents in Mr. Lincoln's office, so I went to get them. He was changing when I accidentally walked in." It was bullshit, complete and utter bullshit, but I was hoping they would believe me.

However, I could see the suspicion on their faces. But I knew, deep down, they didn't truly care about anything other than the lack of professionalism that was shown on my part. Which I will admit wasn't my best move, after being yelled at by a client about the abuse of a woman, and the fact I'm sitting in this office looking over at my superiors whom I hoped to work under one day.

Sighing, Mr. Walters nodded. "This is a professional

setting. I expect better from the both of you from now on. Any other actions such as this, you will be dealt with. Understood?"

"Yes, sir," I say and stand as they dismiss us.

I'm walking out the door and down the hall when a hand lands on my arm. "Thanks for what you did back there," Anthony says.

I snatch my arm from his grasp, and whirl on him. "I did it for me. The next time you decide to be childish and try to jeopardize my career because you want to be petty, I will retaliate in a way you don't want me to."

His jaw clenches as he gets closer to me. "You wouldn't dare."

I laugh hollowly. "I so would. I'm tired of your shit. You're lucky I don't press charges for what you did to my car and trapping me in the bathroom. Which is technically kidnapping. Leave me the fuck alone, Anthony, or I swear to God you'll regret the day you messed with me." Without another word, I turn on my heel and head back to my desk.

Chapter 24

RORY

Sighing in relief I finally leave the office building, completely ignoring Anthony as he walks out of his office, and head to my car that Nico dropped off for me. One thing I was happy about was that I put my dress and shoes in the trunk before Anthony was able to destroy those too. Shaking those thoughts away, I climb into the car and drive as fast as possible to my apartment so I could shower and change. It takes me thirty minutes to get home. I hurry inside tossing my phone on the couch and rush to my room, pull out a little black flowy dress and white heels, then quickly jump in the shower. Once done, I manage to tame my curls in a semblance of a half up half down style and swipe on some mascara.

Once done, I dress and head to the living room where my phone is lighting up. I grab it and see Nirvana calling me. "Hello?" I answer.

"How come I'm just finding out about you and Caden?"

she demands. "I mean I should've put two and two together with how much time you've been spending with him but damn you could've told me." She sounds hurt and I feel awful about it. About the lying.

I chew my bottom lip wondering what I should tell her. It's only fake. I don't even know why Caden agreed to this. "We're just friends hanging out together. He probably won't even show." Not with the way he hasn't spoken to me in days. *Not that you bothered to talk to him either.* My subconscious chimed in.

"Doubtful, I've seen the way you look at him and he looks at you. They're not 'just friends' looks. They're 'I want to fuck you' looks that you two throw at each other." I scoff under my breath and head out of my apartment.

"No, we don't, Vana. We are strictly friends." Nirvana hums under her breath before saying she'll see me soon and hanging up. I shake my head to myself as I rush down the stairs and get back into my car, and I wonder if Caden is going to come and how I was supposed to act. The drive to the club was nerve-wracking as I drove in silence, my thoughts running all over the place. I park and lean my head against the steering wheel taking in a deep breath. I don't know how long I sit there until a knock on my window has me jumping in my seat. I see Nirvana, and she smiles at me as I climb out of the car.

The music was already loud as I stepped outside, hearing the booming bass and the laughter that was coming from the club.

"You look nice," I say, taking in Nirvana's blue dress.

"As do you, my dear. As do you. Caden isn't here yet," Nirvana says, answering my unasked question. I breathe a sigh of relief and let Nirvana link her arm through mine. We walked into the club and I saw the others at a table with drinks already sitting in front of them. I felt awkward as if I was a third wheel to their double date… or was it fifth wheel? I wasn't certain, all I did know is I felt a little out of place. Delaney smiles at me and pats the seat beside her. I take it gratefully and lean into her.

"Hey! How are you feeling?" I ask.

"Fine. Can't really complain too much. I'm glad you could get away for a little bit!" And she did look excited to see me. I haven't been out since her last birthday and that was a year ago. Other than the rage room that ended up being a mess of me freaking out on a car and helping during that wreck. I smile at her, take the drink Nirvana pushes towards me, and take a deep gulp. I needed the liquid courage because being the only one without a date was odd, but they didn't leave me out. Not out of the conversation and not out of dancing. Me and the girls danced, letting the music run through us, and I loved it. When the song ended, I offered to get the next round of drinks. As I walked to the bar a tall man stops me. He is handsome, with light hair and big blue eyes. His smile is easy and charming.

"Hi. I saw you dancing with your friends, and wondered if you'd like to dance with me?"

Before I can answer, a voice sounds behind me. "She has a partner."

My eyes widen, and I turn to see Caden glaring at the man.

The man is gracious about it though and holds his hands up with an easy smile as Caden leads me away. He pulls me into his arms almost angrily before holding me close.

"What the hell, Caden?" I mutter.

"You told me, if we do this, no other women, so that goes for you, too. No other men," he says close to my ear. I can feel his warm breath on my skin as he spoke.

I push him away, glaring at him. "You're late, Caden. Why?"

He sighs, shrugging. "I didn't know how to act. Or if you even wanted me here."

"Why wouldn't I want you here? This was your idea."

He shrugs again, looking vulnerable. "You haven't really talked to me."

Guilt eats at me. "I'm sorry. I was waiting for you to reach out, I guess."

He grabs the nape of my neck and leans down, whispering against my skin, "Dance with me then."

I nod, leaning into him. There's tension in the air as his hands land on my hips moving me against him in the rhythm of the music.

Caden

When I saw Rory I knew I had to say something. I haven't seen her in days and I was starting to miss her. But when I walked in, late as fuck, and saw her talking to another man, something inside of me snapped.

The thought of his hands on her hips, or her hips rubbing against his cock, like they were rubbing on me now filled me with a rage I've never felt before. But here she was now, in my arms. Grinding on me. The music was slow and sensual, building the tension around us. My hands dig into her hips and she looks up at me, without thinking I grab the nape of her neck and kiss her. She tenses slightly before relaxing against me, wrapping her arms around my neck. My tongue thrusts into her mouth and we move to the beat of the music.

It's everything, but not enough. I need to feel more of her.

Someone bumps into me though, breaking the spell we were in. Rory looks up at me, her lips swollen from my kiss and her eyes wide.

"We shouldn't have done that," she says. And I know she's right. Logically I know we fucked up, but I couldn't stop myself. I feel eyes on me and I turn seeing Ravi staring at me with a knowing look in his eyes, and I knew I overstepped. Fucking up before we even started on our plan. Fuck, I made a mess of things.

"I should go," Rory starts. Looking everywhere but at me. Her cheeks are red and I know I fucked up worse than I thought.

"Rory."

She holds a hand up to me and shakes her head. A small smile on her lips.

"It's okay. We both got caught up in the moment. The music was sexy, and the air was hot and we just indulged a little bit is all." Her reasoning made sense in retrospect, but I still didn't like it. And without allowing me to speak, she turned around and left. Pushing through the other people on the dance floor. Leaving me alone with the taste of her on my tongue.

Chapter 25

RORY

It was another few days without seeing Caden or hearing from him. After the kiss things felt different. I know we shouldn't have kissed, and I knew it set us back, but I didn't want to stop this thing with us. I was finished with work for the day and left the building with a briefcase full of cases, but I couldn't get him out of my head. Damn it. With a sad sigh my thoughts go back to Caden as I climb behind the wheel of my car. I needed to see him, to make sure we were okay. Without thinking I pull out of the parking lot and head to his house, my thoughts going a million miles a minute.

It doesn't take me long to get to Caden's, but it feels like an eternity for me. What if he doesn't want to see me? What if the deal is off? Cursing to myself, I climb out of the car and march up to his door and bang on it.

"Are you a serial killer?" his deep voice calls out, stopping me mid-knock.

Clearing my throat, I answer, "Um, no."

It takes him a moment before he responds, "It's open." With a shaky hand, I twist the knob and step inside, kicking my heels off at the side of the door and stare at Caden. He's sitting in a kitchen chair, shirtless, as he tattoos himself. There's ink all over his body, but I don't miss the very distinct scars that pucker out beneath the artfully done pieces.

He glances up at me, dark eyes zeroing in on me before he looks down at his arm. "What are you doing here, Ro Ro?"

"You didn't call," I say, grimacing at the words.

He snorts. "Phones work both ways you know?"

That has me bristling as I walk up to him, dropping my keys and phone on the counter before standing in front of him. "What's your deal? You kissed me."

He doesn't look at me when he answers. "Nothing. I just needed some space."

I huff out a sarcastic laugh. "Well, damn, I didn't realize I was so bothersome." He didn't even want to talk about the kiss. I know I left first, but I was overwhelmed, I wasn't sure where this left us.

He sighs and sets down the tattoo gun, before staring at me, his legs sprawled out in front of him and I'm somehow standing between his thighs. "Not from you, from my thoughts. From my major fuck up with you."

"Oh." I breathe. Embarrassment heats my cheeks and I glance away, swallowing hard, before I point to the tattoo gun. "Can I give you one?" I had to do something in order to get my own thoughts together. To ignore the self-doubts coursing through my mind.

Caden looks taken aback by my sudden change in subjects as he hands me the gun, wrapping my hand around it. I move closer until I'm right against him, but that clearly isn't enough for him because his hands grab my waist and pull until I'm straddling his lap.

Clearing my throat at the sudden closeness, I lean forward to the spot above his heart that was bare and start my drawing. We sat in relative quiet, the whirring of the gun the only sound in the living room until it was becoming too much.

"What was on your mind? Other than the kiss? Which wasn't a fuck up. Like I said, we were caught up in the moment," I say, careful not to defer from the tattoo.

Caden hums under his breath and asks, "Do you really want to know?" His voice is low with caution.

I chuckle slightly, dabbing at the ink with the paper towel he handed me. "I wouldn't have asked if I didn't want to know."

He sits thoughtfully before nodding. "My ex will be at the wedding. Probably with my old friend."

"The one she cheated with?" I ask softly.

"The very one," he sighs. "No one knows she broke up with me. Or that she cheated. Aside from Ravi. I made it seem like we were just in two different parts in our lives and didn't fit together."

"But that wasn't the truth," I finish for him, sitting up on his lap looking at him.

He shakes his head. "No. No, it wasn't the truth at all. After a year she wanted me back but I wasn't in the right mindset. But she wanted him, too. I couldn't do it. Not again. We hooked up." I opened my mouth to ask what he meant, but he held up his hand stopping me. "Not me and him. I don't roll that way. But a threesome. She wanted it, and I loved her with a naivety that embarrasses me. I didn't want to, but I felt like I had to, to keep her happy, and I regret it every day."

"She wanted more than you were willing to give," I whisper.

He nods, laughing bitterly. "And now I'm so fucked up I never want to do that shit again."

I placed the tattoo gun down, so I could grab his face. "Not everyone is like your ex, Caden." He goes to speak, but I stop him by placing a gentle kiss to his lips, shocking not only him but myself. I knew I was going back to that territory from the other night. The one I ran from, but I wanted to comfort him. My mind went to a kiss. Small and to the point. I pull back, my heart racing and I scramble to get off his lap, but one hand grips my hip while the other grabs the nape of my neck so he can pull me flush against him before his lips slam down on mine.

I tense for a moment as his tongue teases the seam of my lips before my body slowly goes pliant against him. The contact sent shivers down my spine as my hands moved up his muscled chest to his hair, pulling hard enough to hear him groan. Then something in him snapped and he was standing and slamming me against the wall.

I groan, my legs wrapping around his narrow waist pulling him closer. Heat was unfurling in my belly as he kissed me. It wasn't a normal kiss either. It was all consuming, intoxicating. His tongue thrust against mine, owning me with a simple caress. Holy shit, how was I going to come back from this? Did I even want to come back from this? No, no I didn't.

Caden

. . .

The taste of lavender was present on my tongue as I kissed Rory. My hands went to her ass as I pulled her closer to me. Her skirt rode up showing the long expanse of skin that had my cock hardening with each tentative stroke of her tongue against mine. Fuck, I needed her. After my dream I wanted nothing more than to possess her. To have her on her knees for me, my cock down her pretty throat. Or have her straddling me and taking every inch of me. I needed her more than I needed anyone else in my entire life. I pull away slightly, placing my head on hers and breathing her in.

"This is against the rules," she whispers.

I huff out a laugh and say, "Fuck the rules. It's taking everything in me not to put you face down on the counter and fuck you until you can't walk."

Her eyes widen and her breathing quickens as my hand moves to the hem of her skirt pushing it up slightly. "Would you like that, Lorelai? Would you like me to fuck you so hard you'll feel me for days?"

"Caden," she gasps, as my hand moves higher up her skirt.

"Answer me," I say lowly. "Do you want me to own your pretty little pussy tonight?"

With a whimper so sweet, she nods and says, "Yes. Yes, please."

A grin tilts my mouth as I reach between her thighs where she's hot and wet. She arches her hips, rubbing against my hand but I pull away and push her flat against the counter. I bunch up her skirt to her hips and groan at the peach lace straining against her ass.

"I've never seen such a beautiful sight before, Lorelai. So fucking beautiful." I grip the waistband and slowly pull them down her slender legs before spreading her wide. "You're dripping wet. Just like the little whore I knew you could be." I run my fingers over her before finding her swollen clit and rub gently.

She moaned, pressing against me. "Please."

I press a kiss to her thigh before standing and whispering in her ear, "Please what? Use your big girl words and maybe I'll reward you."

Rory swallows audibly, her lips swollen from my kiss and her eyes are wide with desire. "Please, please fuck me, Caden." I run my hand down her ass before spearing into her from behind my fingers fucking her tight pussy in slow strokes. She gasps, standing on her toes. "Like this? Is this what you need, baby?"

I pressed two fingers into her, rubbing her in gentle circles, not enough to get her off, and I loved every second of it. The feeling of her clenching around me to the way her hands gripped on the edge of the counter as she rode my hand. But it wasn't enough.

"Please, please, Caden I need more," she cried out. Fuck, the way she said my name had my cock hardening more and my balls tightening for the need to feel her. A part of me wants to tease her, to take her to her limits until she's begging me to stop while arching into me for more. Removing my hand from between her legs, I reach over the counter and pull out the drawer holding my condoms and grab one.

"Wait," she breathes out, stopping all my movements. "If we do this there's no going back," she whispers.

I nod as I free my cock from my jeans and stroke the hard length with the hand I'd had inside of her. "I don't want to turn back. I need to feel you, Rory. We can discuss the particulars again if you'd like."

I rip open the condom and slide it on myself and line up at her entrance, holding myself back from thrusting in the way I wanted to. "Am I going to fuck you, Lorelai? Or do we stop here? The choice is yours." It physically hurt to say that, but I knew I'd do whatever she wanted without argument.

"Don't you dare stop. I need to feel you." That's all I needed. That confirmation, that last shred of decency is out the window replaced by something else, something neither one of us can come back from. Did I care though? Absolutely fucking not. With that I thrust deep inside her.

Chapter 26

RORY

Caden's hands gripped my hips so tightly I knew I'd be wearing his bruises the next day, and some primal part of me shuddered at the thought. But the moment he thrust deeply inside of me I knew I was a goner. I screamed at the fullness of him as he stilled. He was larger than Anthony and, since he was the only man I've been with before, the size difference was jarring.

My hands gripped the edge of the counter squeezing tightly as he stilled, holding me tightly.

"Holy fuck, Rory. You're so tight." His fingers drifted over my skin in smoothing circles, before he leaned down pressing a kiss to the back of my neck. "Are you okay?"

I take a deep breath, trying and failing to breathe through the discomfort. "Can I face you, please?" I didn't mean to say that, but it came out anyway. Without hesitation Caden pulled away from me and turned me around, his hands going to the backs of my thighs to lift me onto the counter. I instinctively wrapped myself around him and groaned when he gently pulled me down on his erection. I groaned again, my head falling back as he moved me slowly up and down him.

"Even better than I imagined," he whispers. My heart is pounding rapidly in my chest and the heat between my legs builds unexpectedly and I can no longer hold onto this easy glide.

Leaning forward I whisper in his ear, "Fuck me the way you need to. For tonight I'm yours." Something snapped inside of him then. He pushed my skirt up higher, baring me to him before he grabbed the front of my shirt and pulled, sending buttons flying all over.

I don't even care as I kiss him. Our tongues thrust roughly against each other and I'm barely aware of us moving until my back hits the cushions on the couch.

Caden pulls back and I stare at him in all his tattooed glory, my eyes drifting lower before he grabs my chin and forces my gaze to his. "I'll fuck you like I need to, and you're going to be my good girl and take it. No matter how rough or how fast. You'll take it because that's what you need."

I whimper, his words making me hotter than I've ever been. I try to press my thighs together to ease some of the ache, but he grips my thighs before bending down and swiping his tongue over my swollen pussy. I nearly scream at the first touch, grabbing at his hair with one hand and his shoulder with the other.

"Oh my god," I gasp. His tongue enters me, thrusting deep, tasting me and one of his hands goes to my clit and pinches it hard sending me careening over the edge crying out his name. He pulls away and thrusts in deep, fucking me with hard strokes. His hands grab mine and pin them down.

"Calling God is a little ironic when what I'm going to do to you is bound to send you to Hell," he says, a cocky smirk on his face. I'm breathing heavily. I can't even say anything as my back arches and my legs tighten around his waist. I'm so close again that I'm unsure of what to do to prolong this feeling. As if he can read my thoughts he slows down and lets go of one of my hands to pull my bra down and bring an erect nipple to his mouth, sucking deeply.

"Caden," I moaned, squeezing his hand.

He looks up at me, his dark eyes bright with lust as his hips pick up the pace again. "Nothing will ever beat the feeling of you squeezing down on my cock, Lorelai." The way he says my name has me coming harder than I ever have in my entire life and, for a second, I'm pretty sure I black out from the pleasure while screaming his name because soon everything fades into nothingness.

Caden

When Rory passed out, I panicked and walked around with my dick in my hand. Literally. Cursing, I discard the condom, zip up my pants, and grab her keys before rushing outside to her car and rummaging through her purse before finding her blood tester kit and insulin. Running back inside I go back to where she's lying on the couch to dress her. When I notice the buttons are all mostly broken, I curse and stand to go to my room and find a t-shirt. When I find a soft enough black shirt I snatch it up and head back out to her.

I try hard not to look at her mostly naked body. To her bare pussy gleaming with arousal, to her small brown nipples still damp from where I sucked them. My cock stirred in my pants making me groan in frustration as I dressed her in my shirt, once she was covered I knelt beside her and set up her kit before lifting up her hand and pricking her finger. As gently as possible I brought it to the strip so the monitor could read her sugars—which were borderline coma numbers at fifty-two.

Sighing, I cleaned off her finger. "I swear to God, Ro Ro, you need to start taking better care of yourself." I stand and make my way to the kitchen, pull open the fridge door and pull out the fixings for a sandwich, then wait anxiously for her to wake up. It doesn't take long before I hear a soft curse, and I hear shuffling. "Before you disappear, come eat," I called out. Not even bothering to look up as I cut a tomato and lettuce.

Footsteps sound as Rory makes her way into the kitchen. "I'm so sorry. I don't know what happened."

I salt and pepper the tomatoes, angry that she isn't taking care of herself the way she should. I slap the sandwich together and slide it over to her, glaring. "Your sugar was low... again. Why aren't you taking care of yourself?"

Rory has the decency to look ashamed as she takes a small bite of her sandwich. She chews thoughtfully, twisting the ring on her finger before finally looking up at me. "I'm trying. I'm sorry. I didn't realize it was so low."

Sighing, I lean forward bracing my hands on the counter. "You're staying the night here. I want to make sure you're okay." Her eyes widen and she shakes her head. Holding up my hand I stop any protests. "You can go back to acting as if we're just friends after you eat and rest. I'll even sleep on the couch."

She takes another, bigger bite before shaking her head. "No, it's fine, we can share a bed." We sat in silence so thick you could cut it with a knife. I watch her, the way her throat bobs up and down with each swallow, the way her hazel eyes dance nervously between me and the front door. She was nervous. I could clearly see that. With a sigh I lean against my counter.

"Speak your mind, Rory."

Her gaze moves back to me. "What?"

"You've got something to say, so say it."

Popping the last bite of sandwich into her mouth she chews slowly before wiping her hands down her skirt drawing my attention to her delicate curves. She clears her throat and asks, "Did you finish?" I can see the slight red blush on her cheeks as she asks.

I stand there and shake my head. "You passed out, Rory. I wasn't about to fuck you when you were not coherent."

"Oh. Do you want me to…" she starts, but her sentence trails off as she looks at my still stiff cock.

Huffing out a laugh, I turn and head towards my room where I proceed to grab a pair of shorts. Rory walks in timidly just like I knew she would. This was a new side of the usually confident woman she presented herself as. "Get dressed and go to sleep, Rory. I don't need you to take care of me. I'm a big boy. If it was bad enough I'd deal with it myself. You're not feeling well. Get some rest."

"You're leaving? I thought you were staying."

I turned to her, noticing the way she held my shirt to her chest. "Do you want me to stay?" I asked, and a part of me wanted her to say no, so I could save what little friendship we had without blurring the already blurred lines. But the moment she gave me a little nod, I knew we'd never be on that friend level again.

"Okay, I'll stay. Let me just get ready for bed." With that I walk into my bathroom and close the door with a finality that echoed into my rapidly pounding heart.

Rory

When Caden closes the door I quickly run back into the living room and grab my phone making a quick group chat.

Me: *I messed up big time.*

Nirvana: *Ooh, I love it when one of you messes up. Takes a lot of pressure off of me and Layla.*

Layla: *Hey! I resent that. I never mess up.*

Sera: *We know you have the hots for Spencer and his old high school friend La.*

Laney: *Let's focus on Rory's mistake right now then come back to Layla's nefarious tendencies.*

Ophelia: *What you did can't be too bad.*

Me: *It's who I did that's bad.*

Nirvana: *I knew it!*

Me: *You can't possibly know who it is.*

Nirvana: *Twenty bucks says it's Caden!*

Me: …

Layla: *Holy shit!*

Laney: *OMG!*

Sera: *You dirty hussy!*

Ophelia: *But how was it?!*

Nirvana: *Give us all the details!*

Nirvana: *And twenty bucks!*

The sound of the door opening had me closing my phone as it began to explode with messages from the girls. I quickly turn it to silent and pull the shirt over my head before running back to the room and jumping on the bed, none too elegantly, and roll into Caden. I stare at the wall mortification burning through me. I glance up and see his brown eyes bright with uncontained laughter.

"Oh. Hi, um, I was just letting the others know I wasn't kidnapped," I breathe out.

He hums under his breath and gently pushes me to my back and leans over me. "I have sisters, Lorelai. I know full well what you were doing."

Heat burns on my cheeks and I look away. "I'm so sorry I…"

He laughs then, turning to his own back. "You're not what I expected at all."

I glance at him in confusion. "What do you mean?"

He turns to stare at me. "You're usually so put together, but you're also really nervous and timid. It's cute. I like knowing there's more to you than the tense lawyer. There's the woman who has a fire deep down, but also someone who is easily ruffled and clumsy." I swallow hard, that was the thing, I wasn't usually like this. It was only around him that I seemed to lose my wits about me. I was calm and collected. I was the one who was always strong but around Caden every wall I've ever built comes down leaving me a complete mess. I wasn't sure how I was even going to come back from this. I turn to my back and stare up at the ceiling wondering why it was him that made me this way.

Maybe because Anthony broke something inside of me and I went for the first guy to show me any ounce of interest. I shake my head, no that wasn't it. Even before all of this came out about Anthony I was drawn to Caden. I would find myself watching him, taking in every angle every laugh line. The way his cheeks dimpled when he was trying not to laugh. The way he smelled, a subtle citrus and honey. It was both intoxicating and comforting. Not the usual overbearing smell that most men had.

Caden turns to his side and slides an arm around me pulling me into him, surrounding me in his warmth.

I glance at him, a curl falling into my face. "What are you doing?"

"Holding you before you bolt out the door."

"I wasn't going to bolt," I lie.

He opens one eye. "You're a shit liar for a lawyer, Ro Ro."

That surprises a laugh out of me. I tried not to lie, and when I did it made me feel awful. I let the tension ease out of my body before softening against him with a soft sigh.

"Fine. I might've bolted."

He lets out a husky laugh. "I know. Now go to sleep."

I lie there in the darkened room and twiddle my fingers.

"What is it?" he whispers, his voice filled with impending sleep.

"Did you like it?" I ask, suddenly remembering what we were doing before I passed out.

"Like what?"

"Your tattoo I gave you." I was in no way an artist, but I wanted him to like it.

His arm tightens around me. "I fucking love it."

Turning in his arms, I pressed my palm against his chest, tracing around the small paw prints and listened to his breathing even out knowing come morning I'll be long gone.

Chapter 27

CADEN

I woke up to the bed empty and sigh, irritation running through me. She really left me. Damn woman didn't even let me wake up. Not that I blame her. Sighing again, I throw my arm over my eyes and curse to the ceiling. The shrill ringing of my phone stops the pity party and I groan, grabbing it and sliding it open to answer. "What?" I demand.

"Wow, what a warm greeting," was Ravi's dry response.

"What do you want?" I ask, ignoring him.

"You're late. Get your ass here now. Training doesn't stop because you want to laze around in bed." I turned my head and my eyes widened at the time. Fuck. I'm late. Cursing, I tell Ravi I'm on my way and hang up. Jumping from the bed I quickly dress and brush my teeth before rushing out the door with a quick goodbye to Skittles. Rory consumed so much of my mind that I was late.

The drive to the station is slower than I would've liked because, for some reason, traffic was a bitch this morning.

Making me later than I already was. I park and grab my gear before running inside where I see an irritated looking Ravi tapping his foot.

"You're late."

Grunting, I stuff my stuff in my locker. "Sorry, Boss. My alarm didn't go off."

Ravi rolled his shoulders and I saw the tic start in his jaw. If it's one thing Ravi hated more than my sarcasm was when I called him boss. A few months ago he had been promoted to captain after Brooks retired and I know that weighed heavily on him.

Sighing with regret, I turn to him. "I'm sorry. Last night was overwhelming and I overslept."

Ravi's face slipped into concern. "You okay?"

I shake my head. "I slept with Rory. I know I said I wouldn't, but shit happened and I screwed up." But I didn't regret it. I wanted her, I still want her. It wasn't just sex, I liked her humor, her penchant for revenge. I liked how warm she was and how authentic. When she came over thinking I was ignoring her it made something in me turn. I was somewhat ignoring her because these feelings I was developing weren't allowed.

Not to mention the fact I was going to see Xena in a few short days. The fact that I told Rory the entire ordeal was enough to show my building trust. Ravi didn't even know all the sordid details and he was my best friend.

"Dammit, Caden," Ravi snapped, drawing me away from my thoughts.

"What?" I ask, dumbfounded by the vehemence in his voice.

He curses and pushes a hand through his short brown hair. "You said it was strictly platonic."

Shrugging, I wrap my hand behind my neck, massaging hard. "It was supposed to be. Shit, I don't even know what happened." One minute she was giving me a tattoo and the next I was kissing her. Or she was kissing me. I didn't really understand how it happened. Shaking those thoughts away I look at Ravi. "If it helps she snuck out before I woke up." Just like I knew she would.

And for whatever reason that hurt. I wanted to wake up next to her, inhaling that vanilla lavender scent that made me relax and want to spend more time with her. Wait, no. I didn't do sleepovers. No, it was good she left. So why did it irritate me so much?

Ignoring the sudden tightness in my chest, I move past Ravi to get ready for drills. He looked like he wanted to say something, but he stopped himself and nodded leaving me alone to wallow. Once done dressing in my gear I climbed into the truck as the sirens kicked on.

"All right! Today's drill is to see how fast you can put out a fire. Last time we did search and rescue but today we need to work as a team in order to stop the spread of fire." Ravi's voice sounded through the mic in my helmet.

Logan nodded next to me and we sat as Ravi gave our orders. "Sato, you're on hose duty, make sure you and Logan work as a unit."

I look at the skinny kid next to me and hold in a sigh. The last time he was on hose he went flying and fractured a few fingers. But I nod as the truck parks in front of an old building engulfed in flames. I jump out, my heart pounding with adrenaline as I grab the hose with Logan and run forward as it kicks on. The rushing water is like music to my ears as it explodes out, pushing me back but not hard enough to send me to my ass. This was the high I always craved. The action, the way the fire burned bright in front of me and the fact that I was the one to control it.

Something so untamed and wild I could have the control and tame it enough to put it out. With both hands on the spout I sprayed the flames, dousing them quickly until nothing but ash and smoke was left on my side of the building. Logan struggled with his side, letting the hose control his movements.

Groaning in exasperation I moved closer spraying the flames until they died down. When the others cut the water I glanced at Logan, eyes narrowed.

"You have to be in control, kid. If you let the hose control you then you don't douse the flames enough and risk the fire spreading," I say, wrapping my hose.

"Two hours and fifteen minutes," Ravi called. I sigh, by that time the fire would've spread and people could've been hurt. Luckily, we were in a secluded part of town that no one was residing in.

I clap Logan on the back. "We should do some weightlifting. Build your stamina." He nods in agreement as we head back to the trucks.

Sighing, I sit down, running a hand through my hair watching as Skittles runs throughout the living room. Tossing a toy between her paws. It's been a week now. One week without seeing or hearing from Rory. Seven long ass days and each day my irritation mounted. I knew she would've ghosted me. Hell, after that moment we had, I expected it. But shit, tonight we were supposed to meet at the hotel. I got my own room, and I was to meet her at the banquet and I've yet to hear a single word from her.

In fact, when I texted her asking if we were still on for the night she sent a fucking thumbs up. A thumbs up of all things. Sighing to myself I decide to pack and head to the hotel at least then I can catch some sleep and not have to worry if I will be stood up or not.

Chapter 28

RORY

I paced my apartment moving back and forth back and forth as my friends looked on.

"Ro, calm down. It's not the end of the world," Nirvana said.

I turned glaring at her as I spoke, "I fainted while we were having sex. Then I completely ghosted him."

"Has he reached out to you?" Delaney asks, rubbing a hand over her rounded stomach.

Biting my lip, I turn away from them, nodding slightly.

"Well? What did you say?" Layla asks, tossing my dress and heels onto my bed.

"I sent a thumbs up to him. And turned my phone off. I haven't spoken to him since." I gasp and throw myself backwards into my chair. "I'm supposed to meet his family in three days."

They stop talking, taking a chance I glance up and see them all gaping at me. Right. They don't know we are fake dating. Swallowing hard I explain everything to them skipping some of the details as to the real reason why. But now I needed to get myself together and finish getting packed.

"So, you're pretending to be his girlfriend because his mom keeps wanting to set him up?" Sera asks, gently packing my insulin and testing kit. After my mishap with Caden I've been on top of my sugars and health and had even started running. Okay, fast walking but I'm getting there.

"Yes," I sigh. "We are helping each other. He's my boyfriend so I don't have to worry about Anthony and the fact he's most likely going to bring his heavily pregnant wife with him." Or the anger that still simmers in me that my intrusive thoughts tell me to dump a glass of wine all over his bound to be pristine suit.

Delaney stands and cups my face. I gaze down at her, being a few inches taller, and take a breath and she breathes with me before giving me a small smile. "You'll be fine, Rory. You're nervous which is valid. You're going on a date."

"Fake date," I interrupt.

"A fake date," she concedes. "And the man you trusted broke something in you. That is okay. You'll have Caden and even though he's a little off sometimes, he's still an amazing guy. He'll protect you and be whatever it is you need tonight. Give him a chance and you'll see."

I nod, taking another deep breath. "Okay. I'll be fine."

"You should just fuck him again," Nirvana blurted out.

I give a shaky laugh and turn to her saying, "No. I think we're past that. He won't want a fainting woman." It was embarrassing enough to tell my friends that I fainted during sex, but it was another reason altogether to do it in front of the man. Not to mention he didn't even get to finish. Even though I offered to help him out he turned me down. Maybe that's why I ghosted him, the fact that he rejected me and I felt like a total idiot. Sighing, I shake my head at those thoughts. They would do me no good tonight.

They all share a look, but glancing at the clock shows I've got very little time to make it to the hotel to get ready before I'm late. Grabbing my things and dress I tell them goodbye before leaving my apartment and head downstairs counting each step it takes to get to my car. It's a hundred and fifty-six steps. A hundred and fifty-six heart beats that has me nervously stuffing my car full of bags before climbing into the driver's seat and turning on my car. But I don't drive away. Nerves have me rooted to the spot until I take another long breath.

"I can do this," I whisper to myself. I won't allow myself to panic, I've been with Caden already. A fake date is noth-ing. So why was I so nervous? Shaking off these thoughts I drive away muttering, 'I can do this' the entire drive to the Four Seasons.

I stare at myself in the elevator mirror for the umpteenth time and swallow hard. I downplayed my makeup going for a soft glow and had my hair pinned up with a few stray curls framing my face. I wore a form fitting champagne dress with matching shoes that had my skin looking like a shiny bronze in this dim lighting. The elevator dinged and the door opened onto the open conference room turned ballroom for the evening.

My heart picked up when people turned to stare but my eyes were scanning until they fell on the lone man standing at the bar. He turns and heat and a sense of peace unfurl inside of me. Caden. He came. He's dressed in an all-black suit with the top few buttons of his shirt unbuttoned showing off some of the ink tattooed onto his skin. He stands straighter taking me in. I step forward out of the elevator and head in his direction.

Caden

My mouth dries at the sight of Rory, dressed in what looks like gold. She looks like the finest piece of art known to man. Her hair is pinned up with little stones with a few tendrils escaping to frame her delicate face. Goddamn, she was perfect. Swallowing hard, she stops in front of me.

"Hi," she says, her voice soft.

"Hi," I repeat. "You look…"

She smiles. "It's nice to know I can make someone speechless." She swallows hard before reaching up and smoothing out the collar of my shirt. "You look amazing, Caden."

I preen at that, the feel of her hands on me after these last few days was like a drug to me. The heat seared straight into my heart and had the organ pounding. But then I remember her ghosting me and a shutter falls in my brain.

"Are you ready?"

She sighs and takes my face into her hands. "I'm sorry for being so distant these last few days. I just needed to get my bearings."

I grip her wrists gently. "And did you?" My voice is barely above a whisper, but I know she hears me.

"I'm scared my heart will fall for you."

I ran my hand up her smooth arm before cupping the nape of her neck. "Don't let it. It was sex, amazing mind-blowing sex. We are still friends. The deal is still on. If you don't think you can handle it, tell me now."

She swallows. "I want more. Have wanted more for days now." It's what I wanted to hear. Hear that she was as stuck on me as I was on her. That she was replaying that night over and over in her head as I was.

Running my thumb over her plump bottom lip I smirk. "All you have to do is ask nicely and I'll give you whatever you want."

Huffing out a laugh she drops her hands. "You're a cocky bastard." Turning to look around us she sighs softly. "I've got to network." Pausing briefly, she says, "If I need you I'll tuck my hair behind my ear."

Nodding, I whisper, "Go network, I'll be here."

With a small smile she stands on her toes and presses a gentle kiss to my cheek before walking away. My gaze is glued to the sway of her hips and I hardly realize someone is next to me before a throat clears.

Gazing behind me, I see an older couple standing a little too close.

"May I help you?" I ask.

The older woman looks at me eyes bright as she smiles. "Oh my, I didn't realize Rory had a partner. How wonderful."

"Oh, I'm Caden Sato," I introduce myself, holding my hand out.

The older woman takes it with a smile. "I'm Olive Frederick, one of her teachers. Rory is an excellent and talented student. You must be really proud of her."

I glance at the woman in question as she talks to another woman around her age or a little younger. "She's amazing," I agree.

As if she can feel my gaze she turns her head and gazes at me, tucking a stray curl behind her ear. Nodding to the couple I say, "If you'll excuse me."

I make my way towards Rory, watching her the entire

way. The woman beside her, a short blonde, stands up straighter beside her and gazes at me.

"Claire, this is Caden. My boyfriend. Caden this is Claire, Anthony's paralegal." I glance at the woman and nod politely, wrapping a protective arm around Rory's shoulders.

"Nice to meet you." It wasn't, but I had to put on this front for Rory. The idea of her being so close to this woman, a woman who locked her in a bathroom alone in the dark bothers the fuck out of me. More than I realize.

Rory places her hand on my stomach and I gaze down at her. She wasn't short by any means but next to me she was, standing at nearly six foot in heels I still towered over her in my six-five frame. "Claire was just telling me about this snake that got loose in the office. Can you believe it?"

I widened my eyes incredulously. "That's crazy, was it caught?"

Claire nods, "Yes the janitor caught it and let it go. It was terrifying."

Rory nods in understanding, but I see her eyes narrow. I follow her direction and see Anthony with a heavily pregnant woman.

"I didn't know he was married," Claire whispers beside us.

Rory turns to her. "You didn't? He must really keep his private life private." Sarcasm is heavy in her tone as the couple gets closer to us. I don't miss the way Anthony's gaze travels over Rory. A look of possession crosses his features and that doesn't sit right with me. Without thinking I wrap my arm around Rory's waist and pull her against me, claiming her in front of the other man. Rory glances up at me with an arched eyebrow but doesn't say anything. If anything, she melts against me more.

"Mr. Lincoln. It's nice to see you tonight," Claire says, her tone stiff.

Anthony barely spares her a glance as he turns to me and Rory. "Rory, I didn't realize you were bringing someone."

"We were allowed a plus one. I brought my boyfriend. And this must be your wife." Her tone is sarcastic and hollow as if she couldn't be bothered with introductions, but I knew better. I knew this was bothering her and I couldn't blame her one bit. I hold onto Rory, being her strength as she faces the man who has caused her so much hurt, and I see the resolve in her eyes. The determination of not letting him get to her and pride unfurls in me. This is the Rory I knew and was coming to care for. Wait, no. No feelings can come into this even if they were pounding at the back of my skull wanting me to acknowledge them. I couldn't, not when she needed me to be at my best to protect her if needed and I would protect her, no matter what it took.

Chapter 29

RORY

I hold out my hand to Anthony's wife and she takes it, shaking it with a bright smile on her pretty heart-shaped face. "Yes. I'm Margo." I nod with my own small smile even though on the inside I'm cringing. She deserved to know what a bastard her husband was. I drop my hand and turn to Caden who is staring daggers at the other man.

"Can you get me a drink while I head to the ladies room?"

He glances down at me, his brow furrowed before he nods, pressing a kiss to my head. It's swift and fleeting, but I feel it straight to my bones and it has me sucking in a sharp breath. This man is going to end up wrecking me if I let him. Excusing myself from the group, I make my way to the restrooms saying hi to the people who stop me on the way. I walk into the restroom and take a breath. It felt like tonight was going slower and slower the longer I was here and it's been all of thirty minutes. I lean against the sink and bow my head calculating how long I have to stay before I can leave. The door opening behind me has me tensing and forgetting my train of thought.

I glance up and see Margo standing behind me. Fuck. Straightening my shoulders I turn on the water and wash my hands, ignoring the way she watched me. Until she scoffed and threw a towel on the counter. "You're really going to pretend you're not fucking my husband while I stand right in front of you?"

Turning off the water, I grab my own towel to dry my hands before turning towards her. "I am truly sorry. I had no idea he was married."

She scoffs, rolling her bright blue eyes. "Everyone knew."

I shake my head. "No. Tonight was the first night we've ever heard of you. I stopped seeing Anthony weeks ago, when I heard you two in his office. If I had known I never would've been with him." And it was true. If I had known I would have left a long time ago. But he tricked not only me but Margo and Claire as well.

"He wouldn't do that." She shakes her head in denial as tears fill her eyes.

My chest hurts for her, for the unborn child. "He told me after I stopped speaking to him that you were in an open relationship. I never knew he was dating anyone since I've known him so long ago."

That catches her attention, "How long have you known him?"

I shrug uncomfortably. "Since I was fifteen."

Margo gasps, covering her mouth. "You're the bright young student he mentioned. You were one of the youngest in the summer class. Oh my god."

She didn't say anything else, just walked out of the bathroom leaving me alone as the door closed with a soft *snick*. I follow after her, worried, but stop when I see Anthony glaring at me as she storms off. I swallow hard and try to walk past him only for him to grab my arm tightly and push me against the wall.

"What the fuck did you say to her?"

Irritated, I pushed his hand off of me and said, "The truth. Someone needed to tell her what her baby daddy is like."

He grabs my jaw tightly, squeezing it painfully until I cry out with pain. "You listen to me, and listen to me well, without me you're nothing. You'd have nothing, you'd be nothing because I made you. Don't fuck it up by getting into my business." I grabbed my knife out of the sheath and point it against Anthony's throat. I got the sheath when Caden gave me the knife, and for some reason I felt the need to wear it wherever I go. He tenses and glares at me.

"What the fuck are you doing?" he demands tightening his fingers against my jaw.

I feel someone behind me, then a hand comes up behind me and grips my wrist pushing the knife deeper. Uncaring that someone could see us. But it's just the three of us, secluded in a tension filled bubble that has my heart rate increasing.

"Are you ready to make him bleed? Or do we stop? It's up to you, *Chīsai doragon*." Caden's deep voice is in my ear making me shiver. I want to make Anthony bleed, I want to hurt him like he's hurt me, like he's hurt his wife, but I just drop my hand gripping the knife in a tight fist. Anthony lets me go and storms off after his wife as I lean against the wall breathing heavily, before standing and making my way to the elevator. On my way I see Caden. He gazes at me and his eyes land on my cheek. I don't say anything as I rush to the elevator.

"Rory," Caden says following after me.

Before I can say anything the elevator opens, and I step inside bringing him with me as the door closes. I slam on the button not speaking willing the damn thing to move faster but it doesn't. "Rory," he starts.

"Why won't this thing go any fucking faster?" I demand, ignoring him and pressing our floor button repeatedly until the elevator comes to a streaking halt sending me falling against Caden. "Son of a bitch," I snap, feeling panic rise up inside of me.

"Don't touch anything else, Lorelai," Caden says, using my full name.

I stop, gaping at him. "What did you just call me?" He's used my full name before and I liked it, but hearing it in a scolding manner had me bristling and anger spiking. "How do you even know my full name? Did my brothers tell you?"

He ignores me and says, "What happened to your face and don't lie to me."

I shrug. "Anthony grabbed it. Doesn't matter." But it did. He showed me his true colors these last few weeks and a part of me was slowly breaking into a full-blown melt down. Caden barks out a harsh laugh. "Fuck that shitty excuse. He put his hands on you."

"It doesn't matter. Stop acting like you care." I was angry, I knew he cared but I was lashing out at the closest person to me.

His head snaps back as he glares at me with heated dark eyes. "Trust me when I say this, I fucking care a lot, Lorelai."

"Yeah, because you need a fake girlfriend for your sister's wedding. I know," I say, irritation beating at me hard. He doesn't say anything, just grabs my hair and pulls my head back before his lips are crashing roughly on mine. I don't even have time to think before I'm pushed against the wall and his hands grab me behind my thighs lifting me up. I give up the idea of fighting off these feelings and fall into him, kissing him back.

These last few days after knowing what it's like to be kissed, to be touched by Caden to having none of it has been torture. So I just stop and lean into his touches.

Caden's tongue thrusts into my mouth, teasing me with what he's capable of. Tasting me thoroughly. My hands grip the back of his hair, and my legs wrap around his waist pulling him closer to me. His fingers knead into my thighs before moving up towards my ass. I gasp arching into the touch before he pulls away staring at me.

"You are the most infuriating woman I've ever met," he mutters.

I huff out a laugh. "Yet you chose me to be your fake girlfriend."

He presses forward his erection brushing against my aching pussy. "Make no mistake, there is nothing fake about what I'm feeling right now. There will be nothing fake about the way I eat your little cunt and make you come on my face."

I reel back stunned and hot. Really damn hot. "What?"

He doesn't say anything, just drops me back to my feet and kneels in front of me, his large hands slowly pushing up the material of my dress to my hips. I swallow hard seeing this man at my feet.

"Caden you don't have to," I start.

His dark brown gaze jumps to mine, and he chuckles darkly. "That little taste I got at home wasn't nearly enough. I need more. Tell me, do you want me to stop? Or do you want me to continue?"

Caden is the first and only person who has ever tasted me, Anthony didn't like doing it, but the thought of this man's mouth on me was leaving me a panting mess.

"Please don't stop," I whimper. He sends me that intoxicating grin of his before he leans down and presses a kiss to my trembling thighs. My head falls back and a small sigh escapes as his teeth nip gently at the sensitive skin.

His hand moves to my ankle and lifts my leg over his shoulder, spreading me wider for him. Then I feel him, his tongue moving up the center of my pussy over the lace of my panties, making me groan.

"Caden," I plead, fingers spearing into his soft black hair. He doesn't respond, just pulls the lace to the side and his mouth is there. "Oh my god," I groan. His tongue spears into me, fucking me before going up to my throbbing clit, taking it gently between his teeth and tugging. I'm a trembling mess gasping and arching into his touch when I feel the elevator start up. Panic seized me and I tried to push him away.

"Not until you come on my face, Lorelai. Now be my good little slut and come for me." I gasp as he dives back in and thrusts his fingers into me as his tongue moves over my clit. I brace my hand against the glass panels and let myself go, moaning his name. With one last stroke of his fingers, I cry out as my orgasm hits me, and hits me hard. Caden stands then and puts my clothes in order before kissing me tenderly. So tender I almost balk at it.

But I don't. I wrap my arms around his neck and whisper, "Come back to my room tonight."

He doesn't get to answer as the doors open and we break apart, seeing a group of people waiting as the doors are pried open. "Oh my, there were people in here the entire time?" one of the fire marshals asked. Caden grabs my hand and pushes past the group of people and heads for the stairs, I can't help the small laugh that escapes me as he takes me not to my room but to his.

"How are you feeling, Ro Ro?" he asks, unlocking his door.

"Good. Really good," I answer honestly.

He turns to me then and nods. "Good. Now get naked and get on the bed."

Chapter 30

CADEN

I take my jacket off watching as Rory swallows hard and slowly unzips her dress letting the material fall to the floor leaving her in a white lace bra, thong and heels. Then I look closer and see a sheath on her thigh with the knife I gave her strapped to it. I groan at the look and almost combust on the spot. I need her now. I move, then step around her to gently pull the pins out of her hair and let the thick mass of curls fall to her shoulders.

"You are a thing of beauty, Rory," I whisper, pressing a kiss to her shoulder. The sweet taste of her is still on my tongue and I'm pretty sure I'm addicted to her now. Yes, we agreed this is a platonic relationship with physical aspects, but I'd be lying if I said I wasn't feeling more. Shaking those thoughts away I reach up and unhook her bra.

"Caden?" she whispers.

"Yes, *Chīsai doragon?*" I say, running my lips over her shoulders, taking great delight in her small tremors.

"Can you be gentle tonight?"

I reel back. "Did I hurt you last time?"

Shaking her head quickly, she turns around. "No. No, nothing like that. I just, I've never had gentle. I think tonight I really need you to be gentle. Please?"

I cup her face gently, still angry that Anthony thinks he has the right to grab her face as hard as he did. I run my thumbs over the sprouting bruises and sigh softly. "Baby, you never have to ask me for anything. If you need something, tell me and I'll make it happen."

She swallows hard and nods. "I need gentle, Caden."

I nod, leaning forward and kissing her gently. I've only been gentle with Xena, but the thought of doing anything other than what Rory needs is abhorrent to me. I walk her backwards until her knees hit the edge of the bed and she falls back. I pull away slowly and shuck out of my clothes before grabbing a condom and sliding it on, then leaning over her to grab her panties and pull them down her long legs. Leaving her in nothing but her silver heels and sheath.

I reach forward and remove the sheath and her shoes,, letting them fall in a heap with our clothes before I settle over her. I kiss her throat, tasting her lavender vanilla scent, moving down to her breasts and pulling a small brown nipple into my mouth.

"Caden," she gasps, her legs wrapped around my waist above my ass and arched into me, running her wet pussy over my abdomen making me groan. "I need you inside of me now."

I move to her other breast and suck gently, running my fingers down her side before gripping her thighs and spreading her for me. I sit up slightly and line myself up at her entrance and slowly, so slowly push into her. She squeezes down on me, making me groan as I push deeper into her. It's a tight fit and I have to stop myself from going too hard and fast. I glance down at Rory and see she's staring up at me with trusting eyes and I know I can be gentle for her.

Once I thrust in all the way, I lean down to press my lips against hers and slowly begin to move. It's intense and the most intimate thing I've ever done. I grab one of her hands and twine our fingers together and begin to move a little harder, thrusting in and out of her. I wasn't fucking her. No, I was making love to her. And the scary part is I wanted to do more.

Light filtered in from the open curtain and I groaned, tossing an arm over my eyes. A weight on my chest had me stopping and I moved my arm and saw Rory lying on my chest fast asleep. She looked beautiful like this. Asleep and uncon-cerned about anything else.

"What time is it?" her sleep-ridden voice jolted me out of my staring. I reach on the nightstand and blink at the bright phone and grimace at all the missed calls and texts I got from my mom and sisters.

"It's eight-thirty," I reply.

Rory groans and slowly sits up, letting the sheet fall to her waist, uncaring that she's naked. "I've got to get ready for today, want to meet downstairs in thirty minutes for breakfast?"

I lean back in the bed and smile at her. "Sure. Is today those mock trials you have to do?"

"Yes. Kaila has been working with me, so I'll be ready."

"Can I watch?" I ask.

She nibbles her bottom lip before nodding shyly. "Yes, but you must sit in the back."

"Scouts honor," I tease, raising my right hand. She scoffs,

but smiles at me as she stands and grabs my shirt and shucks it on and grabs her clothes. "Lorelai," I say, stopping her in her tracks.

"Caden," she says, eyeing me warily.

"Come here." She steps towards me and I pull her down, grabbing the back of her neck and kissing her hard. She melts against me and leans up straddling my waist. Our tongues thrust together and she starts grinding against my growing cock causing me to groan. She pulls away first.

"I've got to get dressed and take my insulin. You now have twenty minutes." With that she jumps up with a little laugh and runs out of the room with her clothes, uncaring about walking out with just my shirt on. Shaking my head with a small smile I lift up my phone and call back my mother.

She answers on the third ring. "Caden? What on earth? I've been calling you for hours."

I sigh and sit up. "Sorry, Mom. I was busy. What's up?"

"Your sister tells me you're bringing your girlfriend to her wedding." I sigh again, my mother loves Xena, I haven't told her the reason we broke up nor have my sisters. I rather not dilute my mother's opinion of people because it wasn't my job to point out how awful a person was. I wished my mom could see what was in front of her, but she was an ignorance is bliss type of woman. My father was on my side no matter what, and I think he never really liked Xena anyways. She was negative and wanted me to work as either a doctor or in an office somewhere like her father and brothers, but that wasn't for me. Never has been and never will be. But my mom? She wanted me to be a traditional Japanese son with a Japanese wife and work a safe job that would keep me out of harm's way. When I told her I was joining pararescue after the Air Force she lost it on me. If I wasn't over eighteen and already in the Air Force I'm sure she would have had a different tune.

When I was held captive, and we didn't know if I was going to die or not, was when I knew I had to stop. But I didn't completely. I went into fire rescue. An equally dangerous job.

"Well, what's she like?" Mom finally asks.

I smile to myself. "She's funny and has a good career. Puts her family and friends first."

"What does she do?" Mom's interest is piqued.

"Right now, she is a paralegal and in her last semester of law school. She'll take the bar in July."

"Wow, a lawyer. This is great. I never met a real lawyer. What kind of law?"

I paused, I didn't know. I hardly knew much about her other than the basics that I learned from Max and as I opened my mouth I saw the time and cursed. "Sorry, Mom, I have to go. I'm meeting Rory for breakfast. I love you, bye." I hang up before she can respond and quickly hop in the shower. I needed to learn more about Rory before the wedding or our lie would be found out way before either of us had the chance to make it believable.

Chapter 31

RORY

I sigh softly as I sip my juice and wait for Caden. It was five minutes after our meeting time, and I was a bundle of nerves. Yesterday was intense. The things that happened with Anthony and Margo. Then there was Caden. The way he made me feel last night was unreal. The intensity of the way he touched me made me feel loved. I know we agreed to a physical relationship, but I was afraid it would go too far. Last night was too far.

"Hey, Rory!" a bubbly voice said behind me, and I smiled as Vanessa bounded over to my table.

"Hey, Vanessa. How are you?"

The redhead sat beside me and sighed dramatically. "I'm ready to see you in the mock trials. I wish we could've done this in the courtroom, but they wanted to do this last minute."

I hum under my breath. "I didn't know they did this to be honest."

"Oh, it's new for this year. It was suggested by Robinson."

I snort, I should've known.

"I'm sorry I'm late," A deep voice says behind me, and I turn to see Caden holding a little plate of complementary pastries and sets the plate in front of me. He looks good, dressed in all black from head to toe and wearing his hair pushed back. It's hotter than I care to admit.

I send him a smile. "It's okay, Vanessa kept me company while I waited." I turn to the woman in question who is gaping at Caden. I hide my smile and nudge her with my foot.

She shakes herself and glances at me and mouths 'wow'. She stands and leaves with a little wave and Caden takes the seat she vacates. "She seems nice," he says, taking one of the powdered donuts.

"She's funny. I like her."

He takes a bite of a donut and stares at me before swallowing. "My mother called. That's why I wasn't here at exactly nine."

I shrug. "It's okay, Caden. You didn't miss anything."

He tilts his head to look at me before looking at the plate. "Eat. I brought you a danish because that's what was left, and you need to keep your energy up." I huff out a laugh and grab the danish tearing off a piece and popping it into my mouth.

He stares at me intensely, as if remembering everything we did the night before. I can't lie and say I wasn't thinking the same thing. My thighs clenched under the table and my heart rate began to pick up. I needed to focus.

Clearing my throat I ask, "So your mother called?"

He eats his doughnut and nods, swallowing before he speaks. "Yes. She was wondering about my new girlfriend that I'm bringing home. Which reminds me, we hardly know each other."

I lean back in my seat and cross my legs. "Ask me whatever you want."

He mirrors my pose and says, "What kind of law are you studying?"

I'm taken aback, but answer anyway, "I work domestic violence cases and familial abuse."

He cocks his head to the side. "Because of Delaney and Nirvana?" he asks, remembering what I told him the last time we talked about this.

"Yes. Because they didn't get the justice they deserved. They weren't protected as children, but I can help those in need now."

"That's noble."

I laugh. "Maybe to some. To me it's what I'm meant to do." He opens his mouth to speak but stops when Kaila sits in the vacant seat at the table.

"Bad news, you won't be doing the trial today. Anthony's wife went into labor, and he rushed her away. I know you worked hard, but the good news is you can enjoy the rest of your day." With that she stood and left us alone, not even acknowledging Caden.

"Damn. Well, I guess that's that," I muttered, turning to Caden.

He hums in thought before standing and holding his hand out to me. I take it and let him pull me from my seat. "What are we doing?" I ask.

"I'm going to take you on a proper date. Get to know you better. Besides, this place is boring. Let's go get some real food and do something fun."

A smile blooms on my face. "I'd like that." A whole lot more than I was willing to admit, but for now I'd just go with the flow.

It didn't take long for Caden to lead me to the car and be on our way to whatever destination he had in mind. I was nervous, excited. I haven't been on a real date in years. Caden places his hand on my thigh and squeezes gently. I look at it and slowly twine my fingers on top of his holding him to me. It's such a simple gesture, but it has me burning up inside. We sat in companionable silence until he turned into the Downtown Houston Aquarium. I sit up straighter and grin.

"The aquarium? I haven't been to one in years!" With excitement I bound out of the car waiting for Caden who laughs. "Come on, come on. There's a Ferris wheel here we should ride before we leave."

"We just got here *Chīsai doragon*. We have plenty of time for the Ferris wheel." I grab his hand and tug him to the front where we pay to get in and start to explore. Walking from tank to tank and having Caden explain different species of aquatic animals to me is the best part of my day. I listen intently as he tells me how sharks aren't really that dangerous to humans unless provoked and how there are some like the lemon sharks that seek attention from people who can see them as we see puppies or babies.

It's a tender moment I never expected to have with him and a part of me is falling for him a little at a time even though I promised I wouldn't. We spent the rest of the day eating some good food and visiting all the attractions. Walking hand in hand Caden finally leads me to the Ferris wheel. We wait for our turn then show our tickets before climbing into the circular ride and sitting. It's dark out now and the lights make the atmosphere feel romantic and almost heady. I swallow hard as the ride starts moving and stare at Caden.

"What's on your mind, Rory?" he asks.

Swallowing thickly, I take that leap and answer honestly, "How I want to taste you." He arches a dark brow and stretches out his long legs.

"Then come here." I go to stand, but he shakes his head. "On your knees. We wouldn't want to be caught."

Heat moves through me as I slowly drop to my knees in front of him, my hands finding his thighs and moving up ever so slowly until I reach his belt. The ride stops halfway, and I take a deep breath as I settle between his legs and undo his belt. The sound is drowned out by the blood rushing in my ears as I reach into his boxers and pull his erect cock free.

"You don't have to do this, Lorelai."

I don't answer him, just swallow him down, taking in his thick length and breathing through my nose. He was hot and hard against my tongue, and I loved it. Fuck did I love it.

"Fuck, Rory. So fucking good for me." I wrap my hand around him, my fingers don't connect but I try my best as I move up and down him. Hollowing my cheeks and swirling my tongue over his swollen head. His hips arch up pushing deeper into my mouth making me choke slightly. His hands come to my face and his thumbs are gentle against my cheeks rubbing in soothing circles before spearing into my hair and holding me against him. I loved it. Taking every inch as far as I could, feeling the way his thighs clenched against my hands. It was too much but not enough.

I pump my hand up and down and he groans softly. "I'm about to come, Lorelai. Swallow every drop." I nod and suck harder moaning against him as he comes hard and fast. I swallow every drop and move back, licking the rest up before slowly moving into the seat beside him.

"You okay?" I ask.

Caden laughs softly and fixes his pants before wrapping an arm around me. "I've never come so hard before."

"That's good. Me and my practice banana are so proud," I tease.

The ride stops and he stands helping me to my feet. "Let's go look at some more animals. The tanks look better at night. Especially the jellyfish."

I nod and step off the ride letting Caden take the lead as we head to the jellyfish exhibit. The way the jellyfish light up the tank is so fascinating, watching them move slowly up and down and seeing the way the lights make Caden look care-free, no longer holding onto the past. It's something I want to capture forever. I look beside me and see a little older woman and ask, "Excuse me?"

She turns and smiles at me. "Yes, dear?"

"Do you think you can take a quick picture of us?" The older woman nods, her gray hair bobbing with each shake. Caden looks at me then and smiles, he puts his arm around me and instead of looking at the camera he looks at me. I glance up at him and smile gently. This is one of the best dates I've ever been on.

"There you go, dear," the older woman said. "You two are a lovely couple. I wish you many years of happiness."

Caden takes my phone back. "Thank you. We appreciate it," he says to the woman, and wraps an arm around my shoulders to lead me away.

He takes me to the concession stand and gets me an order of nachos before leading me to a bench. "So, what was it like growing up with only brothers?" he asks, snagging a chip.

I laugh then reply, "Annoying. They are all so overprotec-tive of me. As if I can't fight my own battles."

"I'm overprotective of my sisters, too. We are supposed to take care of you. It's in the book."

"Yes, well I need to read this book. Because I think it's

wrong. Is it the same book Sorrow mentioned to Delaney by chance?"

Caden shakes his head. "Nah, this is a different volume." He looks at me and laughter darkens his eyes before he leans down and kisses me gently. It gives me hope for the future. But as the saying goes, hope breeds eternal misery.

Chapter 32

RORY

The days passed quickly and now here I was standing in line at the airport so I could meet Caden's family as his girlfriend. Nerves make me irritable and nauseous as I check my bags.

"Are you okay?" Caden asks me.

I nod. "Just nervous. I've never been on a plane before."

He moves back and looks at me. "Wait, really?" I nod. "Damn, it'll be okay. Flying is one of the safest forms of travel there is."

I huff out a laugh. "Did a travel agent tell you that?"

He smirks. "No. Actually it was my little sister Amani. She tells me all kinds of random facts. She's excited to meet you."

I smooth my hands down the dress I'm wearing and sigh when I realize they are shaky. Caden reaches into his pocket and holds out a fun size chocolate bar. I look up at him with wide eyes. "What's this?" I ask, taking the offered candy.

"I always worry if your sugar is going to drop, so I've

started carrying around a little bag of candy with me." His cheeks heat as he tells me this, but I've never felt more cherished or cared for than in this moment. The fact that he cared enough to even have anything on hand was enough to bring tears to my eyes.

After our date to the aquarium Caden has been different with me. More attentive and caring. We haven't hooked up since the Ferris wheel but that didn't bother me. Although my clenching thighs would beg to differ. Swallowing that down, I open the candy and pop it into my mouth waiting for our gate number to be called. We sit in comfortable silence until the PA system comes on calling our gate. Caden grabs our bags and I grab my purse and follow after him. Our time in the airport has been smooth thus far, which is surprising considering all that I know of airports. I figured the movies would be right and they'd be overly crowded and anxiety inducing, but so far it hasn't been.

"Welcome, I hope you enjoy your flight," the attendant said, taking our tickets and letting us board. I gasp when I see how spacious it actually is and I turn to Caden with wide eyes.

"I thought this would be a lot smaller."

He laughs. "No, I got us first class tickets instead of coach. I like to be comfortable when flying and I'm tall, as are you. I want you to be as comfortable as possible."

"Caden, you didn't have to do that," I mutter as I take my seat beside him, stretching out my legs and sighing with relief.

He looks down at me then. "I wanted to, Rory. Besides seeing as this is your first time flying, I want it to be good for you."

When he sits beside me I lean forward and press a kiss to his cheek. "Thank you, *mi vida.*" I whisper the last part, my own face heating.

As I move back, Caden grabs the back of my head holding me to him. "I don't know what you said but I liked it. Say it again."

I swallow hard. "*Mi vida.*"

He grins slightly and leans in, pressing a gentle kiss to my lips before pulling away. "Put your seatbelt on. They're about to go over everything."

With shaky hands I put on my seat belt and listen intently while they go over what to do in a crash, they pull on a mask and breathe through it and that makes my nerves go up. After they finish, the plane taxis and I grip Caden's hand, squeezing tightly. He doesn't say anything, just flips his hand and twines our fingers together, his thumb moving gently back and forth on my knuckles. Soothing this irrational fear I wasn't aware I had.

Swallowing hard, I asked, "What's California like?"

"Palm trees and beaches as far as the eye can see," he responds with a smile on his handsome face.

I nod, relaxing my grip on his hand. "I've always wanted to go to the beach."

"Why haven't you?"

I shrug. "I'm not the strongest swimmer. My dad's tried teaching me, but nothing seems to work with me when it comes to water."

"Maybe if we have time I'll take you."

I smile at him, my heart slowing to a normal rhythm. "I'd like that."

He leans back and smiles at me, showing those dimples I'm coming to love and want to see more of. Without thinking I reach up and place a gentle hand on his face.

"Lorelai," he whispers.

I go to drop my hand but he stops me, grabbing it. I look at him, my eyes wide. "When you say my name like that it makes me think I'm in trouble." I try to tease but it falls on a breathless laugh. The plane jerks then and I grab Caden's hand, squeezing hard.

"It's just turbulence that happens every time it's in the air." The plane slowly levels out and I take a breath trying to stave off the sudden nausea I feel and take a deep breath through my nose before releasing the death grip I have on Caden's hand. The seatbelt light dings and I quickly unbuckle the seatbelt before jumping up. Caden's eyes widen, and I send him a shaky smile before moving past him to go to the bathroom. Nerves are suddenly rushing through me as I run into a flight attendant.

"Sorry," I rushed out. "I'm just trying to find a restroom."

The older woman smiles and points me in the right direction, and I nod in thanks before moving forward. I open the door and slowly lock it before leaning forward and bracing my hands on the sink to take a deep breath. "What are you doing, Rory?" I mutter to myself.

Caden

I glance at Rory as she runs to the bathroom and worry runs through me. Without thinking I stand up and make my way towards the bathroom. Luckily I don't run into anyone as I knock on the door.

"Rory?" I knock gently again, and she opens the door slightly before opening it wide enough for me to walk in. "What's wrong?"

She shakes her head. "I don't know, I just got really overwhelmed and then I started feeling sick and I don't know what I'm doing, Caden."

Her words are panicked and her eyes wild as she looks at me. I take her face gently into my hands. "Shhh. It's okay. You're okay. Tell me what you need, and I'll do it."

She swallows, looks at the door then me. "I need you to distract me," she whispers. I bite back a groan and lift her up, pushing the skirt of her dress up to her hips.

"Can you be quiet for me?" She nods slowly and wraps a leg around my hip, hiking up her skirt. I groan softly at the sight of her little red panties. "Did you wear those for me, *Chīsai doragon?* Did you want me to fuck you on this plane?" I ask, running a knuckle over her lace clad pussy.

Rory's breathing turned heavy as she nodded. "Yes. I've missed the way you've felt." I groan, kissing down her throat taking in her smell with each kiss.

My hands creep up to her breasts and squeeze gently before she lets out a tiny sigh. "Please, Caden. I need…" she pauses, not articulating what she needs before she stares up at me with those dark hazel eyes.

So, I take over, gripping her hips and thrusting up, rubbing my cock against her pussy. "Do you need it rough, baby? Do you want it to hurt to forget everything?"

She nods, arching into my touch. "Use your words, Lorelia."

I hike her leg up higher and press into her, feeling the fabric of my jeans and her panties brush against each other heightening the feeling between us.

"Fuck me, Caden. Make it hurt." Her words were breathless, and it snapped something inside of me as I reached between us and freed my cock from my jeans and pushed her panties roughly to the side and thrust home. I set a hard punishing rhythm fucking into her until her back hit the mirror.

I brace a hand against the wall, clenching my teeth as she

leans forward biting into my shoulder. Her moans are muffled by my shirt as she bites down hard enough I know there will be a mark there. Her mark. I grip her hips hard turning so my back is to the sink and she's riding me. "Look at me," I demand gruffly. Her eyes shoot to mine, and she loses all abandon and rides me hard and fast biting her bottom lip to keep from screaming.

"Should I come in you? Filling you with me so it'll be dripping out of your swollen pussy when you meet everyone?" The words are hushed but hard as I move her on me. "Or should I put you on your knees, so you swallow me down?"

Throwing her head back she moans softly as her pussy clenches down on me. "In me, Caden. Come in me. I'm on birth control and clean." I reach between our bodies and pinch her clit, sending her over the edge and she takes me with her, milking my cock as she comes. I grab the back of her neck and bring her mouth down on mine, kissing her gently. Her arms wrap around my neck and she sighs against me, relaxing finally. When she comes down from the high, I push back and stare at her.

"Are you good now?" I ask.

She nods, her face slightly flushed. "Never better. I'm sorry I bit you. It was an accident."

I look at my shoulder and shrug. "It's fine. I kinda like knowing it's there. But we should take our seats before someone comes knocking." As if on cue a knock rattled the door, we quickly dressed and I opened the door, knowing what this looked like but I didn't care. Nor did I care when Rory flushed the toilet and stepped beside me.

"I was sick," she said, but the flight attendant didn't look convinced. The two of us took the walk of shame, but I broke out into a smile when I heard Rory giggle as if she were just caught doing something naughty. And I guess we did. As we sit down, Rory breaks down into laughter and I join in laughing our asses off.

"I can't believe we just did that," she whispers to me, still laughing.

I shake my head, a smirk playing on my mouth. "I can. I'm irresistible."

"And a bad influence," she teases. That's how the rest of the flight was, her teasing me and us laughing until the descent of the plane. I glanced at her, and I know this is no longer fake to me. I fought my feelings for her for as long as I could, but it's not working. Everything she does brings me closer to wanting more with her. Wanting this to be real. But how do I make it real for her?

Chapter 33

RORY

Caden grabs my bags when they come on the conveyor belt and sets them in front of me. "Okay, my sisters are huggers so be aware of that. My mom is stern, and my dad is a quiet man so they might be standoffish at first."

"Hmmm, and what should I do with the fact there's a really tall, gorgeous woman with them?" I ask, looking ahead and seeing Caden's family. Which I know because I see one of his sisters holding a giant sign that says, *Caden Sato's Family*.

Caden looks and whatever good mood he was in quickly slips away as he stares at the woman who waves at him. "Xena shouldn't be here," he mutters to me.

"How do you want to play this?"

He looks at me and licks his lips. "I want you to hold my hand and don't let go."

I don't even need to think as I lace my fingers through his and squeeze them before taking my bag and walking with him towards his family. His grip on my hand was tight, on the verge of pain, but I didn't say anything as we stopped in front of his parents.

"Mom, Dad, this is my girlfriend, Rory. Rory, this is my mom, Sherry and my dad, Peter."

I smile at them and hold out my hand to shake, but Sherry surprises me and pulls me into a hug, squeezing tightly. "It is great to meet you." The angle is awkward as Caden is still holding my hand, but I don't mind as I hug her back.

"It's great to meet you, too. Caden talks about you all the time," I say. And he does, it's clear that Caden loves his family. Peter shakes my hand and gives a small smile to me.

"It's about time he finds someone. I was thinking he was going to die alone," Amani says, drawing Caden into a hug. I glance at Xena as she says this and see her clench her jaw. I don't know what to do in such a situation, but luckily Jade takes over.

"Rory, this is Xena, my fiancé's sister. Xena, this is Rory, Caden's girlfriend." I hold out my hand to the other woman and she shakes it, tightening her hand slightly as if to prove something.

"I didn't know you were seeing anyone, Cade," Xena says, flicking her pen straight brown hair over her shoulder. She says his name with an intimate whisper that grates on what little nerves I have.

Before Caden can say anything, I respond, "We wanted to keep things quiet for a little bit. I've been so busy with school and work that we haven't been able to come out to meet his parents yet."

Xena's dark eyes meet mine. "Oh, what are you in school for?"

"Family law."

She whistles. "Those student loans must be astronomical."

I shrug and reply, "I wouldn't know. My school is paid off in full. This is my last semester."

"Scholarships?" Sherry asks, looking between the two of us.

"Some, but I also paid it off from working. I got my associates degree when I was in high school and a paralegal technology degree at the start of college. So, I worked as a paralegal while doing my last two years of university before graduating, then transferred to law school."

"That's impressive. Caden, you didn't tell me your girl-friend was so smart," Amani chided.

"I did too," Caden protests, looking at me with pride in his eyes. I smile at him and tug on his hand. He grabs my bag out of my hand and slowly lets go of my hand to pick up his, as if he was telling me it was okay now. I smile again and he sends one back to me making my stomach flutter with nerves and something else. We fall into step behind the others and he whispers to me, "Thank you, *Chīsai doragon.*"

"What does that mean?" I ask, softly so only he could hear.

He smirks. "I'll tell you eventually. Not right now. I like seeing you squirm." He bends slightly so his mouth is against my ear. "Especially when I know my cum is still inside of you."

My cheeks heat up and I nudge him playfully, but he just laughs as we get into a van that is bigger than any I've seen. Caden puts our bags in the back storage area then sits down right next to me, placing his hand on my thigh in a claiming motion. One I wasn't even sure he realized he was doing. But I didn't mind. I knew this was all for show, but for just a little while I allowed the delusion that it was real. That we were real. At least for the next nine days. Conversation surrounded me about the wedding and I leaned my head against Caden's shoulder listening to the deep rasp of his voice letting it lull me to sleep.

Caden

Rory fell asleep against me and I ran my finger over her knee. I knew she was exhausted from being nervous, she told me before we left that she didn't sleep much the night before. Not that I blamed her. Jade leaned into me. "She looked exhausted. When we get home you should let her sleep."

"I might nap with her. It was a long flight." I try not to grin as I remember what we did. Or the giggles we shared like two kids in a candy store.

"Mom has her in the guest room, made it all pretty and left a little gift basket on the bed." That stopped my grin from forming as I looked at the front of the van.

"Mom, she can stay in my room with me," I say, staying as quiet as possible.

She shakes her head. "No, she is in the guest room beside Xena. If I don't let Xander and Jade sleep in the same room, what makes you think I'll let you and Rory stay in the room together?" I grit my teeth. I didn't want Rory out of my sight and definitely not next to Xena. The rest of the drive is in silence until we pull up to my parents' house. I gently nudge Rory and she blinks open her eyes and smiles softly at me. Her hazel eyes are brighter than normal, happier.

"Hi," she whispers.

I smile at her. "Hi. We're here." Sitting up, Rory lifts her arms to stretch before her eyes widen when she sees the house. She glances back at me and I shrug. The house is big and on the outskirts of Beverly Hills with a large wrought iron fence and high pillars. My parents were wealthy doctors who worked their way up in their respective fields. My mom being a cardiac surgeon and my dad being a world-renowned plastic surgeon who worked on those injured in combat, after he himself was, while in the military. I was proud of them for how far they'd come and they did this so me and my sisters could have a better life and we did. Thanks to them.

We climbed out of the van and I stood beside Rory as I grabbed our bags.

"Dinner will be ready in thirty minutes, Caden. Why don't you show Rory where she's staying and get freshened up," Mom says, walking inside the house with a bright smile. I haven't been home since the capture and it was a little difficult to go inside a home I once knew.

Rory grabs her bag from my hand and twines her fingers with mine squeezing gently. "It's going to be okay, Caden," she whispers so only I would hear. Xena stands by the car before walking towards us.

"Cade, can I talk to you, please?" she asks in a voice that I would've dropped anything to do what she wanted. And she knew it, too.

"No. I need to show Rory to her room." With that I walk past her and into the house. I don't give Rory time to explore before I'm taking her upstairs to her room.

She doesn't speak for a while until I close the door behind me and set her bags on the freshly made bed. "So separate rooms?" she guesses.

"My mom is traditional in a sense."

Rory laughs softly and sits on the bed opening her bag and pulling out the little cold bag that held her insulin and looks at me. "I, um, I take this a few minutes before eating." I sit beside her and hold out my hand to her. She slowly slides the bag into my hand, and I watch as she lifts her dress showing her stomach and nods to it. "I put it in the thicker parts a few inches to the side. That's what the doctor told me to do," she mutters.

"Don't be ashamed, Lorelai," I say softly.

She swallows hard. "I'm not used to someone taking care of me."

I squeeze her stomach as gently as possible and inject the medicine, before pulling it away and sliding her dress back down and capping the syringe. "I like taking care of you." And I realized I did. I enjoyed being someone she needed, but I also knew she was independent and didn't always need me. She chose when she needed me, but she was also my equal, a partner.

"Rory," I start but stop when there's knocking on the door.

"Dinner!" Amani said, officially stopping our conversation. Rory smiles at me and stands, looking at me with her hand out. I grab it, but I don't stand, instead I pull her to me with my hands going to her hips.

"I need a kiss before we go," I mutter. She grins and presses a quick kiss to my lips before running towards the door. When she opens the door, Xena is there with her fist raised to knock. I groan inwardly and stand going to Rory's side.

"We're coming," I mutter. I see her glare daggers at me, but I don't care. It's hard seeing her, but not as hard as I thought it would be. With Rory here all my focus is on her. On making her smile, of seeing the crinkle around her eyes when she laughs. I wanted to take care of her, but we only had nine days left. A part of me wondered if I could let her go after all is said and done.

Chapter 34

RORY

Caden leads me downstairs, and I can't help but look around. The house is huge! From the large spiral staircase to the marbled looking floors. But at the same time, it felt homey. Not like a museum like most ostentatious houses like this could be. It wasn't cold and gloomy. In fact, the walls were littered with baby pictures and achievement awards. I stop at the bottom of the stairs and stare at the small picture on the wall with Caden's parents holding a baby with a full head of hair.

"Is this you?" I ask, pointing at the picture.

Caden stops beside me and wraps an arm around me, pressing his chin to my head, holding me to him. It was so intimate, almost natural, that he didn't realize he was doing it. "Ahh, yes, I was the coolest baby ever to live. I had the best hair ever."

I laugh, staring at him before pressing a kiss to his cheek. Was it too much? Perhaps, but I didn't care. Even though this was all fake I couldn't stop with the little touches here and there. I was playing into a game that I was bound to lose and I didn't give a single fuck. Teasingly I say, "Whatever you have to tell yourself at night."

He leans against me, pressing me into the wall. "Keep that up and I'll bend you over later and turn your pretty ass pink."

I swallow hard, clenching my thighs. "You wouldn't dare." It's a challenge and we both know it.

"Oh, but I love teasing you so much. I'd do it in a heartbeat, Lorelai."

I lick my lips and stare up at him breathing in his citrus scent. It was intoxicating. "We need to go to dinner," I whisper.

"Tonight, you're mine, Rory. So be ready for when I come."

My breathing hitched and I watched as he walked away seemingly unaffected. Huffing out a laugh, I follow Caden who is staring at me intently as I enter the dining room. He pulls out a chair for me and I slowly sit, blushing when he brushes his lips across my head. His sisters sit in front of us smirking to each other as they stare at their brother. He pretends not to notice, but the room gets silent as Xena walks in. As if she commands attention from the room as she sits directly in front of me. But her eyes never strayed from Caden, and we all noticed it. Especially his sisters.

Caden, however, ignored her and a part of me wondered if he still had feelings for her or if he truly just didn't care.

"What is Rory short for?" Xena suddenly asked.

Caden took the bowl his mother was passing him and served a heaping pile of shrimp onto my plate before adding it to his as he answered, "Lorelai. But she goes by Rory so that is what you'll call her."

"I was simply making polite conversation, Cade. Or can you not even do that?" Xena goaded.

Caden didn't answer as he put some broccoli on my plate then his.

"What, is she incapable of feeding herself?" Xena snarks suddenly drawing attention to us.

I clear my throat knowing that Caden is only doing this to give himself something to do with his hands. "I can actually, but I'm diabetic and my hands get shaky so it can be difficult for me to grasp things sometimes." Not a complete lie, but it was enough to make her feel like a jackass and mind her own business. Caden coughed slightly as I cast a glare before I saw a small smirk on his mouth. The rest of the dinner is mostly silent, aside from basic small talk, until finally it ends and when I offer to help I'm shooed away. With nothing to do I head to my room to wait for Caden and whatever it is he has planned for me. When I get to my room I can see my phone lighting up and I rush to get it to see it's a slew of text messages from Anthony ranging from begging for forgiveness to cursing at me for ruining his marriage. I sit on the bed and stare at the phone for a few minutes before closing it and flopping back on the bed. There's nothing to be said for him, nor do I want to have any contact aside for my last exam which is happening in a few weeks. All I need to do is wait it out for the next nine days and I'll be golden. As long as I don't get caught up in the small glow that was cast over me with Caden.

I needed to remember this is all an act. That's all it can be.

Chapter 35

CADEN

After dinner my sisters pull me to the side to talk. I don't even know what they're saying as my eyes track Rory as she climbs the stairs bidding goodnight to everyone leaving me alone with my sisters.

"Caden!" Amani scolded me, bringing me back to the present.

"What?" I ask, turning back to them.

"What the hell was that at dinner?" Jade demands, putting her hands on her hips and glaring up at me.

I stare dumbfounded. "What are you talking about?"

Amani huffs out a breath. "The way you talked to Xena, dumbass. You've never talked to her like that before."

I scoff, crossing my arms over my chest to send them pointed looks. "She was about to be disrespectful to Rory and I wasn't having it."

The two looked at each other before squealing in excitement. I flinch away from the loud sound before asking, "What the fuck guys?"

Amani sobers up and grabs my hand. "I've never seen you act the way you do with Rory. Not even Xena had this version of you."

I pull my hand away. "Version of me?"

"Happy, laid back, authentic. You're yourself, Caden," Jade whispers, her brown eyes shining with unshed tears.

I reel back confused. This was all an act nothing more nothing less. I was playing a part for my family, so they didn't worry about me. How was I supposed to tell them that none of this was real... unless it is? Could it be real? I knew I liked Rory as a person, I liked her laugh and when she smiled. I worried about her constantly, but I also knew she could take care of herself. I wanted her with me in my bed and in my arms at night, but could I make this real? Would she even let me after the last toxic relationship she had? These questions have been in my head for days now, but I didn't bring them up to Rory, I mean I wanted to in her room but we were interrupted.

I didn't know. Hell, I hardly knew how I felt half of the time let alone how she felt. Swallowing hard, I excuse myself ready to go find Rory and demand to know how she feels but also hide away from the feelings I was starting to develop. I didn't want to ruin our friendship. But how could I not when everything inside of me burned to go find the woman and claim her as mine. I sprinted upstairs and went to her room, opening the door without knocking and there she stood in nothing but her bra and panties, holding her dress to her chest.

"Caden! Don't you know how to kn–" her sentence is cut off as I close the door behind me and stalk towards her. I grab the dress from her and toss it to the floor before grabbing her face and kissing her. Hard. She stills in my arms for a moment before slowly relaxing against me and wrapping her arms around my neck. Her tongue meets mine in a heated dance, thrusting and caressing against each other, but I can't handle gentleness right now. I need hard. I need to claim her. With a growl, I grab her ass and heft her up so her long legs were wrapped around my hips. She gasps, clutching at me as I walk towards the bed, kissing her harder.

I drop her at the edge of the bed and slowly pull away from the kiss biting down on her bottom lip before standing in front of her. She is flushed and breathing heavily. She looked beautifully disheveled and I wanted nothing more than to ruin her.

"Lie back and spread your legs for me," I finally say.

Rory swallows audibly before slowly leaning back on her elbows and slowly spreading her legs showing me her panty clad pussy.

"So fucking good for me," I whisper, getting to my knees. I brace my hands on her soft thighs and reach up to grab the waist of her panties and pull them down before tossing them over my shoulder.

"I didn't get to enjoy you on the plane, Lorelai. I like to enjoy my pussy." I run my finger up her slit feeling the wet heat seeping from her. All mine.

She moans softly, arching her hips up to demand more. I slap her thigh holding her open for me. "Don't rush me."

She groans falling back on the bed unable to hold herself up as I lick at her swollen clit. I thrust my finger in time with my licks tasting her and fucking her at the same time. She tasted sweet, she tasted like mine. Her juices soaked my hand and something in me snapped. I grabbed her hips and flipped her to her stomach. I quickly undid my pants, taking my aching cock out before thrusting home.

The bed slammed against the wall as Rory cried out in pleasure. Leaning forward I grab her jaw and slam my mouth down on hers. I fuck her into the bed, pinning her down to the mattress. She yanks her mouth away from mine and gasps in a deep breath bracing herself on her hands and knees, arching into my deep thrusts.

I grabbed her hair in my fist and pulled her head back. "That's my good little whore. Taking me so beautifully."

"Fuck, Caden," she gasps tilting her hips up to take more of me.

"That's it, baby, ask nicely and I'll let you come."

"Please, please, Caden. Please let me come."

"That's a good girl, come for me." As if that's all she needed she came with a needy little cry that had me grunting out her name as I found my own release. Rory slouched forward and I pressed a kiss to the line of her spine before rolling away from her and lying on my back. She rolled to her side, breathing heavily before looking up at me.

"What was that for?" she asks, grinning at me.

I reach up and push her hair from her face. "I just needed you."

Her hazel eyes softened as she leaned forward and pressed a kiss to my lips before sitting up to discard her bra.

"What are you doing?" I ask, feeling my cock stir again at the mere sight of her.

She sends me a little smirk before straddling me. "I need you, too. This is our night, remember?" She sinks down onto me and we groan in unison and I know I'm in for a long night.

Chapter 36

CADEN

It's past five in the morning here and I haven't slept yet. I have a lot on my mind, mainly the woman fast asleep in my arms. I glance down at her and smile to myself. She's beautiful, long curly hair tickles my numb arm and her dark lashes make crescents under her eyes, giving her a semblance of innocence in her sleep.

Slowly I extract myself from her warm body causing her to twitch and whisper huskily, "Where are you going?"

I gaze down at her and her hazel eyes are wide as she stares at me.

"I'm just going to get dressed. You should, too. I want to take you somewhere."

She smiles serenely at me, stretching slightly so the sheet pulled down a bit showing off her pert tits that had my cock stirring already, ready for another round. I reach up and cover her up for both our sakes and press a kiss to her forehead.

"Get dressed," I repeat.

She hums under her breath and turns to her stomach watching as I get dressed.

"Does this include you feeding me? I lost all my energy." I smirk to myself as I pull my pants back on.

"Of course it includes feeding you." When I'm done dressing I turn back to her and see her sitting up, raising her arms above her head showing the delicate curve of her spine, before standing up to walk to the bathroom.

"Thirty minutes, Rory!" I called out.

"Yeah, yeah, yeah. Got it," she teases as she starts the shower. Shaking my head to myself I leave her room, stopping short when Xena walks out of her room. Her eyes are dark and shooting daggers at me.

"God, I didn't think you'd ever stop. Don't you have any consideration for the people in the house?" she demands.

I close the door behind me and cross my arms over my chest.

"I never took you as the type who listens," I say in retort.

Xena rolls her eyes. "Seriously, Cade, have you no self-respect. You're disgusting."

"Please save me the holier than thou speech, Xena. You, of all people, have no room to judge what two people do in the bedroom."

She reels back before she steels her spine and glares at me. "I never once enjoyed being called a whore or a slut. If she does, then that says a lot about who she is as a person."

That gets me moving into action, moving into her personal space pointing my finger into her chest, not touching her but she gets the point. "You don't speak about her like that. Ever. She's ten times the woman you ever were. What we do in our bedroom is none of your concern. We may be into a little degradation but make no mistake, Rory owns me. She owns me, mind, body, and soul. Don't ever disrespect her again, do I make myself clear?"

Xena grits her teeth and pushes me away from her. "I'll never respect a woman who willingly whores herself out to a man."

I laugh bitterly. "That's ironic coming from you. Considering you're a cheating slut. You will stay away from her and if I see you anywhere near her I will make sure people know the real reason for our split." With that I turn and head to my room to get ready for one of the toughest battles I have yet to fight. One I very well might lose. Losing my heart in the process. Once I'm in my room I take a quick shower irritation weighing heavily on me from my interaction with Xena. Shaking those thoughts off, I finish my shower and dress before going to get Rory. I walk into her room without knocking and she gives me a dramatic sigh making me smile. Easily melting away all thoughts of Xena out of my head.

"Your no knocking habit needs to get worked on," she teases, pulling her hair into a sexy messy bun that has me wanting to pull it down to see how wild she can truly be and knowing her it was wild and everything I needed.

"You look beautiful," I murmur more to myself than to her. She is wearing skin tight skinny jeans and a light blue sweater that hangs off of her shoulder.

She smiles at me and slips on her shoes. "Are we ready?" she asks.

I nod and take her hand into mine and walk her out of the room and down the stairs. I'm careful of the others sleeping as I open the front door and head outside. It's cool this morning and I worry about my plan before I can overthink it. I open the garage where my Harley sits in all its pristine glory. Rory whistles under her breath and walks up to the large bike and runs reverent fingers over the shiny black and green paint job.

I see my leather jacket on the chair cleaned and I know my mom had it cleaned for me knowing every time I was in town I'd go for a ride.

"She's beautiful," Rory states.

"Thank you." I wrap the leather jacket around Rory's shoulders and grab my helmet and hand it to her to put on before grabbing my other one from the handlebars and climbing on. I pat the seat behind me, and Rory puts her own helmet on before bracing one hand on my shoulder and following my moves to get on the bike. I start the bike and feel it roar to life vibrating through me and my bones, giving me a high I have only felt with Rory. Behind me she gasps and wraps her arms around me tightly as I slowly ease out of the garage. I want to take my time with her as I go down the road leaning in with the dips and turns until I am on the empty California highway.

Rory squeezes my waist tightly and leans in with me and I can hear her excited laughter as we race down the highway towards the beach. The ride ends sooner than I would've liked but as I step off the bike and help Rory down I can't help but be excited with her. Seeing the brightness in her eyes or the way she shakes where she stands.

"That was awesome! I had no idea you had a motorcycle and that they did that!" She waves her hands animatedly and grasps my shirt with her small hands, bouncing on the balls of her feet. "Can we go again?"

I laugh and press my hands to hers, holding her still against me. "Of course. But first we are here. Come on, I want to show you something." I grab her hand in mine and walk her towards the beach.

"Where are we?" she asks, looking around her as we step onto the sand.

"Malibu."

Chapter 37

RORY

My eyes fill with tears as Caden leads us down through the soft cool sand towards the ocean. It was loud, the waves crashing on the surface. Sea salt sprayed in my face, and I soaked it up, breathing it in.

"Can I get in?" I ask.

Caden laughs. "Yeah if you want to freeze your balls off."

I drop his jacket to the ground and strip off my sweater leaving me in my purple lace bra. I shuck my jeans and bury my toes in the sand for the first time before walking towards the edge of the water. It was freezing just by the little bit that got on my feet but I didn't care. I hear Caden huff out a laugh before the rustling of clothes and he was running after me.

He stops beside me and grabs my hand lacing our fingers together before we both run giggling into the water that does in fact freeze our balls off.

I squeal as we go deeper and grab onto Caden wrapping my arms around him and he lifts me up so I'm full-blown koala holding him. It takes a minute for my body to get used to the water, but I don't mind as Caden holds onto me, rubbing his hand up and down my back. We sit like that for a few minutes, in compatible silence just holding each other.

"Thank you for bringing me here," I finally whispered, pulling back to look him in the eye.

"You said you wanted to go to a beach one day. This one is beautiful."

I stare at him for a minute seeing a shutter move over his eyes before it's gone. Leaving his face carefully blank.

"What is it?" I asked, suddenly nervous.

"Rory," he breathes my name. Almost like a prayer or a curse. But it's the reverence that has me tensing. "No, it's not bad."

I swallow hard. "I don't know, you're all serious which means it could be bad."

"I've been thinking."

"That can't be good," I try teasing, trying to hide the fact that my heart is pounding out of my chest.

"Lorelai, I don't think I can do this anymore. The lying, the fake relationship," he whispers softly.

I pull away slightly before nodding slowly even though my heart is breaking slightly. "Oh, okay. Yeah, I get that. It's a lot. I'll, um, say I'm your friend or something and no one will question it, or we can say we got into a fight and I left so it's not awkward for you at your sister's wedding." The wheels are turning in my head as I try to figure out how to play this off.

He looks at me with wide eyes and shakes his head. "Whoa. Let me finish first before your mind takes over," he says.

I stare at him and nod slowly before taking a deep breath and letting him finish.

"I want more from you, Rory. I want this to be real."

My steady breathing stopped, and my eyes widened as the words sank in. "But the rules."

He huffs out a laugh. "Fuck the rules. They were ruined the first moment I touched you, from the moment I tasted you. Fucked you. Lorelai, I want you, I want your good days, your bad days. I want to pull juvenile pranks on people who wrong you. I want to show you off to the world instead of hiding the feelings I have for you."

I'm thrown off balance, shocked, excited. Nervous. I need more from him, I have from the moment I let him touch me. I knew it was a bad idea going into this, but I still played into it all. The fantasy of him and me. Then there is the fact I just got out of a toxic relationship. Could I jump into another one without thought?

"Caden," I breathe out. Wanting to show him I had these feelings, too, but unable to.

"You don't have to give me an answer now, Rory. I know this is a lot for you. Just think about it. Can you do that for me?" He's almost pleading, and I nod, stunned into silence. He reaches behind him and unlatches the dog tags. He's careful with them in the water and slowly attaches it to my neck. "Give this back when you have an answer."

I swallow hard and touch the cold metal before nodding.

"Okay." With that he tugs me close and swims us back towards our clothes before we turn into popsicles.

The ride back to the house was quiet and I was left in my thoughts. When he pulls into the garage I climb off the motorcycle and head towards the door and to my room without saying anything. I just need a moment. But I find my hand going to the dog tags between my breasts and it's like a hot plate searing into my skin. Sighing softly, I step silently upstairs and head to my room and go in closing the door softly behind me. I see my phone on the nightstand and grab it for a much-needed girl chat.

Me: *I have a problem.*

Nirvana: *A dick problem?*

Layla: *Why is every problem with you a dick problem?*

Nirvana: *Sigh… Ravi is holding out on me, it's been a minute.*

Sera: *We'll come back to that one, what's up, Ro?*

Me: *Caden wants to make us official.*

I lean back against the bed and sigh, shucking off my clothes and stepping into the bathroom to turn on the shower as my phone buzzed to life.

Delaney: *OMG that's great. Why don't we sound happy about that?*

Me: *Umm my last relationship was a total shit show.*

Ophelia: *You can't base your relationships on one bad guy, Rory.*

Me: *I can't deal with the pain again. Being used, mistreated and not even noticing it until years later. That's humiliating.*

Delaney: *Honey, what happened? You never really told us.*

Sighing to myself I tell them everything, from the moment he started hinting at more with me to now finding out he's married, and his wife is pregnant.

Layla: *Holy shit, Ro! Why didn't you come to us?*

Me: *It's embarrassing. I should've known better. It's why I can't get into another relationship now, if ever.*

Nirvana: *Caden isn't Anthony, Ro. He's a genuine guy, who seems to really care about you. Don't think about the what ifs and the buts. Think about the time you've spent together thus far, how many more moments you could have like this.*

I read all the messages between the girls and wonder when Nirvana became so insightful, but then again she's a genius who doesn't get the credit she deserves. Wanting the subject off of me I turn to why Ravi is holding out on her and climb into the shower washing away the beach, the one place I've always wanted to go and Caden made it happen. Could I really give him the shot I so desperately wanted to give him, or will it end up in disaster like Anthony?

Chapter 38

CADEN

My eyes track Rory's every movement as she socializes with my family and old friends. She's working her charm on them just like she charmed me. I sip at my drink just watching her. It's been twenty hours since I've been near her wanting to give her space to think but it's killing me.

"You're watching her like a creep," a voice said behind me. I turn and see Amani standing behind me with a flute of champagne in her hand as she tilts her head up at me.

"I don't creep," I mutter.

She snorts. "Could've fooled me. You're practically vibrating with creepiness."

I roll my eyes, but I look towards Rory again. Taking in every inch of her, this time, however, she glances back at me. Her smile is slow and sweet, and I can see she is still wearing my dog tags tucked safely between her breasts. It makes me preen with satisfaction. She says something to the person she was talking to before making her way towards me. Amani leaves me alone with her with a whispered, "Good luck, creeper."

I roll my eyes again and Rory stops beside me. "This is a nice rehearsal dinner. I thought this typically happened the day before the wedding."

I laugh. "My family has a thing for the dramatics plus Jade didn't want to have so much stress on her before the wedding."

Rory nods. "That makes sense." She stares at me before sighing softly.

"What is it?" I ask.

She chews her bottom lip and slowly takes my hand. Then she leads me towards the door and out onto the terrace leaving us alone outside.

"I thought about what you said. I've been thinking about it all day. How I feel with you. You make me feel free and happy. Adventurous." Slowly she takes off the ring she always wears, a dainty little sunflower ring, and slides it onto my pinky. "I'm not ready for something serious right now, but this is a promise that I'm in this with you. I want you, Caden, but can we be casual for now, work up to something serious over time? Move slowly?"

I look down at her hands and wrap them in mine. "Of course, Rory. I'd never rush you to do something you weren't ready for." She smiles up at me, some of the tension she was carrying easing off of her.

"We should go socialize," she whispers. I hum under my breath, slowly running my fingers up her arm towards her neck with the tags and watch as goosebumps pop up on her skin. She takes in a shaky breath staring at me with big eyes that were more green than brown today.

"Can I kiss you during this slow stage?" I ask softly.

She swallows hard and nods slowly as I bend down and press my lips onto hers. Her mouth was soft and pliant under mine and I knew if I didn't pull away right now I'd be sucked into her. She pulls away first, bracing her hand on my chest.

"If we don't stop now we'll end up in a compromising position," she warns teasingly, her cheeks heating up. I smile down at her and run my thumb over her cheek taking in the softness of her skin.

"Would that be so bad?"

Huffing out a laugh, she moves back. The picture of perfect innocence. "Of course. This is a party and I am a guest. I can't have everyone seeing my business because you got frisky."

"Because I got frisky?" I repeat, trying not to laugh.

She nods solemnly. "Yes. I'm a lady, Caden. I must keep my private life private, otherwise what would people think?"

I laughed then pulled her into my chest. "Who gives a fuck? It's you and me out here. I can defile you and worship you all I want." I press a kiss to her throat before pulling back. "But I won't since you're all about keeping your innocence intact."

"That's all I ask," she says with a dramatic sigh before bursting into laughter. "Come on, let's go back before people really do start wondering where we wandered off to."

The ringing of a phone has us stopping and Rory sighs softly, taking out her phone and rolling her eyes.

"Who is it?" I ask.

"Anthony. He's been blowing up my phone since I got here. I never answer. I wish he'd take the hint and leave me alone."

She turns her phone off and shoves it back into her dress pocket with a small frown. "I can answer it and get him to leave you alone," I offer.

She shakes her head and forces a smile. "No, it's fine. I don't want you involved with him. He'll stop once he's bored."

I nod, wanting to respect her wishes but I didn't like the fact he was harassing her. A sense of unease creeped into me, but I brushed it off as concern for Rory and I let the topic drop as she wrapped her fingers through mine and led me back to the party.

Chapter 39

RORY

"I'm going to fucking kill you if you don't make this right. Do you hear me, Rory? Make this shit right or I'll find you and slit your pretty little throat." I listened to the message for the third time, and it had my heart racing and my blood turning cold. There was so much venom in the threat. I was currently in the bathroom of Caden's house getting ready for the wedding when I looked at the hundreds of messages blinking at me through the phone.

My time here with Caden is almost done, the days going by quickly. I sit there on the toilet and take a deep breath swiping the delete button and erasing the message. There was a sinking feeling in the pit of my stomach that had a cold sweat breaking out on my skin, but I quickly stood and stowed my phone away and stared in the mirror. My hair was elegantly curled down my back, my makeup subtle and the green dress flattered my eyes so well that they appeared green with mixes of browns. I'm nervous about seeing

Caden. About what he wants from me, what I want from him.

It's an internal conflict I can't seem to fix and it's getting to me. I know I want him, but with Anthony breathing down my neck… Sighing, I stand and head out of the bathroom. I head down the hallway towards the stairs where I see Caden standing with his back towards me. I stood there for a moment and stared at him, taking in his wide shoulders fitted perfectly in a black tux that had my heart pounding. My heels click on the hardwood floor catching his attention and has him turning towards me. I see his chest expand on a deep breath and he holds out his hand to me as I descend the stairs. When I reach him I grab onto him like a lifeline, holding him to me.

"You look stunning, Lorelai. Absolutely breathtaking. I'm sorry I couldn't tell you that earlier," he whispers. Since he was a groomsman I didn't get to see him before the wedding only after the ceremony.

I feel myself blush and swallow hard. "Thank you. You look amazing too."

He smiles.

"Are you hungry?" he asks, tucking my hand in the curve of his arm.

"I could eat," I say, when in reality my stomach was stuck in knots, and I was on the verge of a panic attack just moments before. But he didn't need to know that. My fingers squeezed his arm tightly as he walked me outside towards the tents where guests are laughing and drinking, generally having a good time and something inside me eases. I don't need to worry about Anthony at the moment, I just have to be in the here and now with Caden.

As I say those words in my head I can feel myself slowly start to relax. The tension eased out of me and I felt Caden look at me, I turned to stare at him with a small smile on my face. "Forget food for now. Let's dance."

He smirked and led me to the dance floor where couples danced. He pulled me into him, his hands going to the small of my back and holding me close.

I laid my head on his chest and listened to his strong heartbeat as he held me. It was soothing and left me feeling calm.

"Thank you," I breathe out softly.

His hands move up my back in gentle movements before he responds. "For what?"

"For bringing me here. For everything you shared with me."

He laughed softly. "Rory, I want to share a lot of things with you."

I nod against his chest. "I'd like that."

"Yeah?"

I huff out a small laugh. "Of course. You're easily becoming one of the most important people in my life. These last few weeks have been different in the best way possible. I want more of it. I just need to go slow."

His hold tightens against me. "I'll go as slow as you need me to."

"I know." And I did know. I knew that he'd do what I needed him to do, and he wouldn't mind it at all. So, I knew I had to give him something in return.

"I want to try this, Caden. You and me. Just know I come with a lot of baggage."

He stopped swaying to the music and pulled away slightly to look down at me. "You're serious?"

I nod. "Of course, I am. Why wouldn't I be?"

He shrugs, looking slightly embarrassed and nervous. "Because you've been through a lot, and I don't want to pressure you into anything you don't want to do." He sighs softly. "I want you to want me the way I want you."

Reaching up I cup his face. "I want you, Caden Sato. All of you. The good and the bad. I might be scared and a little apprehensive at times but I'm all in. Just go slow with me."

His smile is slow in coming but when it does it reaches his dark brown eyes and lights them up. It steals my breath and makes me want to see that smile for as long as possible. Without thinking I stand taller and press a gentle kiss to his lips. He doesn't hesitate to deepen the kiss and he doesn't care that we are surrounded by people, nor do I. Because at this moment it's just me and Caden.

"Get a room!" someone calls, and I pull away laughing as Amani dances next to us and for the next few hours we dance, eat, and have fun nothing could take this from me. At least so I thought.

Chapter 40

RORY

The shrill ringing of my phone had me jerking awake from my sleep disoriented and confused. A strong arm is wrapped around my waist and the sound of the ringing stops until it starts again.

I groan and toss an arm over my eyes before reaching over the nightstand and grabbing my phone. Seeing it's a call from my school, I answer it quickly.

"Hello?" I whisper into the receiver.

There's a silence on the other end of the phone before I hear my name. "Lorelai Phelps Flores?"

"This is she." My heart is pounding out of my chest as I sit up, effectively waking Caden. He stares at me in question and I mouth, *my school.* He nods in understanding as he sits up with me, pressing his bare back against the headboard.

"Miss Flores I don't usually make calls to students regarding their grades and classes, but I saw your transcript and as you're supposed to graduate this year I'm a little concerned about your family law class. Have you not been turning in your work?"

I sit there in stunned silence as I listen to the woman on the other end of the line. "Miss Flores?"

I clear my throat. "Of course I have. The last time I checked I had an A in the class. None of my work is missing and I'm always at the lectures."

"Do you have proof? Because if you don't pass this class you don't graduate."

"I have every assignment and proof I turned it in, yes." Anger boiled up inside of me as the reality of the situation set in. After another few minutes of talking, I hung up the phone and sprang into action pulling on my clothes and started putting my clothes back in my suitcase.

"What's going on, Rory?" Caden asks, standing to pull his own clothes on.

I huff out a bitter laugh. "Fucking Anthony failed me. I need the class to graduate, and he failed me. I need to go to the campus and figure this out."

He nods. "It's okay, we'll figure it out. Just pack and I'll see about switching our flights."

He's already on his phone before I can object, and I realize I don't want to object. He brings me a certain level of peace that makes me want to be around him even when my mind is chaotic like right now. I can't do anything but nod at him. Tears burn the backs of my eyes at the thought of my hard work being taken away from me because of a vindictive man.

"All right we have our flights changed to today. We need to leave in the hour if we want to make it."

That pulls me up short. "You're coming, too?"

He gives me a *What do you think?* look that has me staring at him with an open mouth. "You can't go! You have stuff to do here!"

He stands and comes towards me cupping my face gently. "Where you go, I go. You need me now. I was there for the wedding and did my part. Now, let me be there for you."

I take a deep breath and nod. There was no use in arguing with him when we didn't have a lot of time. So instead, I turn my back on him and get back to packing as he leaves the room to do the same. We weren't supposed to be sleeping in the same room, but he snuck in every night. The sound of the door opening had me turning to see Xena standing in the doorway glaring daggers at me. I sigh, not in the mood for her shit.

"What is it, Xena?" I ask, stuffing a pair of shorts into my bag.

"You're leaving early." It was a statement, but I could hear the judgment in the undertones.

"Yes, something came up. So, if you'd excuse me." I motion for her to move out of the room, but she doesn't. Throwing up my hands, I sit on the edge of the bed completely exhausted already. "What do you want, Xena?"

"You're not good enough for Caden." She doesn't beat around the bush and that has me laughing slightly only it's with anger. Annoyance.

"And let me guess, you are?" I ask, at my wits end.

She shrugs her slender shoulders. "I've known him since elementary school. He was my first love, my first kiss, my first lover. He was my everything. And I was his."

I scoff under my breath and say, "Yeah, until you fucked his best friend behind his back."

I see her tense as if she thought I didn't know why they actually broke up. And that snaps something inside of me. "Yeah, I know the full story so don't try that woe is me shit on me. It won't work."

"You have no idea what you're talking about," Xena snaps.

"No, you have no idea what you're talking about. You broke something in Caden. Something he doesn't think is fixable, but I intend to fix it."

"Please. You can't fix someone like Caden. He needs stability, someone who will be there for him at all times."

"No, he needs a partner not another parent. You can't tell him what to do. He's a grown ass man. He is special and he deserves better than you talking about him as if he were a petulant child."

"You don't get it, Rory," she started, but I cut her off with the raise of my hand.

"No, you don't get it. You broke something in him. You stole his trust. And for what? A few moments of pleasure. Caden wanted you to have everything you wanted because he loved you, but you didn't love him the way he needed to be loved. You loved yourself. You're selfish. I'd never do what you did. For one reason he doesn't like to share and if I asked for anything like that he'd make sure I had no reason to ask for such an asinine request again. Hell, he'd break up with me because of it. He's something special and you lost out on it. That's your problem not ours. Get over yourself, Xena."

A throat cleared and I looked up at Caden standing in the doorway. Xena started crying and stood closer to Caden who looked repulsed and moved to the side closer to me.

"We need to go, Rory," he said, his tone gentle with a softness in his eyes I hardly see. I swallow hard, grab my bag and phone before pushing past Xena who was sputtering after us. Caden doesn't talk as we leave the house and I don't expect him to. There's so much on my mind and I don't even know where to begin with this mess I somehow created. Caden's fingers wrap around mine as we sit down, some of the tension eases out of me and I silently pray that every-thing is okay.

Chapter 41

CADEN

She stood up for me. Called me something special. Xena had a controlling personality, even as kids things had to be her way. My feelings for her clouded my judgment and left me following after her, taking the scraps she was willing to give. Naively I thought it was love, but I was wrong. What I felt now, for Rory, was love. This burning intense need to have her near me. To have her surrounding me in every aspect, to hear her laugh, to take on her demons, that was love.

I don't know when I fell in love with her, maybe it was when she called me after she was trapped in the bathroom, or when she cried during our first movie together, but I knew now I was in love with her. I could feel the way her hand shook in mine, the way she worried her bottom lip. She was anxious. Squashing down my feelings, I spoke.

"It's going to be okay, Rory."

She turned to me. "What if it's not? How can he do this to me?"

I face her fully and am honest with her. "Anthony is a narcissist. He will do anything if it puts him at the top. You took something from him, so he's taking something from you. He knows you value your education and worked hard to get where you are, so he's taking it from you because then he can feel powerful and hold it over you."

She blinks her big hazel eyes at me, wet with tears before she takes a deep breath. "She deserved to know the truth."

I nod in agreement. "She did. But Anthony isn't going to see it that way." And he wouldn't. To him she was just a pawn in his game and if he was willing to fuck her education up how far is he willing to go? Not wanting to think about that right now I turn in my seat still holding her hand and send out a text message:

Me: *I need a favor.*

Ravi: *What favor could that possibly be?*

Me: *I need the ETA of Anthony, Rory's ex, at all times. I don't trust the man as far as I can throw him and he's up to something.*

Drew: *What do you think he's going to do?*

Me: *I don't know but I want everyone to be on alert for him.*

When I get the affirmative I shut off my phone and lean back in my seat looking out the window twisting the small ring on my pinky as my thoughts turn to whatever it is that Anthony is planning and how I can stop it before he does anything drastic.

Chapter 42

RORY

The plane ride felt like it took forever. It wasn't as fun as the first ride and I hated that our little vacation, though it was for a wedding, was cut short. Everything felt like I'm running on fumes of depression and anxiety. After everything we've been through Anthony was still out to get me for something he did. It's not about getting even, it's about his pride. I broke it when his wife confronted me and now everything was falling apart.

Dring the plane ride, Caden and I sat in complete silence, both lost in thought as he absentmindedly rubbed my hand with his thumb. I wondered if he even noticed he was doing it or if he just wanted to give me comfort, because all the way to the school he kept my hand firmly in his. I felt my heart beating faster and faster the closer we got to home. Then it dawned on me. It's Sunday, why on earth would the school call me? I mean, yes, some weekends have some office hours but not by the time I'd get there.

Something was wrong. "He's messing with me again," I mutter to myself with a short huff of laughter. I run agitated fingers through my hair wincing when it catches on a knot before I glare ahead.

"What?" Caden asks. And for a moment, I forgot he was here before I turned to him.

"Anthony. He's fucking with me again. The school will be closed by the time we get there. Why would he do this?" I ask.

Caden is silent for a moment before he curses. "He wants you back home."

I nod, suddenly scared and anxious. "But for what reason?"

Caden

I run Rory's words through my head over and over again until I decide to send out a group text saying to meet at my house ASAP because something was really wrong. I don't know what Anthony is planning but I can say whatever it is I don't like it one bit. I was so worried about Rory it didn't even occur to me that this whole phone call didn't sound right at all. No school would call on a weekend and about a student's grade. At least not that I was aware of. But it was like rubbing salt into the wound Rory already had. So, what was Anthony thinking? His thought process concerned me because he did the one thing he knew she couldn't ignore.

The ride to my house was silent and I could see Rory panicking. Her knee was shaking and she was biting her nails. Gently I reached over and grabbed her hand and held it tightly in mine, giving her my strength as best as I could before our Uber dropped us off. I got our bags from the trunk and walked inside where Skittles was running in circles chasing her tail.

I set our bags on the ground and stopped short when a knock sounded on the door.

"Go sit down and relax. I'm going to figure this out," I tell Rory.

She stares at me, tears shining in her eyes. "What is going on?"

I grab her face, forcing her to meet my gaze. "None of that. No tears, baby. Not for that fuckwit. I promise you I'm going to figure this out and I'm going to fix this."

She shakes her head, her curls bouncing around her scared face, she still wore the dress from the wedding, and she still looked incredible. But I didn't say any of that, instead I pointed to my room and gently pushed her near the door.

"Go get changed into something comfortable." She nods and presses a kiss to my cheek.

"Thank you." With that she turned and went to my bedroom as I opened the door.

"This better be an emergency," Spencer said as he walked in, followed by his friend Elijah and Sorrow, Ravi and Max.

"Where's Drew?" I ask, closing the door behind them.

"Fuck if we know. He's been MIA lately," Max replied, looking at the suitcases then at the closed door of my bedroom before arching a red brow at me.

"I can explain," I mutter, just as Rory steps out of the room wearing a pair of my sweats and my t-shirt. And fuck if I didn't love seeing her in my clothes.

She stares around her and waves awkwardly. "Hi."

"Hey," the men chorused before turning to me.

"Anyway, the reason I called you here is because Anthony

is up to something. I need to know his whereabouts like yesterday."

Spencer is in working mode now, pulling out his phone and typing away.

"What makes you think he's up to something?" Sorrow asks, sitting at the counter.

"He had someone call Rory and tell her she failed a class, a class she was required to complete, and told her to come to the school today to figure it out. But it's Sunday, the school is closed on Sunday."

Rory clears her throat softly before turning to me. "I don't think he'd hurt me. Yes, I technically screwed up his plans with his wife, but he wouldn't hurt a fly. I mean come on, the man is scared of garden snakes. He couldn't hurt a fly."

I shake my head. "Anyone desperate enough is capable of hurting someone, Rory. Especially if they have a motive."

"His way of hurting people is mentally not physically. I'm telling you I've known him for years." She was adamant but something wasn't sitting right with me about this. He was up to something that needed her here but what was it? What could it possibly be?

"And how well did you really know him?" I ask, because she didn't know him. Not the real him. Not the married man who preyed on an innocent girl who wanted to make something of herself. He took advantage of her, lied to her, to his wife and still has the audacity to call her and try to ruin all her hard work.

Rory takes a deep breath and nods. "Fine, I didn't know him as well as I thought I did. But the subject still stands. I don't think he has it in him to hurt anyone."

I sigh, running a hand through my hair. "I believe you, Rory. I do. But I won't risk your safety with someone who is clearly going off the rails."

Rory sighs in defeat and nods slowly. "Okay. I think I'm just going to step outside for some air."

"Rory..." I call but she just shakes her head and walks out the door. Groaning, I throw up my hands and look at the other men in the room. "What the fuck happened?"

"You basically said you don't trust her judgment."

I pinch the bridge of my nose. "No. I don't trust him. He wanted her back in town for a reason and I don't trust it or him."

"You have every right to that but she might not see it the way we do," Ravi said.

"Delaney didn't. She's too trusting, all of them are when they shouldn't be. We really should have a talk with them and train them to defend themselves better. The one session wasn't enough," Sorrow muttered looking down. He hasn't been the same since Delaney's attack and he's more protective than I've ever seen him, and I finally get it because when the one woman you love is in danger you'd do anything for her. That's why I started planning to search for Anthony before he found her. But nothing would prepare me for what was to come.

Chapter 43

RORY

I didn't think before I left Caden's house in full-blown panic mode. I didn't think before I called Seraphina.

She answers on the first ring. "Hey, girl! Did you finally decide to keep Caden and make a million babies with him?" she teases causing me to give a hiccupping sob. "What is it?" she asks, turning serious.

"I... can you come pick me up?" I ask. She was the closest to me and I needed to leave. To be able to breathe and feel like I was able to gather my scattered thoughts.

"Yeah. Of course. I'll be there in five." She hangs up and I start walking down the street. The next few minutes feel like forever until I see Sera's car pulling up beside me. I can see Darcy in the backseat sleeping and a sense of peace flows through me as I get into the car. Sera doesn't say anything as she pulls away until we are far away from people as she drives down the river. It's a few hours later, it is starting to get dark, and I feel my phone vibrate. I look at the screen and see Caden's number and I send it to voicemail.

"Where are we going?" I ask.

"The cabin. I figured you'd be able to breathe away from people. I'll send a group text to everyone, so no one worries too much."

I nod and turn my head to the window and watch the river and trees until we get to a roadside pharmacy. Seraphina pulls up to the pharmacy and sighs, "This one doesn't have a drive thru, so I have to run in and get it. Will you be okay with Darcy?"

I glance at her and see worry in her dark brown eyes. "I'm fine, Sera. It's just been a long few weeks."

Sera nods, gripping my hand gently. "It'll be okay. We'll figure everything out." I nodded but I wasn't convinced. My life was ruined, my career was over. All because I was stupid.

Sera looks in the backseat where her daughter was sleeping and says, "I'll be right back."

"Okay," I mutter, tilting my head back and closing my eyes. My eyes aren't closed long before my door opens. "Did you forget your purse?" I ask, blinking open my eyes before I gasp.

Sera isn't there in the car, it's Anthony. His face is grim as he pulls me roughly out of the car. I scream scratching at his hand as he pulls me toward another car. I fight until he just lifts me up and walks me to the passenger seat and shoves me inside slamming the car door behind him. I try to yank it open, but the child lock is on and I can't open it. Panic seized me as I bang on the window but he's fast and climbs into the driver's seat and drives out of the parking lot. Leaving me alone with him. I look behind me and see Sera running out of the store, her phone to her ear.

"Let me go!" I shout at Anthony, but he doesn't listen to

me, just turns the radio up really loud leaving me screaming into nothingness.

Caden

I'm driving to the cabin when Sera's phone number pops up on the screen. I sigh wanting to put it to voicemail, but I don't. I answer it instead just as I pull into the cabin's lot where I see three men standing outside. Beside me Sorrow sighs as we see Rory's brothers standing there as if waiting for their sister.

"Are you going to answer the phone?" Elijah asks from the back seat.

Cursing, I slide open my phone. "Hey Sera, we're at the cabin where are you?"

"He took her. While I was in the pharmacy he snatched her out of the car." She was speaking so fast that what she said didn't fully register.

"What?" I ask.

"Anthony took Rory. He snatched her out of the car! I'm following behind them, but he's driving faster than I can. Caden, I don't know what to do."

"Send me your location now. Don't lose sight of them, do you hear me?" Sera takes a shaky breath and agrees before sending me the location.

"What the hell was that?" Max asks as I swerve out of the lot and back onto the main road. I can see Rory's brothers pile into their car and follow, sensing that something is off. I don't answer. I can't. My heart is pounding so hard, and fear is a bitter taste in my mouth as I follow Sera's location as fast as I can. My fists grip the steering wheel hard as I race down the empty roads before I see a silver car and a white car up ahead. It has to be them. Time seems to stop as we all watch the car go over the railing and into the choppy river.

"No!" I shouted, but it was too late. The car was gone.

Chapter 44

RORY

A few minutes earlier

My heart is pounding as Anthony speeds through the streets, uncaring of the car that is so obviously following us. I'm terrified as I try to talk to him.

"Please, Anthony, let's talk about this." It was useless, because he just shot me a glare so dark it had me shrinking into my seat. I glance around me and slowly press my finger onto the window button and slowly let it down, blowing cool air into the stifling car. Anthony curses and tries to reach over me. But I held him off with my hand and let it down all the way, knowing his car windows didn't roll back up without it being done by hand. I reach out of the car and reach for the handle ready to launch myself out of the car when he swerves, sending me flying into the dashboard as the car careens off the road and into the dark murky waters of the river.

My heart is in my throat as I scream in fear as the car disappears into the water. The Nueces River is deep, around eighty feet, and the river right now is choppy, sending the car twisting and turning in the shallow water. Ice cold water fills the car fast, sinking it faster than I'd like. But I know I have to fight. If I don't fight I'm dead and I'm not ready to die yet. With strength I didn't know I had, I unbuckle my seat belt and force myself out of the window and into the water. It's shocking to my system leaving me sinking until I force myself to swim up towards the light, but I'm not a strong swimmer. Never have been, and I know when I'm running out of air. I can feel my lungs burning with each burst of energy I use up trying to swim towards the surface. As I break the surface I take a gasping breath, before I'm pulled down into the water again. Water fills my mouth and nose as I'm pulled down by my ankle. I panic, fighting for my life as I kick at whatever has me. My arms are burning as I swim higher and higher until I'm back on the surface coughing, and trying to get the loose tree branch I see. I can hardly breathe as I pull myself out of the water and onto the branch. A part of me hopes Anthony didn't make it, but as I glance into the dark water and see him break the surface, I knew I didn't have enough time.

Groaning softly, I push myself up and take off into the woods.

Caden

. . .

I can't breathe as I stop the car and climb out running towards the wrecked guardrail. The car was long gone and I felt my heart break in a million pieces. "Fuck! We have to get her!" I shouted.

I'm ready to jump in when strong arms are surrounding me stopping me from jumping into the river.

"Let me go! I have to get her! I have to save her before it's too late!" I'm basically crying now as I fight against the hold the arms have on me.

"We can't just fall into the river, it's dangerous," the calm voice of Ravi says. But I could hear what he wasn't saying. It was too late. There was no way someone could survive that. He pulls me away as flashing red and blue lights show up blinding me as I look into the murky water. Cops pile out of their cars and the sound of a helicopter is loud as it circles ahead of us making it nearly impossible to see or hear my own thoughts.

"What the fuck happened? Where is Rory?" Nico demands climbing out of his car. No one says anything as police officers surround the area and I can't help but feel like this isn't the end. Not of Rory and not of the two of us. She's still alive. I can feel it. I just needed to get away from everyone, but I was stuck giving my statement as they started searching the water.

It was getting dark and I was afraid they wouldn't find anything and as the hours dragged on the more I started to panic.

"We've got something!" someone called out. The large crane that was being used pulled out a white car and I felt my heart stutter in my chest.

"We got a body!" That was when my heart stopped. Was it Rory, was she dead? Were my instincts off? My breath stalled when the trunk was opened and I saw the limp body of Anthony's wife. I almost sink to my knees but just because that wasn't her doesn't mean anything. She could still be in the river.

"I'm sorry, but there's nothing else we can do until morning. We will get back to searching once it's daylight. I'm sorry," the officer in charge said to us and they went and collected evidence but I knew in my gut Rory was still alive. But where was she? My gaze traveled to the woods, and I nudged Sorrow pointing to them. He nods and we slowly motion to the others. Because if she was still alive she'd have run to safety. The only place that is is through the woods to hopefully get back to the main road. Nodding to myself I slowly enter the woods, uncaring that there's a whole investigation going on. My main priority is Rory. She always will be.

Chapter 45

RORY

My breathing came out in short gasps as I ran through the dark woods. The sound of my feet hitting the ground was overly loud in my ears as I tried to dodge any trees in my way and keep out of Anthony's sight. Caden was right. When Anthony was desperate enough he'd do anything. I should've listened to Caden, but my instincts told me he was trying to control me when, in reality, he was trying to protect me. Now, here I was alone in the woods with a madman following after me.

"Rory! Come out, come out wherever you are!" Anthony shouted, causing me to stop. I pressed myself against a tree and took slow deep breaths. As quietly as possible I sank to the ground and found a large branch and wrapped my fingers around it.

"Listen, I just want to talk to you," Anthony continued. "I want to apologize for everything. You know, for not telling you I was married. She's gone now. Out of the picture and we can be together again. Try this out for real this time."

I close my eyes briefly, but they pop open when I feel hot breath on my neck. Tears burn my eyes.

"Boo," Anthony whispered, and I swung the branch connecting with his jaw. He reels back and I take off running again pushing myself harder, but he's faster than me and tackles me to the ground covering us both in dirt and leaves. I groan in pain as he straddles me.

"Stop running from me," he demands, grabbing at me to hold me down, but I wasn't having that.

I shake my head and grab a fistful of dirt and throw it into his eyes. He curses and pulls back letting me go, and then I'm up and running again. But it doesn't last long before he's on me again and this time he's standing on my leg, putting a painful amount of pressure on it. I scream in pain the moment I feel the bone snap. Tears leak out of my eyes as the pain radiates up my body until I'm just screaming. He puts his hand over my mouth silencing me and I took the opportunity to bite down on it. Hard. Just like with Caden when we were doing those lessons.

He curses and grabs my neck, squeezing as I fight him. I scratch at his face, beating at him as dark webs cloud my vision. I feel the dog tags at my neck snap, and I stop and grab them. I curl my fingers around the cold metal and whip it up as hard as I could, slapping him in the face with it.

He looks stunned and lets go of me, his hands going to his face giving me time to draw in a breath before I roll to my stomach and force myself up and limp my way forward. My leg is sore and any pressure on it has me crying out. I don't get far before I'm grabbing a tree and trying not to sink to the ground.

"You should've listened to me," Anthony whispers, wrapping his belt around my throat. I struggle, fighting him off as he tightens the leather against the base of my throat. I can't breathe as he pulls tighter. This is it, this is how I die, strangled to death in the woods because of my choice to leave Caden's apartment. I should've listened to the men. But it was too late now. My vision blurred and the air in my lungs was giving out, I was dying again. I stop struggling and sink to the ground as spider webs begin to overtake my sight. But then a shot rings out and Anthony is falling away from me. I fall to the ground, the belt falling from my throat, and I take a deep gasping breath while grabbing my sore throat making sure I could breathe. I glance up and see Sorrow rushing forward with Caden hot on his heels. I can see the relief on Caden's face, and I start crying. It's not a little crying, it's full-on body sobs as relief settles inside of me.

"Shhh, I got you," Caden whispers, grabbing me.

"You were right," I sob.

"None of that. We can talk about this later. We need to get you to the hospital."

I gasp in pain as he lifts me up and I slide my arms around him. "No. No hospital. Get Drew. Please."

"Anthony is gone," Sorrow reports.

I look up at Caden and see rage flash in his eyes before he nods. "Fine. Let me take you to the house."

I nod and hug him to me as I cry, uncaring that we have Sorrow here with us. Neither man says anything, just let me have this moment and Caden keeps his arms around me holding me to his chest as if I weighed nothing and he wanted nothing more than to make sure I was okay.

"Don't let me go," I whisper brokenly.

"Never," he promises.

Chapter 46

CADEN

Running through the woods was something I never thought I'd do again. Going on a rescue mission with the guys again. It never occurred to me that this would happen again. We fell into step with each other as we always did, and we split up to find my woman.

Then I heard a scream and knew Rory was alive, but if I didn't get to her soon she'd be taken from me. When I saw her with that belt against her throat I was gone. I shot at him without caring if I killed him or not. I'm still pissed he wasn't dead, but as I held Rory in my arms I knew nothing else mattered. The way she held onto me had me holding her tighter as we navigated our way back. The cops were gone leaving the rest of us alone. They thought Rory was dead. Not wanting to worry about that now, I head to the car where I see her brothers waiting, all of them pacing around it. Wondering if they were ever going to see their only sister again.

When they see us they converge on their sister spouting questions and hugging her in my arms, but she never dropped her arms from my neck.

"You came?" she whispered.

"Of course we came. You're our sister and you needed us," Marco said, his voice thick with emotion.

"Rory!" Seraphina gasped, rushing to her friend.

"I'm so sorry," Rory started, finally dropping her arm and I see her fist is closed around something. When I get a closer look I see it's my dog tags.

"Let's get you to Drew. I'm worried about your injuries," I say, finally giving her a reprieve from the questions, and it was a long drive back to her home. As if none of her brothers could bear parting with their sister they climbed into my car and Sorrow and the others take theirs.

"I called Drew he should be at my house, or we can go back to yours," I tell Rory who is sitting by her brothers trying to prop her leg up as best as she could.

"I think it's broken," she mutters.

"Can it bend?" Rio asks.

Rory snorts, pushing her wet hair out of her face. "I'm not going to risk trying to bend it. It hurts like a son of a bitch though. So does my throat."

I glance at her and see her hand go to her bruised throat and that rage I felt before boils to the surface, but I push it down. I know this isn't the last time we'll see Anthony. I know Rory is trying to be strong, but I can see the way her hands tremble and the cracks in her voice whenever she talks. She's scared and she has every right to be. I'm pissed at myself for not realizing she left when she was at my house, I'm angry that I let her get hurt.

It's my fault we almost lost her. That her family almost lost her. In my moments of wanting to protect her I let her get away and it's my fault she's hurting now. Swallowing hard

I moved my eyes back to the road driving the three hours back to Drew's apartment.

Rory

Caden is silent all the way to the apartment, and it sends worry down my spine. I can feel him pulling away and I hate it. This is all my fault. I should've never left Caden's home. I should've waited until I knew I was safe. My bad judgment got me to where I am. I want to speak, to say something to him, but I can't with my brothers hovering over me. So, I sit back in silence watching Caden's every move. The way his eyes would travel to me before jerking away as if he couldn't bear to look at me.

When we got to the apartment Caden stops the car and climbs out of the car followed by my brothers. I don't move, not just because I can't but because I need to process everything. To process the fact that I don't know Anthony as well as I thought. That I was used and groomed to fit into his perfect pretend world and left almost dead. He was going to let me die in that car even if he would've died with me.

I took in a shaky breath as my door opened and Caden leaned in to grab me, but I stopped him. Pressing my hand to his chest.

"You're angry," I mutter.

"Lorelai," he sighs softly.

"Caden."

He braces his arms on the roof of the car and nods, the anger and fear written on his face. "Yes, I'm fucking angry. I'm scared. You almost died, Rory."

"But I didn't," I whisper. I was lucky I didn't die. I was so close to it twice.

"But you could have. You could be sitting there alone in those woods dead, and it would be my fault," he snaps.

I reeled back, stunned. "Your fault? It's no one's fault but my own. I left. I shouldn't have. I should have stayed and listened to you, but I got overwhelmed and left. And he followed me. How, I don't know, but he was going to get to me no matter what. We both know that."

He shakes his head. "I should have protected you better. Why couldn't I have protected you the way you deserve? I almost lost you and I don't really even have you. Rory, this isn't what I want. I need you to be safe and sound at all times."

"Stop. Caden, I'm a grown woman. I knew what I was doing. I don't need a bodyguard; I need a partner. You have to know that. Please stop talking as if you're going to leave because you promised me."

"Lorelai," he whispers softly.

"No," I say and shake my head. "No. We already made this official. We aren't going to let Anthony break us before we can even start."

He sighs but doesn't say anything else as he lifts me from the seat and brings me towards Drew's apartment who is already setting up everything in the living room. He glances up when we walk in, arching his black brow at us.

"How the hell did you survive?" he asks, not one to beat around the bush. I appreciated that he never sugar coated anything and said what was on his mind because it means he wasn't afraid of getting all the details or scaring me. He saw me as a person not a victim.

Caden set me on the couch, careful of my leg and I knew they were waiting for me to explain it all. The front door opened, and Delaney rushed in, uncaring that the others were here waiting for an explanation nor my wet clothes as she wrapped me up in a strong hug. Then I promptly burst into tears.

Chapter 47

CADEN

Rory bursts into tears as soon as Delaney wraps her in a hug, and it makes something in me want to snap. I want to be the one holding her, but I know it's for the best as her friends take over Drew's apartment fussing over her. All of them were scared of what could have happened to her.

"All right, all right. I need room to work," Drew said, taking charge of the situation as I stand back. There isn't much privacy that we could give Rory, but she doesn't seem to care that she has to have her pants cut off. No one really looks at her until she sucks in a deep breath, and I turn to see her leg. It's bruised and swollen to twice its normal size. I watch as Drew puts his gloved hands on her leg.

"I don't think it's broken. It's probably fractured, but he didn't add enough pressure to break it," he says as he makes a temporary splint to stabilize her leg better and so the swelling can go down.

"How'd you get out of the car?" Max asks, leaning against the wall across from me.

Rory shrugs then hisses out a breath when Drew moves her leg. "Stop being a baby," Drew admonishes.

Rory rolls her eyes before turning back to the people in the room, looking at them before coming to settle on me as if she were explaining the whole ordeal to just me.

"Through the window. When he was driving, I felt this strong need to roll it down, and it's one that can't be rolled up because it's broken. Once it's down, it's down."

"So, you swam out the window," I say, watching her.

"Yes. But he somehow got out. He was on the swim team in college, so he had an advantage over me."

"If the car is filled with water the pressure of the river would balance out with the car and he could've opened the door," Nirvana said. We all stare at her, and she shrugs.

"It takes a car seconds to sink, seconds you wouldn't have had without the window being open," Sorrow adds, telling us just how close we were to losing her.

"I know. Then he pulled me under the water, and I knew if I didn't fight him I'd die, and I wasn't ready to go. I have too many people who need me, who I care about." Her eyes never leave mine as she says this, and I sigh softly not wanting to rehash this because I know it's painful for her. For all of them.

"You're one tough woman," Elijah says randomly, startling me away from Rory.

When the hell did he even get here? Spencer is beside him and Layla and I wonder what's going on there before I step next to Rory and place a hand on her shoulder, rubbing gently. "She always has been."

Elijah nods. "Yes, but who can say they survived this? It's crazy. And he's gone. Don't you think he'll come back to finish the job?"

It was one of the concerns that plagued me when we found Anthony gone. But at the time I just wanted to make sure Rory was safe. That's all that mattered to me now, but I know deep down she was scared of Anthony.

"We'll be ready for him this time," I say, because I'd be damned if I lost her again.

Chapter 48

RORY

Finally, we are back at Caden's house after hours of discussing what happened tonight and I'm exhausted. I knew Caden was going to freak out and leave but surprisingly he didn't. Now I lie in his bed freshly showered with my splinted leg propped up on the bed as he lies silently next to me.

Wanting to say something, I whisper into the darkened room, "I broke the rules."

"What?" he asks, turning his head to look at me. I turn to face him, fingering the cold metal now safely placed back around my bruised neck.

"Our rules. I broke them."

He huffs out a laugh. "Yeah, I'm pretty sure we both did."

I shake my head. "No, the major rule."

He swallows audibly. "Rory."

"I can't help it," I whisper. "It was hard not to fall, Caden."

"You've experienced something traumatic today."

"Stop. Let me say this. I need you to know that these feelings have been building for a while now. Something I fought so hard not to let happen, but I wasn't strong enough."

"Rory," he whispers, cupping my cheek.

"I've fallen in love with you, Caden," I say. I've been trying to ignore those feelings but being alone in the woods made me realize how precious life is and that I can't fight these feelings any longer. He was the reason I stayed alive. The fact that I didn't want him to hurt when I was gone or the fact that my family needed me still. I had to fight and fight I did.

He closes his eyes, soaking in what I just said before opening his eyes again to stare at me with so much love that it steals my breath away.

"I love you, too, Lorelai. So fucking much it hurts. I know I said I wouldn't love anyone again, but you dug your way into my heart. I don't know how you did it, but you did, and I couldn't be more grateful." I smile at him and lean forward pressing a kiss to his lips. He rolls me to my back still kissing me gently before he settles down over me. Our tongues move languidly against each other neither one of us in a hurry. I run my hands up his chest slowly pushing his shirt up.

He pulls away slightly, breathing heavily.

"You sure? Your leg."

I nod. "Show me I'm alive. That I'm with you. Please, Caden."

He leans down again and fastens his mouth to mine, kissing me deeper and harder. He gently spreads my legs after pulling down the shorts I'm wearing and runs his fingers over my overly heated skin. I gasp softly, arching into his touch. Caden kisses down my throat to my collarbone before lifting my shirt and tossing it over his shoulder before latching onto one of my nipples. Nipping at it and licking away the sting.

Groaning, I grab his head, holding him to me as he brings me pleasure.

"Please," I gasp when his fingers travel between my legs, stroking my pussy ever so gently.

"Use your words, Rory. What do you need?"

I arch up my hips wanting more. Needing him. "I need you inside of me."

"That's my girl," he mutters against my skin before he kicks off his pants and positions himself at my entrance. Very slowly he pushes inside, stretching me more than I think I can handle before he's seated deep inside me. I clutch at his shoulders, gasping for breath as he holds still, stroking my hair gently.

"Look at me," he demands softly.

I glance up at him and he starts to move, thrusting deep and hard making me moan in pleasure.

"Tell me again," I say, needing to hear the words from him. Needing that reassurance that I'm not in this alone. He smiles at me before kissing my lips, his hips still moving at a slow pace.

"I love you, Lorelai." Just those words had me gasping for breath. He held onto me, his hands gripping me tightly as he made love to me. And it was making love. Slow and hard. Just the way we both needed. He thrusts deeper causing me to gasp when the orgasm hits me, my body no longer my own but his. Through it Caden makes love to me. Holding me on that brink that ultimately has me falling, crying out his name, and saying I love him.

Caden

. . .

Rory lays soundly on my chest fast asleep. Slowly I disentangled myself from her and get up, pulling my pants back on, and heading to the kitchen for a drink. It's well past three in the morning, but sleep eludes me.

I'm by the sink drinking water when I hear it. The subtle click of the lock disengaging and the door opening. I don't move, looking as if I'm unaware of the intruder. The intruder moves into the kitchen and stops when he sees me standing there.

"I wondered when you'd show up again," I muttered.

"I see," he says. But he doesn't make a move. Not yet. My back is still turned to him as I sip my water and he finally makes his move towards me. I turn, then throw the water at him, slamming the glass into his head and letting it crash against his skull.

Anthony curses and brings out a blade before rushing me and pushing me against the counter. I grunt when my back hits the counter, before I slam the heel of my hand into his chest sending him falling backwards. He falls to the floor, and I descend on him, punching him in the face over and over again, before I feel the knick in my skin as he slams the knife into my side. Cursing, I fall away holding the injury.

"Rory isn't worth your life, Sato. She's not worth anything," Anthony gasps, wiping at the blood on his face.

"She's worth everything," I say and grunt, pushing myself up but not taking the knife out. I don't think he hit anything vital but the bleeding if I took the knife out could kill me.

"She's a good lay I'll admit, but she's useless."

"Then why go through all this trouble to kill her? What about your wife? They found her in the trunk of your car."

Anthony's eyes darken. "She ruined everything. My

career, my family. She wanted to leave me, but I couldn't... I wouldn't let her. She's mine."

I heard a shuffling noise and I knew I had to keep Anthony's attention on me. "Why'd you kill her?" I asked, wincing as pain laced through me.

"She killed my baby," he whispers.

"Anthony," Rory says, her voice soothing. I glanced up and saw her holding a gun towards Anthony wearing nothing but my shirt and it was a beautiful sight.

He turns and laughs and shakes his head. "Put the gun down before you hurt yourself, Rory."

"Get away from Caden."

"Your little boyfriend? Oh, we're just having a chat." He moves over to me and without warning pulls the knife from my side causing me to cry out in pain and then all I hear is the sound of the gun going off. I stare in shock as Anthony goes down onto his knees before falling on his face. Rory drops the gun and rushes to me, her face pale.

"Oh my God. Caden, what do I do?" she asks, putting her hands on the wound trying to stop the bleeding.

"Drew," is all I manage to get out. She nods and helps me stand before grabbing her phone and keys and helping me down the three flights of stairs. Her neighbors come out of their apartments and see what's going on but neither of us pays any mind as we rush outside to the car. Sirens sound in the distance and I know things are about to get dicey and I didn't feel up to dealing with the cops.

"How are you doing *mi vida?*" she asks, putting me in the backseat.

"Never better," I reply.

She nods as she starts the car and drives us to Drew's as she calls him.

"Drew, Caden's been stabbed. I don't know how bad but there's blood everywhere," she pauses as he speaks but she shakes her head. "No, he told me to bring him to you. Drew, I killed someone. I can't be anywhere right now." Her voice is panicked and I try to sit up to comfort her but she sends me a glare that has me lying back down.

"I'm almost to your apartment, please. Please help him." The last was said on a broken sob but I don't hear anything else as the world goes black around me.

Chapter 49

RORY

I rush to Drew's apartment and stop the car outside where I see Drew and Sorrow standing there, I get out of the car quickly and towards the back of the car where Caden is lying unconscious. I try to limp to him, but the men are already there helping him out.

"What happened?" Sorrow asks, putting pressure on Caden's wound.

"I-I don't know. Anthony showed up and there was a fight. I think he stabbed him." I was panicking and I jumped when I felt a hand on my shoulder. I turned and there was Max who smiled kindly at me.

"He'll be okay. Come in and sit down." I nodded and let him help me to the apartment and sat down. Drew and Sorrow brought Caden to another room and left me alone with Max who stood by the door watching everything around him.

I sit in silence shaking my head. God, how could I let this

happen? I was going to go to jail for murder and Caden was lying on a table bleeding out because of me.

"If you shake your head any more it'll dislodge from your shoulders," Max suddenly says.

I look up tears streaming down my face. "I killed him."

"Who?" he asks.

"Anthony. I shot him three times. Then I left."

"It was self-defense," Max says.

"The courts won't see it that way. Then there's Caden. What if he's seriously hurt?"

"Nah," Max shakes his head. "It's mostly blood loss. Caden bleeds like a stuck pig. Always has. But he's one strong bastard and is going to pull through."

"How do you know?"

"Because Caden wouldn't leave you unprotected, even if Anthony may be dead, he's going to be there."

I shake my head. "Caden has all of you, too."

"Yes, Caden has us. But until recently he was a shell of his former self. You brought him back. You're his salvation he didn't even know he needed."

I sit in silence waiting for news on Caden as I let Max's words consume me. Was he right? I don't know how long I sit there before Drew comes and tells me Caden is going to be fine, and I could see him. I walk into the sterile room that is eerily identical to a hospital room. I turn to ask Drew about it, but he's gone leaving me alone with Caden. I sit next to him and run my fingers gently over his hair. "Caden," I whisper. Hoping he'd hear me.

Caden

. . .

I grunt as I try to move my hand and curse. It was useless. The damn thing was covered in ugly scars and hardly worked. How was I supposed to go on with this?

"It'll get easier," a voice sounded behind me.

I didn't turn as Ravi entered the room. There was no reason to. I didn't want to see him. I wanted to see none of them. Anger and embarrassment ate at me. How was I supposed to face the men, my team after I failed to protect them?

"Caden."

"Go away, Ravi," I finally say, tossing the little ball away from me.

"Don't do that, Cade," Ravi says, picking up the ball I threw and putting it back where it was supposed to go.

"Stop trying with me. I don't deserve it. I need space. I need to not be here. I shouldn't be here," I muttered to myself. I almost died. We all did but I should've known something was wrong. My gut should've warned me and maybe just maybe we wouldn't be here. Stuck on a constant loop of agony. For six weeks, six long agonizing weeks I sat alone debating ending it all, but something kept me going. The anger at Xena, at myself. Hell, even the guys. I was angry at everything.

But something held me back from ending it.

The sweet smell of lavender and vanilla wafted through me, washing away the blood and gore.

"Caden," a soft voice whispers. It's no longer Ravi. It's her.

"*Chīsai doragon,*" I mutter, slowly blinking my eyes open and seeing her beautiful face above me. Her hazel eyes are more green than brown now, bright with unshed tears. "Don't cry."

She gives a hiccupping laugh. "What does that mean?"

I smile, at least I think I do before whispering, "Little dragon."

"Little dragon?"

"Hmmmm. You have the spirit of a dragon but you're little. Thus, little dragon."

"*Mi vida*," she murmurs.

"Now what's that mean?" I ask, running my fingers over her forearm watching as goosebumps rise on her brown skin. I enjoy watching the way she reacts to me and how I can affect her so much.

She swallows hard. "My life." Her words are whispered, and it takes me a minute to realize what she said.

"Am I your life?" I ask, stroking her arm with gentle fingers.

"A part of it. A big part of it. It happened fast, but I can't picture it without you in it."

"*Chīsai doragon*, you're everything to me."

She laughs softly. "You're high."

"That may be, but I've never told you a lie. I love you."

"You're in this bed because of me, Caden," she whispers brokenly.

I shake my head, groaning at the ache there. "No, I'm in here because of Anthony." The name gives me pause. "You shot him."

She nods. "I did. I already called Kaila and told her what happened. She's going to help me with any trouble I may be in."

"Trouble? Why would you be in trouble?" I demand, trying to sit up but wincing when my side twinges in pain. She shouldn't be in any trouble with the fact that she was protecting not only herself but me too. How would that consist of her being in trouble? My thoughts are jumbled before she speaks.

She pushes me down on the bed and sits beside me. "Caden, I left the scene of a crime to get you here. I didn't know if you were going to die, and I panicked after shooting him."

"Shit," I mutter. Reality is finally kicking in. What just happened to us. Hell, this was a shit day.

"Yeah," she says, curling her hand in mine.

"Everything is going to be okay; you know that right?" I ask after a moment's silence.

"I know."

"I love you, Rory."

She turns to me with a smile. "I love you, too."

Chapter 50

RORY

Three weeks later

I sigh softly as I climb out of the car and grab my crutches. After Anthony showed up to my apartment I messed up my leg more by walking on it and running. So, I had to be put in a cast and crutches for the next six weeks. But the good news is I'm not a murderer.

Anthony was shot in the arm and leg, nothing major, but he couldn't leave the apartment. I did get fined for leaving a crime scene and have to do community service once my leg is better but that's all. Anthony is in prison for the rest of his life with the attempted murder of me and the murder of his wife, which makes me sad. A part of me feels like it's my fault, but I know it's not. I mourned her when I found out, I still mourn her and hope her family is doing okay.

Shaking off those thoughts I rush forward toward Heidi's, excitement and pride coursing through me.

I open the door and push my crutches inside. "Today's the day!" I called.

Layla pops her head from around the corner and squeals in delight. "I can't believe it's finally happening."

"I brought the champagne and whiskey!" I say showing the bag. She comes forward and grabs the bags before giving me a tight hug.

"Thank you for being here," her voice is thick with emotion, and I feel tears prick my eyes.

"Nothing could keep me from this event, LaLa," I replied.

"No, no, no tears. Today's a happy day," Delaney says, coming from the back to put a tray of cupcakes in the display case.

I laugh pulling away and go to the corner to sit down as the others do the last-minute details before opening. A line was already forming outside, and I could see Layla becoming increasingly more nervous. I watch as Elijah steps behind her and rubs her shoulders gently. I arch an eyebrow to myself but turn away when my seat is pulled back and I'm lifted from it. I laugh as Caden steals my seat and sits me on his lap uncaring that there's a line of people outside or that our friends are around us. I don't care either.

"Hey RoRo," he says, kissing the side of my head.

"Hey yourself. How's everything looking?"

"Great! We tasted everything, we got the coffee machine working, everything is in working order and they finally decided on a place for the jukebox."

I smile at him and press a kiss to his cheek. "Thank you for helping this morning."

"Of course, *Chīsai doragon.*" I loved when he called me that. His little dragon. A fierce warrior that would fight no matter what. It reminded me of the knife he gave me, the one that was currently strapped to my thigh, and I loved it.

The day goes on like that until it's closing time, and we can all finally settle down. Layla pops open the champagne I brought and pours us glasses and gives Delaney some cider before holding up her glass. "Thank you guys so much for making today happen. I couldn't do this without any of you."

We all cheered for her, and I looked around at my friends and smiled. This is what I could've missed out on. If I didn't fight. If I didn't take a chance on Caden. I look at the man in question who is talking and laughing with Ravi and, as if he can feel my gaze, turns and looks at me. *I love you.* He mouths.

I love you. I mouth back. And I do. They said I was his salvation, but I think he was mine. He rescued me when I couldn't rescue myself and I loved him all the more for that. He was my best friend, my lover, my person and I wouldn't have it any other way.

I walk towards him, and he wraps his arm around me.

"Good?" he asks.

"Never better."

I've never been so happy to break rules before, but loving Caden was worth it. Worth all the anguish, the fear, and the heartache to lead us here to where we belong. Together in each other's arms.

Kenzie Young

Kenzie Young is a pen name I chose when I was in Junior High. I began writing in 8th grade after I was given an assignment to write a short story based on a single sentence. My passion for writing began then. I'm originally from the South and moved after graduation. I met my husband and now have three dogs and two cats. I love to read romances, along with my mom and my sisters, and now I'm writing my own!

Visit her website here:
https://kenzie-young.mailchimpsites.com

Don't miss these exciting titles by AUTHOR and Blushing Books!

Rescue Me
Saving Sorrow – Book One
Surviving Him — Book Two

Blushing Books

Blushing Books is one of the oldest eBook publishers on the web. We've been running websites that publish spanking and BDSM related romance and erotica since 1999, and we have been selling eBooks since 2003. We hope you'll check out our hundreds of offerings at http://www.blushingbooks.com.

Blushing Books Newsletter

Please join the Blushing Books newsletter
to receive updates & special promotional offers.
You can also join by using your mobile phone:
Just text BLUSHING to 22828.